NOV 0 5 2015

D1006600

NEAR ENEMY

ALSO BY ADAM STERNBERGH

Shovel Ready

NEAR ENEMY

A Spademan Novel

ADAM STERNBERGH

 CROWN PUBLISHERS
NEW YORK

This is a work of fiction. Names, characters, places, and incidents either
are the product of the author's imagination or are used fictitiously.
Any resemblance to actual persons, living or dead, events, or locales is
entirely coincidental.

Copyright © 2015 by Adam Sternbergh

All rights reserved.
Published in the United States by Crown Publishers, an imprint
of the Crown Publishing Group, a division of Random House LLC,
a Penguin Random House Company, New York.
www.crownpublishing.com

CROWN is a registered trademark and the Crown colophon is a trademark of
Random House LLC.

Library of Congress Cataloging-in-Publication Data
Sternbergh, Adam.
  Near enemy : a Spademan novel / Adam Sternbergh. — First edition.
  I. Title.
  PS3619.T47874N43 2015
  813'.6—dc23   2014024991

ISBN 978-0-385-34902-4
eBook ISBN 978-0-385-34903-1

Printed in the United States of America

Jacket design by Will Staehle
Author photograph: Marvin Orellana

10 9 8 7 6 5 4 3 2 1

First Edition

For RC

NEAR ENEMY

I hate to bother you,
but I am talking about evil.

It blooms.
It eats.
It grins.

—ANNE CARSON,
"The Fall of Rome: A Traveller's Guide"

I.

1.

Voice on the phone said a single name.

Lesser.

Woman's voice. Hung up quickly.

Money cleared an hour later.

I wrote the name on a scrap of paper. Put it in one pocket.

Box-cutter in the other.

Simple.

And no way to know, when she said that name, that it would go so wrong.

2.

This used to be a city of locks.

Every home, at least five, down the door, like a vault.

Chain lock.

Rim lock.

Fox lock.

Knob lock.

Deadbolt.

Funny name, that last one.

Dead. Bolt.

Neither word exactly conjures security.

But no one bothers with that many locks in New York anymore. City's safer. Or at least emptier. No end of vacancies. And no one bothers to burgle anymore. Nothing left to burgle. Everything's picked clean, and anyone who still lives in Manhattan and has something of real value to protect—family, dignity, vintage baseball-card collection—does it with a shotgun, not a deadbolt. So the real problem, for the burglar, isn't getting in. It's getting back out.

After all, if you apply enough force, deadbolts give.

Shotguns take.

The richest folk still have lots of fancy stuff, of course. They just don't keep most of that fancy stuff out here.

Out here, all they need is a bed and a connection.

Everything else they keep in the limn.

And if you're that rich, rich enough to go off-body all day, to tap in and slip away into the limnosphere, then you probably live in a glass tower somewhere, sealed up tight, behind code locks and round-the-clock doormen who watch the street with shotguns propped on their knees.

Where you don't live, if you're rich, is in a place like this: a squat, sprawling, crumbling tenement complex like Stuyvesant Town. A few dozen forlorn lowrise apartment buildings scattered over several city blocks on the east side of downtown Manhattan, just close enough to the waterfront to smell the river. Brick towers clustered around central courtyards, grass long ago scoured to brown. Communal playgrounds left to ruin, slides warped, swings hanging lopsided on one chain, iron rocking-horses splotched with raw-rust sores, stricken by some rockinghorse plague. The apartment buildings themselves are about as inviting as a low-security prison, except without the tennis courts or fences or guards to give a shit if anyone tries to escape.

Now everyone's escaped.

Courtyard's a ghost town.

Lobby left wide open.

Waltz right in.

Stuyvesant Town was built decades ago for the middle class, back when there was such a thing as a middle class. Eventually sold by the city to private interests. Left to rot after Times Square. Now basically a free-for-all, home to squatters, deadbeats, homesteaders, claim-jumpers, freeloaders, and bedhoppers.

It's that last kind I'm after, by the way.

Bed-hopper.

One hopper in particular.

I have to admit. I miss this.

I've been distracted lately. On a kind of hiatus. Family business. Since I seem to have a family now. Of sorts.

It's complicated.

But this?

This is simple.

You ask. I act.

Cause and consequence. Old as Cain and Abel. Old as the universe.

And not many things feel that simple anymore. Not in my life. Not in New York. Not in the universe.

Save this.

You may think it's cold and cruel, and you're right. On both counts.

Cold and cruel.

But then again, so is the universe.

Just ask it.

Apartment number scrawled on the scrap next to Lesser's name.

2B.

End of the hall, under a failing fluorescent.

Turns out our friend Lesser's less trusting than most. Has double deadbolts and a rim lock besides. So I pull out the lock-picking tools I keep hidden in my hair—

Kidding.

Heft a twelve-pound sledge from my duffel bag.

Let the duffel drop.

Before I swing, I spot a business card wedged in the door-jamb.

Pluck the card out.

Read it.

PUSHBROOM.

No number.

No nothing.

Just Pushbroom.

I pocket it.

Get back to work.

Heft the sledge.

Open Sesame.

Knock three times.

Jamb gives first.

Thank God for cheap doorframes and negligent landlords. And neighbors who know which noises to ignore.

I kick the door in, then wonder if Lesser's got company.

Don't have to worry about waking Lesser. He's a notoriously heavy sleeper. Not the picture of health, either. He's fat, and generally smells like there's places he can't reach to wash.

I met Lesser once through my friend Mark Ray, but mostly I know him because he has something of a reputation, at least with the hard-core tap-in crowd. Some kind of whiz kid, used to be a hotshot at something. But he pissed it all away to become a bed-hopper, waste his days peeping on other people's dreams.

Inside the apartment, I hear snoring. I follow it down the hallway, like Pepé Le Pew trailing perfume.

I used to love Bugs Bunny cartoons as a kid. Wascally wabbit.

Hated the Coyote though. Really hated the Road Runner.

That was some pointless desert bullshit.

Le Pew I could take or leave.

I find the bedroom. Nudge the door.

No furniture. One visitor. Skinny kid, junkie thin. Camped out bedside, watching Lesser, like a worried relative on vigil.

Lesser's bed is no more than a cot. Coils of wires, homemade solder-job, like a grade-school science project gone awry.

Bought myself a word-a-day calendar, by the way.

Awry. Yesterday's word.

Lesser's under, snoozing in the dream. Occasional snorts let us know he's still alive.

Light in the room is the color of rusty water. Newsprint for curtains. All the windows papered over. Old headlines scream at the world unheeded, like crazy sidewalk prophets.

The End Is Nigh.

Lesser's naked, by the way.

It's a hopper thing. Some like to do it in the buff. Bigger kick, apparently.

The other kid, the skinny one, just sits there, staring, gape-mouthed, as a stranger walks in carrying a sledgehammer. Maybe this happens a lot.

So I put down the sledge. Gently. Hold a hand out.

Name's Spademan.

Kid blinks once. Sign of life.

I'm Moore.

Funny. Lesser and Moore. Fat and skinny. Like a comedy duo. And no shake. Fair enough. I put the hand away.

Can you give me a moment? I need to talk to Lesser.

I don't think he'd want to be disturbed.

Trust me, I'll only take a minute.

But I'm supposed to watch him.

I don't think you want to watch this.

Skinny gets the hint. Grabs his things. Army rucksack and a surplus khaki coat, still has the soldier's name stitched on it.

Bows to me once as he leaves, like a geisha. Which is weird.

Once he's gone, I reach into my pocket.

Find my box-cutter.

About the time I get the blade extended, Lesser bolts upright, awake, already screaming. Louder than a five-alarm fire.

Rips his tubes out.

So that's messy.

Still screaming.

Tears off the sensor pads, yanks out the IV. Also messy.

Still screaming.

It's called the wake-up call. Senses coming back online. The sudden shock of the real-time world.

Slaps at himself like he thinks he's on fire.

Still screaming.

Skinny ducks back in. For some reason.

Maybe curiosity trumped the survival instinct. Or maybe he's genuinely concerned for his friend. Though that wouldn't explain his quiet exit a second ago.

Who knows. Hopper logic. It's—what do they call it?

Oxymoronic.

Today's word.

Bed-hoppers hop from dream to dream in the limnosphere, unseen. They're like peeping Toms, except worse, because they're basically inside your mind. They peep on your fantasy, the one so twisted that you'd only ever dare to act it out in the limn, in total secrecy that costs top dollar.

It's those dreams that hoppers are interested in. Because that's what hoppers do.

Hoppers watch.

For that reason, they're not too popular. Trouble is, if they do it right, you never even know that they're there. They just watch, undetected. Like Scrooge, from that old Christmas story.

Ghosts of Perverts Present.

Hopping is highly illegal, of course, but if you get caught, you don't end up contending with cops. People hire private dream-sweepers. They're like bouncers, but less gentle. Sweepers catch you bed-hopping, they make you regret your actions. In a memorable way.

And not out here.

In there.

That's why smart hoppers usually hop in pairs. Have a buddy

out here to keep watch, like old Skinny here. Someone to tap you back out if you get detained. Otherwise, I've heard tales of hoppers who got held in the limn for weeks, leg-breakers working on them round-the-clock. Won't let them wake up, won't let them tap out, and if there's no one out here keeping watch, then the sweepers can just whale away. Take their time. Weeks on end. Mark Xs on a calendar. Leave different marks on you.

The sweepers can't kill you. After all, you can't die in the limn. But sweepers find a way to use that to their advantage.

Then again, if the person you peeped on is especially vengeful, they might skip the sweepers altogether.

Hire someone like me.

Someone to find you out here, in the nuts-and-bolts world.

Where punishments tend to be more permanent.

Lesser's still screaming, by the way.

I assume he ran into some limnosphere heavies. That maybe I caught him in the midst of a lesson and he only just barely broke free. Which is bad timing for him, given the fact that I'm here.

Frying pan. Fire. Etcetera.

Finally Lesser stops shouting. Slides into stuttering.

Mumbles something.

What he's saying:

Not her not her not her not her not her not her not her.

Not here.

3.

Damn.

Quick house call turning into a fifty-minute couch session. With me in the role of therapist.

And here I forgot my turtleneck and pipe.

Frankly, I could still finish my business and get home early. But I'm curious.

Not her.

Not here.

So I pull up a chair and send Skinny to the deli for a six-pack and a quart of milk. Press two twenties into his palm, which is one more than he'll need. Hope the tip means he'll come back, looking for more.

He comes back.

Brings me a six-pack, a quart of milk, and a turkey-on-a-hard-roll besides. In case I'm hungry.

I'm starting to warm up to Skinny.

Crack the carton.

Milk calms hoppers.

No, I don't know why.

Six-pack's for me. Skinny's on his own.

Lesser sits up in the bed, guzzling milk.

Cascade of white splashes off his chest. Runs down his belly. Pools over his privates. Covers them up.

Small mercies.

Then I ask Lesser to spill exactly what he saw.

Finance dude. Orgy. Saturday nights. Like clockwork.

Milk bubbles on Lesser's lips as he speeds to spit the story out.

I've hopped it plenty of times before. So easy to get in it's almost like he knows you're coming, wants you there, gets off on someone watching.

Skip to the punch line, Lesser.

Lesser wipes his lips. Looks around. Realizes he's naked in a darkened room with his skinny friend and a quasi-stranger. And, for some reason, a sledgehammer.

Puts the empty carton down.

Can I have my robe?

Lesser, I thought you'd never ask.

Lesser's out of the bed, in an overstuffed chair now, in his robe. Terry-cloth. Underwashed. Seen better days. Hopefully better bodies too.

Lesser's only early twenties, but he's flabby enough for fifty. Stringy chin-length hair. Skin the color of the great indoors. Complexion like drywall.

He continues.

So I slip in, full-on cloak-mode? I can see him, no one can see me, unless they're looking for me, which they definitely aren't. Not in a room that's so full of distractions. We're talking wall-to-wall centerfolds. Oiled-up curves in all directions. Like some vintage Playboy-mansion shit. And this dude—

Lesser leans in, like he's telling us a secret.

—this dude has a thing for amputees. Total weirdo fetish. So half of these ladies are, like, legless. Armless. I don't know. A few—

That's interesting, Lesser. But I'm guessing that's not what sent you out here screaming.

No. So. Any case. Finance dude. Buff as shit. In there, anyway. On the outside, he's, like, seventy. But in there, dude's a Golden God. Like he just surfed down from Olympus—

Lesser—

Okay. So orgy. The usual. Room is decked out in this kind of, I don't know, Victorian drawing-room wallpaper. Couches everywhere, the old-fashioned kind, with velvet. Dude is *jacked*. Really overdoes it on the cock length. God, these coots and their fantasies. I'm talking *javelin*—

Lesser—

Sorry. So all proceeds as expected. Then there's a knock at the door. And—dude seems surprised. Not scared, exactly. Not yet. Just—curious. Maybe a little annoyed. At first.

Okay.

So the door opens, and holy shit—there's like—first the temperature drops. Like sub-zero. And these—the centerfolds? They start just—glitching out. Freezing up. Like the whole program's seizing. So of course finance dude is super-pissed now. Because this is a mad-expensive construct—

But who's at the door?

Lesser crosses his arms. Holds himself. Looks around.

I gotta go. We can't stay here. We gotta go.

Stares back at me.

We gotta get out of here.

Lesser, who was there?

Black eyes.

Says it twice.

Black eyes.

Black guys?

No. Black eyes. Just her eyes. Floating there. You couldn't see her at all. She was cloaked. Floating. She was wearing—what do you call it—

Lesser gestures. Full-body. Head-to-toe. Searches for the word.

—you know, like a ghost.

A ghost?

Yeah. A black ghost.

I puzzle it out. Find the word.

You mean a burqa?

Lesser nods.

Yeah. A burqa. So all you could see were her eyes. These black eyes.

Lesser shivers.

This banker dude, he just starts *laughing*. Completely naked. Starts laughing, like this is some present someone sent him to spice things up. Like some prank. This woman in a burqa. She isn't moving. Just watching him. And he, like, walks right up to her, totally naked, this javelin dude. And he looks at her and says, *What's this? A present? For me? Well, then, let's unwrap it.* He leans in real close. Says to her, all low-like, *I'm going to* peel *you.*

Then what happened?

Lesser's eyes empty. Answers in a whisper.

Oh. She peeled him.

Skinny pipes up.

Oh shit.

Lesser spooked now.

She had this blade—

Barely croaking out his story.

—this curved blade. Just cut him right down the front. Just *skinned* him—but left him alive—

And then what?

I mean, everyone else there is *freaking*. Centerfolds just *glitch-*

ing. Two or three start scrambling for the exit—I don't know, I think maybe two or three of the women were real? I mean, attached to someone real, out here. Girlfriends, call girls, I don't know. But they're shrieking, yelling *Security! Security!* like that's going to help, and this woman's got some fucking curved, I don't know, like, sword that she's pulled out. From beneath her robe. Blade's all bloody now. She just *split* him, man. Down the front. And this fucking *skin*—she's holding his fucking *skin*—

Lesser stops. Gags. Throws up milk.

Splatters on the hardwood.

Wipes his mouth.

Proceeds to paint a vivid picture, despite the occasional retching.

Woman in a black burqa. With a bloody blade.

Floats among the centerfolds.

Makes new amputees.

What then, Lesser?

What *then*? What *then* is I'm scrambling and fucking signaling *this* shitstain to tap me out—

Points to Skinny.

—I'm fucking screaming every safe word I know—

And that's when you tapped out?

No. No, not right then. But thank God he started pulling me back—

What happened?

What happened? She blew up.

Lesser relives it. Voice rasping now.

She just reached her arms around the banker and then she blew herself up—

We watch it flicker across his face like a movie screen.

—everyone everywhere. Body parts. Fucking fire. I'm on fire—

Skinny flinches.

Holy shit—

—and I'm fucking screaming, they're all screaming, and I'm *burning*—

Story ends. Movie's over.

Last frame of the horror film looping on Lesser's blank face.

Lesser and Moore have both more or less lost it.

Moore crying. Lesser babbling.

Don't you see? If she's figured that out—

I press him.

Lesser, figured *what* out—

—if they can bust in to a construct, blow it up, and kill you like that, blow you to shit, then we're all fucked. Don't you see?

Who, Lesser?

That *dude*. The banker—

But Lesser, he's not dead. Not really—

Trust me, man, I've seen a million deaths in the limn. This was different. Someone cracked it—

Lesser, that's nuts—

—and if they could bust in there, and do that, and now that dude is dead for real—

But you didn't die, Lesser. You're fine. You got out—

Don't you get it? It's bad enough when they blew it all up out here. They blew this fucking city up. Don't you remember? Out here—

Lesser, you're out. You're okay—

—limn's the last place we have. But now if they're in there? In the fucking *limn*?—

You'll be okay.

—if they can find you in the fucking *dream*—

Lesser—

—find you in there and fucking kill you there too? Then no one's safe. No one's safe. Don't you see?

Obviously, after that, I let Lesser live.

Hard to hear a story like that, then say, Great. Thanks. Just one more thing—

Plus I want to figure out exactly what Lesser saw in there. Because what Lesser's describing, in his babbling way, shouldn't be possible.

To be killed while you're inside the limn.

But then, no one understands that better than a hopper like Lesser. And he certainly seems convinced.

I ask him one last time.

Who was it, Lesser? Who did you see in there?

He pauses. Says nothing. Like he's thinking. Weighing something. Then says simply.

I don't know. I don't know.

What about the banker?

Just some guy I peep on. Don't know his real-time details.

So how can we find out if he's actually dead?

Lesser looks up at me. Still spooked. And still certain.

Trust me. He is. I know.

I leave Lesser with Skinny and another twenty dollars. Don't know why. Maybe buy some Band-Aids.

Then I head back to Hoboken, thinking about what he said.

Not her. Not here.

Terrorists blew this city up twice. The real one, I mean.

World Trade and Times Square. Both left a lingering impression. And the last one left a toxic aftertaste.

It's been quiet for a while. What with everybody dreaming.

But if they've found a way to break into the dream—

———

Personally, I'm not much for the tap-in.
    I did my time in the beds but it didn't stick.
    I prefer the nuts-and-bolts world.
    Aches and pains. Bricks and mortar.
    Treasure it, really.
    But I take Lesser's point.
    This crippled city can't live without its crutch.

4.

Mark Ray picks me up the next day, early Sunday morning, at my apartment in Hoboken, for our weekly drive upstate. I tell him Lesser's story, then ask him to explain what it means to me.

Turns out his explanation is very short.

It's not possible.

You sure about that?

He laughs, then steers our rented minivan toward the mouth of the Holland Tunnel.

What's the first rule of the limnosphere, Spademan?

Mark says this like he's talking to a child.

You tell me, Mark.

You can't be killed through the limn. That's the first and only rule. Not even a rule, really. More like a law. Like gravity.

I thought anything was possible in the limn. I thought that was the whole sales pitch.

Anything but that.

Why not?

Mark gets serious. After all, he's a bed-rest junkie. So he can only joke about the limn for so long.

Says solemnly.

Because if you could find a way to kill someone through the limn, Spademan—to find someone in there and kill them so that they died out here? That would be the end of it. The limn would no longer be viable. If it was that dangerous? Game over. They'd have to flip the switch and shut the whole thing down.

———

Mark's a former youth pastor, hails from Minnesota, with a moptop of unruly blond curls, so he looks like the heartthrob lead singer for some '60s surfer band, the guy all the girls would swoon over. Sadly for them, girls aren't his preference. Misplaced guilt over that is what drove him out of the ministry. Away from the church. Toward New York and full-time bed-rest.

Good heart, though. Good person. Probably the best one I know, though that might be faint praise, given the kind of people I know. And he would probably take issue at the compliment. Mark's hard on himself that way.

Grips the steering wheel with two tattooed hands, DAMN written across the knuckles of one fist, ABLE across the other.

DAMN and ABLE.

DAMNABLE.

Pretty much sums up Mark's life philosophy.

He slows the van as we get closer to the Holland Tunnel, inching us past the rows of cops keeping watch. Finally one waves us through and we speed up and plunge into the shiny swallowing brightness of the tunnel. We could easily just drive straight north through Jersey, hook up with the Thruway once we're far from the city, since we're headed to upstate New York. But like a proud Manhattanite, Mark wants to show off the rebuilt Holland, fully restored and back to full capacity, ribbon cut just a few weeks ago. The Holland Tunnel spent most of the years since Times Square half-closed and under construction, ever since a Times Square copycat barreled a wood-paneled station wagon packed with homemade explosives down the tunnel's windpipe, got halfway to Manhattan, then blew the car up.

Took out a tour bus, two taxis, and a tiny chunk of the tunnel's ceiling.

But when you're a tunnel buried under a hundred feet of water, a tiny chunk of the ceiling is enough.

Tunnel flooded. Then lay abandoned for a long while, waiting for federal funds that weren't forthcoming. Then the city finally pumped it out and patched it and reopened it at half capacity, the occasional cars braving the darkness with fingers crossed and highbeams on.

Cars full of people packed up and leaving New York.

Then this year the mayor made a big deal of restoring it. A more cynical mind might suggest the mayor's newfound interest in infrastructure has something to do with his reelection campaign. Or the fact that, for the first time since Times Square, he's facing a real fight this fall. Supercop named Robert Bellarmine. Tabloids dubbed him *Top Cop*. He's head of the city's antiterrorism task force, appointed after Times Square to try and stop the bleeding. Return a few punches, which he did. Not sure how many of those punches landed on actual terrorists, but they definitely sent a message.

Now Robert Bellarmine's back with a new message.

As we exit the tunnel into Manhattan, we pass a huge billboard that reads BELLARMINE FOR MAYOR.

Serious scowl under a bristling black mustache and, below that, a campaign slogan that looms two stories high.

VOTE BELLARMINE. SLEEP TIGHT.

Every Sunday Mark and I take the same drive upstate. Mark picks me up in Jersey, then we head north out of New York. Always rents the same car for us too. Big white minivan, even though it's just the two of us. Says he likes the legroom. Rents it from this discount place, one of the last few that still bother to operate in the city. None of the national chains stuck around, so you settle for dicey mom-and-pops like this one.

Check-Off Rentals. Slogan stenciled on the side of the mini-van.

CHECK-OFF: ONE LESS THING TO DO ON YOUR TO-DO LIST.

Personally, I'd prefer to splurge on something sporty, but Mark likes his minivan. Likes to call it a magic wagon. I told him no one ever calls them that anymore.

Not true, he said. I do.

So every Sunday, we head upstate in our magic wagon. Usually we don't talk much. Enjoy the scenery. But today I have questions. I lay out the rest of Lesser's scenario.

Mark shakes his head.

Like I said. Not possible.

But I've seen you bust into constructs before.

Sure. That woman crashing someone else's construct is not the issue. Killing that someone is the issue. I mean, you can slice and dice a person all you like in the limn, that doesn't mean he's got a scratch on him out here. You sure this guy she attacked is even dead?

I'm not even sure who he is. Some banker with perversions.

Mark laughs.

That hardly narrows it down. Look, you can't kill someone through the limn. Period. So your banker probably woke up somewhere in a high-end bed with a nasty headache and a few second thoughts. Unhappy, but unharmed.

Mark's right. I've done enough tapping to know, way back when I used to tap in. You can punch me in the limn, and I'll feel the punch, and the pain, might even taste the blood, but it's not real, it's all in my mind, sensations piped directly to my brain. Chances are your body and my body are miles away from each other out here, in the real-time world, strapped into our respective beds. And no amount of damage in there is actually going to kill me out here. Limn won't allow it. It will spit me out first.

So I ask Mark.

What if I pull out an ax and chop your head off? In the limn?

Won't kill me.

You just run around without a head?

Sure. For a while.

What if I toss you into a wood chipper? Like in that old movie?

Doesn't matter. Construct just ejects me eventually, Spademan, once the scenario is no longer viable. You'd still be there but I'd disappear. Wake up in my bed.

And what about those tricks you do?

What tricks?

Like with the wings.

Mark smiles.

Look, if you tap in enough, you get good at stuff like that. Conjuring things. You can't alter the basic construct but you can alter your presence in the construct. Choose your appearance. Give yourself different attributes. Like wings, for example. That part is baked into the limn, like an added feature. I once saw a guy reattach an arm that had been sliced off in a sword fight, just through sheer force of will. I have to admit, it was impressive.

And who sliced his arm off?

Mark shrugs.

He got cheeky.

Explain one last thing to me, Mark.

What's that?

If all that's true, then what exactly did Lesser see?

Mark frowns. Watches the road. Frowns deeper. Then says.

I don't know.

Because Lesser's seen a lot. My guess is he's not easily spooked.

I know. That I can't explain. I mean, Lesser knows his stuff. He's a special kid, Spademan.

Why? Because he knows how to peep in on other people's dreams?

Mark looks at me. Like he's surprised I don't know this part.

Spademan, Lesser's not just some random bed-hopper. Lesser's the one who found the glitch in the limn that makes bed-hopping possible.

We drop the conversation, continue north, watch the city shrink in the rearview. Manhattan gives way to the Bronx gives way to Westchester gives way to the woods. All of it more or less empty now.

Woods are prettier, though.

As we drive, Mark finally asks me the question I know he's been itching to ask me.

Why in the world were you talking to Lesser anyway?

We just ran into each other.

Mark's skeptical. Understandably.

He's a good kid, Spademan. He doesn't deserve whatever you had in store for him.

This time I frown.

Who does?

After that, we drive in silence. Then Mark spots our exit, turns off the freeway, and takes us deeper into the woods.

The whole time, Mark's lost in thought. Seems puzzled. Definitely troubled. For all his self-diagnosed faults, he's a choirboy at heart. Doesn't drink. Doesn't smoke. Rarely curses. So maybe that's why I find it alarming when he finally pipes up.

Bottom line, you can't die in the limn, Spademan. Lesser must have been wrong. He must have misunderstood.

Mutters this last part to himself, almost like a plaintive prayer.

Or at least I really fucking hope he did.

5.

Ever since Times Square, upstate is thriving.

Village of Beacon.

Case in point.

Beacon's a onetime whistle-stop town with an optimistic name that more or less died when all the factories closed down. Sat fallow for a long while. Eventually cheap rents attracted artistic types. Then came Times Square. Then the big New York exodus.

Upstate towns started swelling again.

Beacon most of all.

Suddenly it's a boomtown. Which is also a funny phrase.

Boomtown.

Different context, same name could apply to New York.

Lots of back-to-the-land types live in Beacon now. People who figured, Fuck the toxic city—let's move to Green Acres and start again. Found a farm. Take up needlepoint. Loose the kids to run around barefoot. Make public declarations to live limnosphere-free. A whole village unplugged. Communal rules tacked to the town-hall door, decided by a show of hands. Hippie paradise, or what used to be called hippies anyway. These types are more clean-cut. Better funded. Drive hybrids. Still wear overalls, but bespoke.

Happy hamlet on a river, more or less cut off from the wired-up world. Not much to not like. And a great place to relocate.

Or, in our case, to relocate a friend.

———

We skip Main Street.

Drive straight through town without stopping.

After a few more miles, find a side road that no one would ever think to notice. Follow that road for a bit to a dirt turn-off that's little more than tire tracks in the soil. Not listed on any maps, and fuck GPS. We turn right and head down a passage choked by dead limbs. A few good-sized rocks in the mud ruts to ward off the curious.

It's another bumpy twenty minutes before we even see the house.

Cedar cottage, tucked into a hidden pocket of the woods. You'd never spot it unless you knew to look.

Mark turns in the long dirt driveway, inching forward, branches scratching like beggars at the windows, then pulls the van around back to park.

She's already in the doorway by the time we mount the porch.

What happened? You guys decide to stop in town for souvenirs?

Wipes her hands on her flower-print skirt. Leaves flour prints. Sees our skeptical faces. Smiles.

Yes, I'm baking a pie.

Raises one flour-dusted finger.

And if either of you says a word about it, you won't get a fucking slice.

Wild curls hogtied in some mockery of a ponytail.

Hard to tame.

Just like her.

Persephone.

Exiled in her backwoods hideaway.

Inside, the cabin smells of cabin. Knotted rugs and rocking chairs. Drop-leaf table with a frail lace tablecloth and an honest-to-God kerosene lamp in the center, kept in case of blackout. Power's spotty this far out from the civilized world.

Lamp's not exactly childproof, though. I'll have to mention that.

Look at me. Babyproofing.

Place is small but cozy. Turns out Persephone's got a homesteader streak. Bakes a pie every so often. Even embroidered a sampler. As she'll be the first to tell you, these days she's got plenty of time on her hands.

Sampler's hung over the door. Her favorite Bible verse.

2 Thessalonians, chapter 3, verse 3.

The Lord is faithful. He will establish you and protect you against the evil one.

Verse edged in needlepoint flowers and thorned ivy. Persephone's touch. A deft stitch. She notices me noticing. So I ask her.

And who's the evil one?

She folds her arms across her chest.

I don't know yet. I just hope I do by the time he darkens my door.

It's a good verse.

Yeah, I liked it as a girl. Last year I actually thought about getting it as a tattoo. Right here.

Traces her finger along the inside of her right forearm.

So why didn't you?

She shrugs.

Not safe to get a tattoo while you're pregnant.

So why not now?

She looks over at her daughter. Smiling baby, sitting up on a blanket, playing in the corner. Beautiful girl. Light of the world.

I have to set a good example, right?

6.

When I first met Persephone, a year or so ago, she was pregnant and on the run. From her father, or so she told me. Also told me he was the one who'd put her in a family way.

Funny phrase. Family way.

Turned out to be a lie. She was pregnant, but not by her father. I forgave her the lie, though, because the truth about her father turned out to be much worse.

Her father was a preacher. His name was T. K. Harrow. And he'd collected an extensive catalogue of sins in his life. A few of them ancient and familiar. A few of them impressively inventive.

For starters, he'd hired me to kill his own daughter.

But that didn't work out so well for him.

T. K. Harrow was a famous evangelist and head of a megachurch called Crystal Corral, nationally known, widely influential, and completely corrupt. He's now enjoying his eternal rest in a quiet graveyard in Vermont.

Knife through the heart at the hands of his daughter.

Twist ending.

He never saw it coming.

Okay, I confess.

I helped.

Railroad spike. Through the forehead. In his bed. While he was tapped in.

So she stabbed him in the limn while I killed him for real out here. Which means I killed him in the way that counted. But we had to kill him in both places, at the exact same moment. Only way to trap him in the loop.

The loop was Persephone's idea, actually. There's a theory that if you're killed out here while you're tapped into the limn, then your very last moment in the limnosphere loops. Your consciousness persists as a last burst of electricity, living that last moment in the limn forever. Seems unlikely to me, but then again, in Harrow's case, it didn't much matter.

See, for him, the best-case scenario is that he's dead and buried out here.

That's the best-case scenario.

Worst case is that he's dead and buried out here, while in there he's stuck forever, the last electrical spasms of his expiring brain dying in the limn, over and over again, at his daughter's hand.

Either way, it's an outcome I can live with.

Official cause of death was a heart attack.

Funny diagnosis, given the spike wound. But they needed something to tell CNN.

So that's what his church announced, and all the news channels ran with it. The official story was that T. K. Harrow died peacefully in his sleep after a lifetime of saintly service and has now gone on to his heavenly reward.

That was the official story. Though that version took a hit when the first of his victims came forward.

See, Harrow ran an operation on the side called Paved With Gold. Big initiative. Lots of converts. Pitched as heaven, right now, in the limnosphere. The idea was to create a glorious afterlife, here on Earth, that overeager converts could tap into today, without having to wait until after their actual lives.

Why wait?

That was the pitch, anyway.

Harrow promised his flock a sneak peek at heaven.

Delivered something different.

If he liked you, he tapped you into a dream. Not your dream, though. The dream of one of the church's richest donors. Then Harrow trapped you there. As the donor's plaything.

A creep named Milgram, Harrow's right-hand man, worked out all the technical details.

Milgram's also passed on to his eternal reward, by the way.

Box-cutter to the windpipe. No family plot or tidy burial. Met his end in an incinerator.

Just flames, which is all he deserved.

And Paved With Gold's been shuttered now. The compound down South has been razed to the ground, and the Crystal Corral church, the one Harrow left behind, underwent an extensive purge under interim leadership. The whole Paved With Gold endeavor was denounced as a rogue operation, blame laid squarely at the feet of Milgram, which was convenient, since he's dead, so he can't protest too loudly.

All the victims of Paved With Gold, and there were many, dozens of them, spent a few weeks as national cable-news curiosities. Trotted out for tearful interviews. Consoled by outraged pundits who'd pound their fists on shaky stage-scenery desks and wonder what this country was coming to. A group of the victims even banded together and launched a class-action suit against Crystal Corral.

Settled quietly. Fat damages in exchange for nondisclosures.

Victims went silent. News story went dormant.

Some of the survivors got shuttled off to therapy.

A handful hanged themselves.

But just a handful.

May God, or Whoever, rest their souls.

————

And Crystal Corral survives. Somehow.

Even prospers.

No thanks to Simon the Magician.

Simon was Harrow's other lieutenant, his head of security. Calls himself Simon the Magician after a real-life biblical-era charlatan. And like his namesake, Simon the Magician is a man of flexible ethics. He betrayed Harrow, and had a hand in Harrow's end, then made his own play for power. Nasty fellow, with a sadistic streak.

Also, Simon is the father of Persephone's child.

Twist number two. The one I didn't see coming.

After all that, Simon and I don't really get along.

Thankfully, Simon's not around much these days. Last I heard, he's too busy angling to ascend to Harrow's throne. Though I also heard he's having some trouble making the sale. As it turns out, many of the Crystal Corral's devoted followers, goodhearted folk though they may be, aren't quite ready to be led to the Promised Land by a man of color.

Which must be driving Simon the Magician crazy.

Since every man ever mentioned in the Bible was a man of color.

As for Persephone, after her father's death, she stayed near New York City.

Hoboken, to be specific. My place.

I slept on the couch for months.

While Persephone got bigger. Then bigger.

Then popped.

Gave birth to a beautiful baby girl.

New York native. Manhattan-born. I'd pushed for Jersey but got outvoted. So when the time came, I ferried pregnant

Persephone across the river to St Luke's. Escorted her to Emergency.

Afterward, in the hospital room, Persephone held her newborn girl, swaddled in blankets, and cried. Then laughed. Then announced she was naming her Hannah.

Another Bible story. Hannah, the woman who prayed to God to let her have a child. Which He did.

A miracle, they say.

Hannah.

Translates as God has favored me.

Plus, it's a palindrome. Same backwards and forwards. Persephone likes that. Thinks it's lucky.

And it turns out Hannah has another meaning too, Mark Ray told me later. In this case, it seemed especially appropriate.

Persephone's given name is Grace Chastity Harrow.

Persephone's just her chosen name.

Now her daughter's given name is Hannah.

Which also translates as Grace.

Grace Junior.

At that point, I figured we'd all part ways.

Keep in touch. Swap hugs. Promise postcards. Once Persephone got back on her feet.

I'd get my bedroom back. Go back to the day job.

Back to being a bullet.

Killing people.

Simple.

Once I knew Persephone and Hannah were safe somewhere.

After all, New York's no place to raise a child. And the rest of America's still big. And still functional. For the most part.

Amber waves of grain and purple mountains, etcetera.

But Persephone decided she wanted to stay. Her and Hannah. Make a go of it.

Can't say I understood, but it's her family.

Tried to set her up in Hoboken. Except we found out there were complicating factors.

See, Harrow may be gone, but Harrow still has plenty of followers. And his flock heard that Harrow's eldest daughter, the runaway, was still alive. And that she'd had a child.

Turns out a few in the flock blame Persephone for orchestrating Harrow's downfall. And a few of them consider her to be the rightful heir to his church. And a few of them even seem to believe her child is some kind of chosen one, destined to deliver the world from, well, take your pick.

All of them are crazy, by the way.

A few of the crazies found their way north in the weeks after Hannah was born.

Tracked her down. Tracked them both down, mother and child, to my apartment in Hoboken.

These were the members of the flock who saw Hannah as some kind of usurper.

Usurper.

Interesting word. Had to look it up.

Apparently it means you think you have good reason to kill a baby.

Either way, these followers showed up in Hoboken.

Half dozen of them. Well armed. With bad intentions.

Unlucky for them, I happened to be home at the time.

Which is how Persephone wound up here, outside Beacon, stashed in the woods. Safe at her safe house. For the time being, at least.

As for what comes later, I don't know yet. We're still figuring that part out. In the meantime, Mark and I drive out every week to visit. Keep her company. Bring her groceries.

See Hannah.

I confess. I'm biased.

But best I can tell, she is the perfect child.

Cherub's face. Rascal's laugh. Eyes that don't miss anything.

Tangle of toffee-colored curls. Like her mother. Like her father. Got her curls coming and going.

Persephone's white. Simon's black.

Hannah's both.

Little Einstein too. That's already obvious.

And stubborn. Just like her mother.

Hannah's just over a year old, so she doesn't talk much yet. Kid of few words. Which I can respect.

Mostly babble, though I could have sworn I heard her say Spademan once.

Persephone calls me her uncle.

Uncle Spademan.

Have to admit.

Has a certain ring.

7.

We sit out on the porch and eat pie.

Hannah's in the corner, playing in her playpen. Mark's sprawled out in a wicker chair, china dish balanced on his lap. Only crumbs left on the dish.

Me and Persephone share a porchswing.

Truth is, porchswings never factored into any life I ever pictured for myself.

Porchswings and box-cutters. Strange marriage.

But I sit on the porchswing with this makeshift family and watch the peaceful woods. Listen to the soothing sounds of crickets and tree frogs and Persephone complaining loudly once again.

Like all families, we squabble.

Maybe more than most.

Persephone slumps and pouts. Kicks her feet. Rocks the porchswing. Makes the same plea all over again.

Two hours from the city and we can't even go in for a visit? Can't even take a grocery run into town? Spademan, staying out here was supposed to be temporary.

It is temporary.

What the fuck? We've been out here almost a year. That's not temporary. That's penitentiary.

Hey.

What?

I nod toward Hannah.

Language.

Persephone smirks. Stage whispers.

Fuck you.

She has a point. I pay Margo, my old nurse friend from Hackensack, to drive out a few days a week and check in on Hannah. Provide some company. Play cards with Persephone.

Crazy Eights. Old Maid.

Somehow I don't think that's helping.

Peresephone sits up straight on the swing and lists off her grievances.

There are still museums open in New York, Spademan. You know that, right? You've heard of those? Museums?

Like what?

I don't know. The big ones. The Frick. Maybe MoMA. Look, I know it's not really your thing, but museums are good for kids. Hannah needs stimulation. She needs friends. Eventually she'll need school. God, I need friends. I need *something*. I'm nineteen, but out here I feel like I'm ninety. You know what I did the other day? I started quilting a fucking quilt, Spademan.

Quilting is a lost art.

She slugs my arm. Porchswing sways. Then she pulls out a pack of cigarettes.

I frown.

Since when did you start smoking?

She taps one loose.

Helps pass the time.

I nod toward the baby again. Persephone scowls.

It's fine, Spademan. We're on the porch.

She digs out a matchpack. Tries to strike one, but the damp matchheads won't spark. She chucks the matchpack in the underbrush, then growls.

This fucking humidity is killing me.

I pull out a Zippo, spark it, and she dips her cigarette in the flame. Then I hand her the lighter.

Keep it. I have plenty. And it might come in handy.

She shrugs and pockets the Zippo, then takes a long pull and exhales like a forlorn sigh. Watching her smoking reminds me of being nineteen, restless and invincible, which for me is about twenty years ago.

Correction. Fifteen years ago.

Let's not get ahead of ourselves.

She takes another drag. Exhales slowly. Then spills it.

So I heard from Simon.

Really.

Yep. Called my cell. I could barely hear him. You know how hard it is to get a signal up here?

Why did he call you?

Spademan, it's his daughter too. If he can't visit, at least he can check in.

What did he say?

He told me once he deals with the situation at Crystal Corral, he can come out here and rescue me. Sweep me off my feet. Take me away from all this.

I don't want him near you.

She takes another pull.

I don't particularly want him near us either, but I'm going fucking crazy up here.

Look on the bright side.

What bright side?

Hold my fork up. Tines licked clean.

You're getting really good at making pie.

She sneers, slugs my arm again, harder this time, not smiling, then she flings her pie-smeared china plate like a Frisbee off the porch and into the woods.

Stay the night at least. There's a guest room.

I have got to get back. I have someone I need to see.

Persephone, disappointed.

Sure. Of course.

Mark pipes up.

I can stay. As long as you remember to return the minivan.

Tosses me the keys. I tell him thanks, because I know, despite his protests, that it's a burden for him to be away from the beds. Even a few days hurts.

I tell Persephone.

See? Now you've got some company. You can teach Mark to play Go Fish.

One last hug. Then I'm off.

Hoist Hannah.

Pleasing heft.

Tell her.

Be good for your mother.

She giggles. Of course.

Plays me for a chump every time.

On the way out of town, I stop in Beacon, at a hardware store. Ask about an A/C unit. Not surprisingly, they're sold out. Clerk tells me there's a heat wave coming. They're expecting a shipment, so he says he'll put one aside for me once they come in. Asks for a delivery address, which I'm not about to give him. So I pay up, then tell him to hold the unit when it arrives and I'll have a friend drive in and pick it up.

Make a mental note to call Mark about it.

After all, it is summer.

And I'm not a monster.

Not all the time anyway.

There's one other reason I stashed Persephone near Beacon. Before everything ended with Harrow and Milgram, they dangled a bit of information, hoping to buy me off. Information about a seventh man involved in the Times Square bombing.

A motorman.

Subway driver who may have helped in the attack on the train that exploded about an hour before Times Square. Milgram thought I might be interested.

Since my wife was on that train.

And while I didn't take his bait, I was definitely listening.

The clue-gathering part of my job is not the part I've ever been good at. The Colonel Mustard in the Library with the Candlestick part.

I played that game as a kid exactly once, by the way, with my dad, back when he was still alive. I was maybe ten, sitting at the kitchen table. My mom was half playing, half finishing the dishes.

About forty minutes into it, my father finally got fed up, tore open the little envelope, and read all the cards out loud: Mrs Peacock in the Kitchen with the Wrench. Then he tossed the cards on the table and said, If anyone needs me, I'll be the Father in the TV Room with the Beer.

In his defense, it's a stupid game.

And I never did get much better at it.

Still, I did a little digging on the motorman.

Found a lead.

Thin lead.

But a lead.

Just a name. A few details. And an address.

Guess where.

So on my way through Beacon, I plan a detour past his house.

Just want to talk to the guy.

Just talk.

Nothing untoward.

Not really.

Not yet.

Roll the van past slow.

Driveway's empty. Lights extinguished. No one's home.

And no time for me to wait around, since I need to get back to the city and check on Lesser's banker.

Motorman will have to wait. Lesser's case is still nagging at me, and I want to put that whole thing to rest.

Was supposed to be simple. Might still be.

Because if I track down Lesser's banker and find out he's still alive, still tapped in and dreaming blissfully, that means Lesser was wrong, and the attack he witnessed was just a hoax or some kind of prank, and I can drop the whole thing and simply finish the job on Lesser.

Finish Lesser.

Then again, there's a chance I go back and find out that the banker's dead, and Lesser was right, and what he saw was real, and someone's found a way to kill you while you're in the limn.

And if that's true?

Forget Lesser.

Because I'll have bigger problems. We all will.

City's crippled, but this would kill it.

Watch it spiral into panic.

Into chaos.

Into worse.

8.

Unlike Mark, I don't bother with the scenic route.

Drive the ugly Major Deegan Expressway instead, right down the gullet of the Bronx.

City's quiet.

Skyline's stoic.

You'd barely know it's slowly dying.

Upside is, I make very good time to Chinatown.

Park the minivan in an alleyway. Lock it up tight. Lots of sticky fingers in Chinatown.

Autolock beeps as I click the fob. Then I pull out my phone to call Mark about the A/C unit. Terrible reception, so I have to tell him twice. Then he reminds me that he doesn't have a car.

You took it, remember?

Of course. Fuck. I forgot. So I tell Mark.

Okay, listen, maybe I'll call Margo, have her pick it up next time she's headed out there. Could be a few days, though.

I heard we're expecting a heat wave, Spademan.

Tell Persephone I'll do my best.

Hang up with Mark. Add another errand to my to-do list.

Then think back to the good old days.

Spademan, alone in Tribeca, early morning, walking the cobblestones.

Taking phone calls.

Killing people.

Carefree.

Before I suddenly found myself with a family.

In Chinatown, I drop in on Mina Machina.

She's the former life partner of Rick the tech-head, an old friend of mine who's no longer with us, thanks to Simon, which is another thing on the long list of things that Simon has to answer for. As for Mina, she's also a crack limn technician, a so-called gizmo, just like Rick was, maybe even better, definitely more unreliable. She used to be a serious tapper, but she swears she gave it all up after Rick was killed. Now she's head-clear, she claims, and running Rick's Place, his old flop-shop, one of the many discount tap-in joints you'll find in emptied-out Chinatown. Huge open floor full of beds, just tricked-out cots really, laid out in rows like a battlefield hospital. She changed the name of the place, though. Too many memories, she said.

Rechristened it the Kakumu Lounge. For a classier clientele.

Told me *Kakumu*'s Japanese slang for *tourist dream*. The dream you have when you're away from home.

Only the Japanese would have a word for that.

Mina used to have a witch's nest of waist-length staticky black hair, long bangs, kind of her trademark, but now it's all shorn to the skull.

Sign of mourning, she says.

I admit, it brings her eyes out nicely.

Like I'm a hairdresser now.

We sit in the cramped reception room on a couple of beanbag chairs. I sink slowly and ask Mina about my banker, the one that Lesser peeped on. From Lesser's description, the banker definitely doesn't sound like the type who'd frequent a Chinatown flop-shop. No doubt he's got his own luxury setup in a penthouse somewhere, a nurse, a top-notch bed, the whole works. But hoppers gossip, notoriously, and gizmos and hoppers talk. And if someone has a particularly weird or notable fetish like, say, orgies with amputee centerfolds, that tends to get around. Tends to trickle down, even to Mina.

She scratches her shorn head. Thinks a minute.

Still exhibits a bit of that tapper's cognitive delay.

Dressed in all black, also for mourning. Long black cloak. Black socks in bamboo sandals. Heavy eyeliner. Even heavier than normal.

Still has that cross-shaped scar on her forehead too, though it's faded a bit.

Another souvenir from Simon.

And yet another thing he has to answer for.

Mina thinks.

Then Mina speaks.

And ever since she quit the tap, with her, when it comes, it comes in torrents.

Yeah, I heard of a guy, banker dude, big money, you know the amputee thing is not that uncommon, but, as you know, some people get off on knowing they're playing with the real thing out here, so this guy, he likes to hire amputee call girls, real ones, then tap them in, for that extra bit of verisimilitude.

Amputee call girls?

Mina shrugs.

Hey, it's a thing.

Then she tells me the name of the banker she heard of who pays top dollar to recruit these call girls. Name's Piers Langland. Lives at Astor Place, so she heard, in that fancy glass condo tower, the one that's made out of wavy blue glass and kind of looks like it's melting.

Astor Place is not such a long walk from Chinatown, and it's a nice day, so I thank Mina and head out, figuring I'll stroll over and pay this Piers Langland a visit, ask a few questions, while the memory of him getting skinned and then blown up by a suicide bomber in the limn is still fresh in his mind.

Stop on the street corner and pull out my phone. Dial directory assistance. Ask the automated operator to patch me through to the main desk at Langland's building.

Doorman answers. I ask for Mr Langland.

Short silence.

I'm sorry to be the one to tell you this, sir, but Mr Langland passed away peacefully in his bed just last night.

Accept the doorman's condolences.

Then snap the phone shut.

Could be just a coincidence, right?

Which is right about the moment when a police cruiser makes a noisy U-turn on Canal Street, jumps the curb ten feet in front of me, and looses a pair of loud whoops from the siren just to make sure it's got my attention.

Driver waves me over.

Driver looks Hispanic. The other cop, a black woman in dark sunglasses, her cap tugged low, sits silent in the passenger seat. The first cop, the driver, is hatless with a military haircut, crisp and precise, and the elbow of his waving-over arm is propped out the driver's-side window. It's so hot out that he's wearing regulation short sleeves. Arm's tattooed to the elbow. It still always surprises me to see cops with sleeve tattoos.

His ink is fancier than most, though. No girlfriends' names or hula girls or ribboned banners reading MOM.

Just snakes and flames.

I approach the patrol car.

Can I help you, Officer?

Spademan, just get in.

I could run, but I'm not much for track and field.

Besides, they've got a car. And they're cops.

So I get in.

Slide into the backseat, which is sealed up, hot and airless as a kiln, with at least an inch of scratched Plexiglas separating me from my chauffeurs. Full of lingering odors from former occupants, who were either scared into soiling themselves in the backseat or just smelled that way before they got inside.

Either way, backseat's foul.

Summer heat isn't helping.

Cop car makes another screeching U-turn on Canal that acquaints me abruptly with the other side of the backseat.

I spend the rest of the drive to midtown wondering how the cop knew my name.

9.

Cop cruiser takes the empty FDR north at full lights and sirens. Not necessary, since there's no traffic.

But cops do love their lights.

After Times Square, the NYPD took a lot of blame and a lot of abuse, and deserved at least a little of both. Times Square wasn't like the first time, on 9/11, when everyone in uniform came off as selfless heroes. When Times Square happened, it had been nearly twenty years and countless foiled plots since 9/11, so people had forgotten how to be properly scared. Now they were just jaded and pissed. And unfortunately for the NYPD, safeguarding the city is the kind of job that, even if you fuck up just once, you've failed.

They fucked up twice.

First the subway bomb. The one that killed my wife.

Random incident maybe. Hard to predict. Hard to stop. But still.

Then came Times Square, an hour after that.

Dirty bomb. Long plotted. Dots that should have been connected. Money transfers, online chatter, all leaving traceable trails in the ether.

Bad guys' fingerprints were all over it, in hindsight.

Radioactive fingerprints. Practically glow-in-the-dark.

Of course, second-guessing is easy. First-guessing is what counts. And with Times Square, they simply guessed wrong.

Cops, feds, everyone.

A national tragedy.

All the car bombs that came after just felt like a bad hang-over, like bad news on top of bad news.

At first, there was a lot of sword rattling, of course. Press conferences with stoic cops in full dress uniform in front of a row of crisp flags. Strident vows of stepped-up vigilance. Fists hammering lecterns to drive home the point.

We. Shall. Not. Let. This. Pass.

Podiums took a real beating that year.

From the mayor, and the governor, and the president, all the way up the food chain, endless promises about new funding, extra training, renewed resolve. Then the city hired Robert Bellarmine, the crack expert in black ops, to come in and revamp the local effort. Took the mike in his bad suit and bristly black mustache and introduced himself in a squeal of feedback and cleared his throat and promised different tactics and different results.

Meanwhile Times Square withered. Tourists disappeared. Businesses pulled down the iron grates. And the first trickle of locals drained out of New York.

Everyone having been given an excellent reminder of how to be properly scared.

Cop cruiser takes the Thirty-Fourth Street exit at a careen, tires whistling on the asphalt. Driver spins the steering wheel one-handed.

Pigeons scatter.

Cruiser screams up Park Avenue, practically airborne. Light bar sows red. Every traffic light clicks to green. You'd think they had the dying president in the backseat, clipped by an assassin's near-miss.

Instead of just me.

Just a garbageman.

And more businesses shuttered. And more locals left.

And it turns out that, despite all the president's speeches and the prime-time telethons hosted by handsome movie stars, the rest of the country was going through some pretty hard economic times of its own, and wasn't all that interested in saving New York. The rest of the country didn't have much appetite for funding new barricades and hiring new cops and sinking even more federal taxpayer funds into guarding a broken city they never really liked in the first place and definitely no longer gave a shit about ever visiting again.

And at some point in there, between the car bombs and the budget crisis and getting cursed out daily on the streets for fucking up on the job twice in twenty years, the cash-strapped, overstretched, outnumbered, and underappreciated NYPD officially stopped giving a shit.

Which is why, only three years after all the handshakes and press conferences and sword rattling and presidential promises, the mayor called a smaller press conference. Just a roomful of local reporters. And he announced a different initiative, an innovative public-private partnership, as he called it, that would allow the few large businesses that were still standing strong beside the city to invest directly in New York's defense, as he said. The Strong City Initiative was what he called it, as he pulled down a velvet cloth to reveal a logo printed on a poster board. Two hands shaking in front of a resurgent skyline. One hand in a cop's uniform. One in a business suit.

Basically, the mayor put the NYPD up for sale.

Cops still work for the city, officially, but now they're paid for by private interests.

New York's Finest. Going cheap.

Don't get me wrong. There are still a few good cops out there.
So I've heard.

Look forward to meeting one someday.

In the meantime, whole sections of Brooklyn haven't seen a
cop in two years.

Queens too. The Bronx. Whole chunks of northern Manhattan.

You see a cop car up there, you figure they took a wrong turn
and got lost.

Either that, or they're out on some other sort of errand.

Moonlighting.

It's okay, though, because, as the second part of the mayor's
Strong City Initiative, he announced he was relaxing the city's
gun laws. Completely.

Let the citizenry take a more DIY approach.

Next day, shotgun sales soared.

Ride's over.

Cruiser pulls up beside Grand Central Terminal.

Driver gets out and opens the door for me. I take note of his
badge: Officer Puchs.

His lady partner, in the sunglasses, circles around the cruiser
to flank me. Her badge: Officer Luckner.

I unfold myself from the backseat, only slightly bruised by
our journey.

Still no word on why we're here.

They just escort me inside.

Grand Central.

Last remaining jewel in the city's tarnished crown.

And I have to admit, it hasn't lost its allure. Looking out from
the balcony over the main concourse can still stop you short.

A majestic landmark.

Even empty.

10.

Correction.

Almost empty.

Single man in a suit waits for me by the big clock in the middle of the concourse floor.

Checks his watch.

Doesn't trust the big clock, apparently.

Cops march me down the stairs to meet him. Sound of our boots on the marble floor ricochets.

Train-schedule boards all cleared. Ticket booths shuttered.

Which is weird.

Should be a few commuters, at least, even on a Sunday afternoon. After all, Penn Station's long since been shut down. And there's just weeds and rubble where Port Authority once stood. So Amtrak, LIRR, Metro-North, all the trains have been rerouted to Grand Central.

City only needs one train station now.

Even if you have to cover your mouth when your train arrives, run through the lobby, and hope for the best.

Man in the suit holds out his hand for a handshake.

Mammoth wristwatch rattles. One of those chain-link kind. Face as big as a compass.

Ostentatious.

Sunday's word.

Spademan, pleased to meet you. My name is Joseph Boonce.

Pinstriped suit that's very well tailored. Has to be, since

he's about a half foot shorter than me, at least. Maybe five-six. Maybe. So either he gets his suits custom-made or he shops at whatever the opposite is of a Big & Tall store. White-blond hair is cut close and conservative. He looks young. Not yet thirty. What's the word?

Wunderkind.

The kind of guy who's probably respected or resented by everyone in the office. Or both. Either way, his whole getup's meant to convey extraordinary competence. Dress for the job you want, etcetera.

Though my guess is he already has the job he wants.

He somehow hoists his wristwatch skyward and points toward the atrium's famous ceiling, arcing a hundred feet overhead. Storied mural of the Zodiac, played out across a painted green sky.

Starts his speech.

We fought hard to keep this place intact, you know, to preserve it, when the rest of the city was going down the shitter. They had to fight once to protect this place from the wrecking ball, believe it or not, way back in the 1970s. Bureaucrats wanted to level it, build something more modern. But they fought to save this place back then, and we've had to fight for it now. Save it from everyone, on both sides of the battlefield. Savages who won't be happy till this city's burned to cinders, and bureaucrats who want to tear everything down and start again.

His eyes meet mine.

And yet it's still standing.

His eyes smile. Face follows.

Pleased to meet you, Spademan. I like to take my meetings here. I have them shut down the lobby for me. I find it makes for a memorable first impression.

Motions to Puchs and Luckner. Tells them they can open up again, let the people through. Puchs gives a sign to someone unseen. Schedule boards flutter back to life. Footfalls of the occasional commuter echo, people now loosed to hurry through.

Then Boonce waves away Puchs and Luckner, who retreat to stand sentry.

Turns to me.

So, Spademan—you like oysters?

The Oyster Bar in the basement of Grand Central is still open for business. At the lunch counter, a few lonely weekend travelers poke at fifty-dollar bowls of oyster bisque, based on that classic recipe: half an oyster and half a quart of cream.

Boonce and I head back to the backroom, the saloon, which is empty, of course. Ancient maître d' bows to Boonce then shows us to our table, smack-dab in the center of the room. Only table in the place set up with a white tablecloth.

Saloon is nautical-themed. Model sailing ships tacked up on the dark wooden walls. Angry swordfish glued to plaques, posed to look like they're still putting up a fight. Fake ship portholes for windows, but they don't look out onto anything.

Boonce flaps his linen napkin, then smooths it on his lap.

So I assume you know who Robert Bellarmine is.

Sure. I know his name from the Atlantic Avenue sweep.

Boonce smiles.

The sweep. Yes, if that's what you want to call it. More like a massacre, if you ask me. But it sent a message. Which I guess was the point, right?

Boonce fiddles with his silverware. Rearranges it. Tells me.

Well, I work for Bellarmine.

If you're a cop, Boonce, why aren't we having this conversation at a police station?

Boonce adjusts his fork just-so. Looks up at me.

I'm off the books.

Then he pulls out a handheld and lays it on the table, screen-side down.

Spademan, I'm about to show you three photos. I think they're photos you're going to want to see.

Okay.

But before I do, I need to know something. I need to know that we can work together.

Okay. Work together on what?

He smiles. Taps a finger on the backside of the handheld.

Let me put it this way. If I show you these photos, and share this information with you, and we don't work together, that's going to be a problem.

Okay. Why don't you start by showing me the photos?

He turns over the handheld. Shows me photo number one. A crisp surveillance photo of Lesser, taken at Stuyvesant Town.

I assume you know who this is. Jonathan Lesser.

Sure. I know him. Bed-hopper. Fond of peeping.

Boonce grins.

Good answer. But he's not just any hopper, mind you. He's king of the hoppers, basically.

Boonce swipes his finger to bring up photo number two. This one I don't recognize. It's another surveillance photo, taken on the street, of a young man in a tweed suit with round glasses. Looks Middle Eastern. Egyptian, maybe. Frail kid, fragile as a bulrush. Bad burns stretched across one side of his face like a handprint from a lingering slap.

Boonce asks me.

Does this person look familiar to you?

No.

Well, let me introduce you. His name's Salem Shaban, aka Salem Khat, aka Sam Khat, as his friends like to call him.

Why Khat?

It's a drug. You chew it. Looks like twigs and leaves.

Sorry, but his name doesn't ring a bell.

How about the name Hussein el-Shaban?

No.

You sure? It was in all the papers.

I don't read the papers.

Well, Hussein el-Shaban was a minor terrorist. Right-hand man to a right-hand man. Killed in Egypt a few years back. Drone strike. Wife too. Whole building full of people, actually. But his wife was an American citizen, which got some bleeding hearts ruffled stateside. More important, el-Shaban also had a son.

Let me guess.

Boonce gestures to the photo.

Shaban Junior here survived the drone strike, barely, got pulled out of the rubble, and now he's living here, in Brooklyn, running a perfume shop on Atlantic Avenue.

I thought no one lives on Atlantic Avenue anymore. Not after the sweep.

Shaban's trying to change that. Encouraging Muslims to move back to the neighborhood. He's become something of a celebrity, actually.

How is he even living in the States?

Boonce fidgets with his wristwatch.

Like I said, his mother's American. Trust me, he's on every watch list, including mine. But he used to be some sort of computer whiz kid and he got shipped over here on a special visa. There were . . . back-channel accommodations. The punch line is, he gave up all that tech-whiz stuff when he suddenly found religion. Became a devout Muslim. Then became an activist.

I examine the photo again. Kid looks harmless. Bookish even. Smooth cheeks, save for the burns, which curl across one cheek and wrap around his throat. Tweed suit's baggy, maybe two sizes too big.

I say to Boonce.

He looks fifteen.

Boonce chuckles.

Don't let the babyface fool you. His father also had a daughter, but guess what? The daughter's dead. Rumor is, Salem Shaban murdered her, his own sister, back in Egypt. Honor killing. That's what they call it. She got gang-raped, so naturally, he killed her. And he didn't stop there. Found the rapists too. Killed them. Found their wives. Killed them too. And their kids, in a couple of cases. Little kids, I mean. Cut quite a swath.

Okay. So why not just arrest him?

Hey, I'm NYPD, not Interpol. Plus, it's all rumor. Records from Egypt right now are, shall we say, spotty. You probably saw the reports on TV. Things are a little chaotic over there.

Like I said, I don't follow the news.

Boonce smirks.

Well, let's just say I hope you had a chance to visit Egypt back when the pyramids were still intact.

Points to the photo of Shaban again.

This kid's taken it upon himself to lead a crusade to repopulate Atlantic Avenue. Pretty small-time right now, but it's growing. Plus—and here's the kicker—he knows Lesser.

How?

Best buds from the whiz-kid days.

Okay. Now what does any of this have to do with me?

Boonce picks up the handheld. Swipes again. Then says.

Don't forget. I've got one more photo to show you.

Turns the screen back toward me.

I assume you recognize this asshole.

I examine the photo. It's blurry, but, yes, I know him. Because this one's me.

————

It's a photo shot in the Stuyvesant Town lobby. Security camera, judging from the overhead angle. I'm toting my duffel bag on my way to see Lesser on Saturday night.

Waiter in a white coat arrives with two steaming bowls of bisque that I don't remember either of us ordering. Boonce thanks the waiter, then gestures toward the curved wooden walls of the saloon, with their useless blind portholes.

You know what I like about this place, Spademan?

What's that?

No windows. So no one can see in.

Takes his spoon and skims his bisque.

Because that's my job. That's what I do. See into every room in the city.

Blows on the spoonful.

And I do see everything.

So are you here to arrest me?

Boonce smiles.

Not arrest you. Recruit you.

Then he takes another sip from his bisque.

Look, Spademan, to tell you the truth, I don't much care what you do. You find people, I find people. It's a living.

Swallows the spoonful. Frowns. Puts the spoon down. Pushes his bowl aside, barely touched.

Leans in.

I love this saloon. Last bastion of a whole different city. Only trouble is—

Cups a hand to his mouth. Stage whisper.

—the bisque sucks.

Leans back.

I just need to know what Lesser saw, Spademan. Or what he thought he saw. Because I know he told you. And I figure you're just about the last one he talked to about it.

So why not just ask him yourself?

Haven't you heard, Spademan? Lesser's disappeared. Poof. No trace.

So where'd he go?

Boonce rattles his watch as he crosses his arms.

That's what I was hoping you'd tell me.

Waiter whisks away both bowls of bisque.

I shrug.

I wish I could help you. But I don't do missing persons. I talked to Lesser last night but then I left him at his apartment.

Boonce checks his watch again, jostling its jeweled face free from under his starched French cuffs. Boonce is exactly the kind of fancypants who still wears cuff links. NYPD shields, no less.

Looks up. Seems pressed for time. So he delivers his pitch.

Unlike some people, Spademan, even people I work with, I'm not ready to give up on this city. I'm not ready to leave it to be ransacked by savages, or crushed under the wrecking ball. I grew up in New York, in Hell's Kitchen. Used to skip school to go watch movie matinees in Times Square. After Times Square happened, I signed up to become a cop, work antiterror, because how could you not? And I'm not going to let what happened happen again. Not on the streets. And not in the limn.

He leans in.

Lesser's a special kid. You know that, right?

So people keep telling me.

He is. And he was working on something special, Spademan. Something special and very dangerous. That's why we were watching him. Rumor was, he'd worked out a new hack for the limn. One that goes way beyond bed-hopping.

Which was?

I think you know, Spademan. Or at least you have an inkling.

You think Lesser found a way to kill a person while they're in the limn.

Boonce leans back. Grins.

Now, as we both know, that's not possible.

But you think that's what it is.

Well, if anyone could have done it, it's Lesser. Like I said, he's a special kid.

But he's just a hopper, Boonce. Why would Lesser want to kill anyone in the limn?

I don't know that he did it. I just think he figured it out. Then I think maybe he let his secret fall into the wrong hands.

Shaban?

Maybe. But think about it, Spademan. If Shaban found a way to use what Lesser knows? To pick people off through the limn? That's huge. Especially given what the city's facing right now.

You mean the election. The one your boss Bellarmine is running in.

Boonce stills his hands. Smiles.

So you do read the papers.

I skim.

Boonce kneads his knuckles. Seems on the edge of genuine concern.

Then you should understand, Spademan, that the limn's just about the only thing that makes this city viable. People have already got plenty of reasons to leave. Limn's the only reason they've got to stay.

Not everyone.

No. But most. The ones with money, anyway.

So what do you want from me?

I'd suggest you start with finding out who exactly Lesser was peeping on. And what that person's current condition is. Because God help us all if that poor person is now dead.

Which is interesting. Because it means Boonce doesn't yet know about Langland. Which means there's at least one thing in the world that I know that Boonce doesn't already know. I don't tell him that, of course. Instead, I ask the obvious question.

Why me?

Why you what?

Why me for this job, Boonce? You seem to have plenty of resources at your disposal.

They see us coming, Spademan, they scatter. And I need to know what Lesser knows, but he has no real reason to tell me. You, on the other hand—you've proved yourself persuasive. And I believe that you can find him. You found him once already.

Fair enough. Now why do I want to help you, exactly?

Boonce grins at me like a patient hunter sitting in a blind, waiting on his well-built trap to spring.

Because there's a few more things that I know about you, Spademan. I know you have a woman stashed in a cabin upstate and that there are a bunch of religious nuts currently combing the woods trying to find her. I know you think you can protect her, and I know you're secretly worried you can't. Which you should be. Because you can't. But you know who can?

You.

Look, you can walk out of here right now, back to your life in Hoboken. But know this: I have the keys to the rooms in the city that no one can see into. That's who I am. You work with me, I give your lady-friend safe passage back South or wherever she chooses. Hell, you can all live here, together, in the city, stress-free, if that's what you really want. I can make that happen. If you find me Lesser. That's what I'm offering.

Trap sprung, he takes a pause. Jangles that watch again. Then adds the kicker. What salesmen call the sweetener.

That's my offer to you. To her. And to her little baby girl.

I can't promise anything, Boonce.

I don't want promises, Spademan. Just Lesser.

And what will you do with him if I find him?

Don't worry about that. Though I'm assuming you weren't headed to his apartment last night to deliver him flowers.

He holds out a business card. Nothing on it but a number.

When you find him, call me here. Direct line. Day or night. Consider this my Batphone.

I pocket the card.

I'll keep in touch.

Boonce rises, makes a big show of peeling off a fat tip for a meal we didn't have to pay for, then escorts me back out to the grand concourse, where Puchs and Luckner are still standing guard. Then Boonce smiles the smile of a slippery salesman who just closed a difficult deal without a moment of doubt that he'd do it.

Offers a handshake to seal the agreement.

Then says, with a wink.

An actual wink.

Spademan, welcome aboard.

11.

Officer Puchs asks where I want to be dropped off, so I tell him Union Square, which is close enough to where I'm actually headed, but not so close that they can follow me there. I don't buy most, or any, of what Boonce is selling, and I know he's only telling me half the story at best. But the truth is, if he can help Persephone, that's worth something to me. Get her and Hannah set up somewhere secret. Somewhere safe. With a yard. Maybe swings.

Could do worse.

Plus, I admit, now I'm definitely curious. If you can actually kill someone through the limn.

Boonce certainly seems to believe it. Boonce and Lesser both.

And if it's true, what Boonce said, that there are terrorists who've found a new way to blow this city apart, from the inside out, after what they did before, then maybe there's a part of me that wants to know that too.

Maybe even have a hand in stopping it.

Never had that chance last time around.

Patrol car squeals to a stop out front of the plaza in Union Square. A few forlorn panhandlers, stranded around the base of the stoic statue of George Washington on horseback, take notice and rouse themselves, drifting plaintively toward us, palms upturned.

I exit the backseat, say thanks to Puchs for the ride, and Puchs doffs his cap from the front seat.

Have fun with the punks.

Then he flips on his siren and peels out just for fun.

Panhandlers scatter.

I figure I'll start my search with Langland, the dead banker, the one part of the puzzle I've got tucked in my pocket that Boonce doesn't know about yet.

Once I'm clear of the square, I pull out my phone and make a call. Used to be, when I needed information, I called a journalist friend named Rockwell. Unfortunately he's not around anymore. Took a bullet on a barstool, meant for me.

Good man. I still miss him.

And turns out Rockwell had an intern.

Never knew that until she tracked me down after he was killed, claiming I owed her a job.

Young kid, early twenties, smart as a pistol and an expert at combing the old abandoned Internet. Hails from Sri Lanka, she told me once, and when I asked her where that is, she said, Picture the farthest place in the world.

Okay.

It's a mile past that.

She favors zootsuits with shoulder pads. Wallet chain and wingtips. Shaved head, save for purple bangs that droop over her eyes. Says she takes inspiration, fashion and otherwise, from Malcolm Little, who was Malcolm X before he changed his name to X. Then she asked me if I knew who Malcolm X was.

Told her I read *The Autobiography of Malcolm X*. Found it on a bus once. Good read. Missed my stop.

She goes by the nickname Hymen Roth, by the way. That's her street name. Like a rapper, she said.

When she first told me that, I winced, and she said, What? You never saw *The Godfather 2*?

Told her that's not why I was wincing.

Now I just call her Hy.

She and her cohort call themselves Netniks. Hang out at a clubhouse in Williamsburg, a safe haven for self-proclaimed info-chaos activists, the types who rummage through the ruins of the Internet, seeing what trouble they can unearth.

Turns out she's the best of them.

Unearths plenty, for a price.

First ring. Hy picks up.

Spademan, you know I don't do phones.

I don't have time to come to Williamsburg. Just let me give you a name.

You better be on a burner. What's the name?

Piers Langland. He's a banker.

Got it.

I want to say thanks, but she's already hung up.

Kids today.

No time for niceties.

As for me, I head to Astor Place. Use the walk to compile a list of people who might be interested in making Lesser disappear.

Turns out it's a long list.

First up: Langland, the banker with a secret, who'd be plenty pissed to find out some geek had been peeking through his curtains.

Trouble is, Langland's already dead.

Peacefully, in his sleep. Supposedly.

Which brings us to whoever Lesser saw in the limn that night. The woman in the burqa, the one who crashed that banker's construct and blew him up. Maybe she found out Lesser witnessed the whole thing and decided to hunt him down and do the same to him out here. Except whoever's behind this seems to want to make a statement. Probably relish a witness, someone to come back here and tell the world.

Which is exactly what Lesser did. Maybe he served his purpose. Still, it seems doubtful they were done with him. If you're going to create a canary in a coal mine, it seems strange to strangle it after just one chirp.

So on to suspect number three: Whoever hired me to kill Lesser in the first place. Obviously, she has motive. But then, if her plan was to snatch him up, why hire me to kill him? Could be she got antsy, sent someone else to finish the job, except twenty-four hours isn't much of a window to let me finish.

Which leads me to the last person on my list, which is any and all of the people who've ever been crossed or violated or spied on or humiliated by Lesser or any of the hundreds of bed-hoppers he unleashed, once he invented his creepy little limnosphere parlor trick. Imagine you went into the limn to act out all the desires or appetites or twisted predilections you didn't want anyone to ever know about.

Then you find out someone was watching. Playing witness.

Might ruffle feathers.

Raise ire.

Inspire revenge.

No need to make a list of all those people. Just grab a phonebook and riffle through. Decent chance you'll land on someone with a grudge against a hopper.

Just kidding.

There's no such thing as phonebooks anymore.

When I get to Astor Place, the day shift's just ending, so the sidewalk out front of the Sculpture for Living is swarming with nurses, done for the day.

That's what they named the condo tower when they built it, by the way.

Sculpture for Living.

Must have made sense once.

The nurses pooling out front aren't the old-fashioned medical kind. They're the type of nurses that wealthy people hire to watch their beds while they tap in. You can spot them by their uniforms, timeless white outfits, very traditional, with white skirts and white stockings and white hats with red crosses bobby-pinned to swept-up hair. The limn is expensive enough already, but if you tap in a lot, and you're already rich, a nurse is a nice extra perk. Someone to tuck you in, watch your vitals, keep you safe and dry and well maintained while your body withers as you drift in a dream in the limn.

Nurses work in shifts, round the clock, and now a cluster of them is huddling on the sidewalk over cigarettes, trying to smoke off the tension of the day. A few others check handhelds or hail cabs, a herd of which is just now inching up and sniffing around for fares.

I grab a seat on a park bench opposite the condo tower and consider the building.

Langland, my banker, lived in the penthouse. And I figure there's only three armed doormen and a tower full of plain-clothes security standing between me and a chance to poke around his apartment.

As I ponder that challenge, I sip a lukewarm street-cart coffee and skim the headlines of a discarded *Post*. Front page features a big photo of Bellarmine, under the headline: BELLAR-MENTUM! TOP COP SURGE AS POLLS TIGHTEN.

Wonder how news of a terrorist infiltration in the limno-sphere would affect Bellarmine's rising polls.

Might spike them, actually. If people get scared enough.

After all, that's Bellarmine's whole campaign.

Sleep tight.

Across the street, I spot Bellarmine's opponent, the city's

honorable incumbent mayor, smiling and waving at me, or at least that's how it looks from the placard plastered on the side of the abandoned bank. Mayor doesn't look too concerned about his electoral prospects just yet.

Dollar-sign graffiti spray-painted across the mayor's smile. Someone's idea of a campaign contribution.

I flip through the paper. Search for Sports. Spot a small item on Crystal Corral.

MEGACHURCH MILLIONS AT STAKE AS SISTERS SQUABBLE.

Skim the news.

Turns out Harrow had four daughters. Persephone's the eldest. The other three are still teenagers, the youngest just barely. All wards of the church now, and they're staking a claim on their late father's kingdom. No doubt causing plenty of headaches for Simon the Magician.

Can't say I'm sorry to hear that. Or that I care much what happens to Crystal Corral either way.

Toss the paper aside and settle back on my bench. Turn my attention back to Langland's building.

Watch the nurses.

The nurse is the way in.

Only question.

Which nurse?

The nurses come and go, dressed in their crisp white outfits. I'm hoping to spot some standout feature. Something telling. But they all wear the exact same uniform.

All but one.

Almost miss it.

The discreet black armband.

And then there's the shiny limo, waiting to pick her up at the curb.

Maybe she works in the penthouse. Certainly seems well compensated.

And newly in mourning.

I ditch my coffee.

Let's start with her.

12.

The nurse pauses by the limo for one last rummage through her
purse, like she forgot something upstairs, which gives me my
opening.

I step up. Swing the limo door wide for her. She looks surprised, but says thank you. Then I ask her.

You have time for a coffee? My treat.

She shoots me a suspicious look.

I'm afraid I have to get home.

Just a quick one. And maybe a few questions. About your em-
ployer, Mr Langland.

I nod at her black armband.

My condolences, by the way.

Thank you. That's kind. But I don't like questions.

That's okay. I don't like coffee.

She lets slip a slight smile.

What are you, a reporter?

Just a concerned third party. It will be painless, I swear.

She looks me up and down. Considers. Then taps the limo
window and tells the driver.

Frank, swing back around and pick me up back here at eight.

Driver nods. Starts the engine. Given it's only six, I'm en-
couraged.

The nurse turns back to me.

Frank knows judo. Should you try anything funny.

I wouldn't dream of it.

I know judo too. Frank's a good teacher.

Black belt?

She shows me the full smile.

Let's hope you don't find out.

The nurse declines the offered coffee and suggests we go for a drink instead. Says she knows a bar down the block on St. Mark's, a place underground called the Plowman. It's dark. Below street level. No music. I like it. And from the bartender's greeting, my nurse has been here before.

We take a seat at the bar and I say to the nurse.

I'd buy you a drink, but I don't believe in buying anyone a drink until at least I know their name.

Makes sense. I'm Nurse.

Care to be more specific?

Just Nurse. For now. Does that still get me that drink?

Sure. What's your preference, Nurse?

She sets her white leather medical bag up on the bar. Smooths her skirt out. Lifts her eyes. Says to me.

Size me up, then take a guess. Let's see how good you are at reading people.

I flag the barkeep and order two Wild Turkeys with extra ice. When they arrive, I take two cubes from my glass and plop them into her shot. Then raise my glass.

Cheers.

She smiles.

Bourbon. Good guess.

Not just any bourbon. This is a special drink I invented myself. Even has a special name.

Really? What's that?

The Cold Turkey.

She laughs. Despite herself. Raises her glass to meet mine.

To Cold Turkeys.

We clink. She sips. I ask.

So did I do a good job of reading you?

Another sip. Another smile.

Well, I'm still here, aren't I?

We talk a bit. Not about Langland. About Nurse.

She looks about thirty, maybe thirty-five, about my age, though with nurses and their uniforms, it's hard to tell. Dark hair the color of strong coffee, pinned up in the regulation style. Green eyes. Greener than most. That's obvious, even in the bar light. Red lipstick. White pantyhose. The standard nurse getup. Looks better on her, somehow.

We chat. I tell Nurse my mother was also a nurse, which is true, though she was a real one, the kind who worked with the sick. Nurse seems impressed. She tells me she never trained as an actual RN, just decided to skip the hard part and get her certificate to work as a tube jockey.

Tube jockey—her words. Laughs when she says it. I know I'm getting somewhere with her when she finally takes off the hat, the one with the big red cross on it. Unpins it carefully. Lays it gingerly on the bar, next to her bag.

Looks at me.

Long day.

Leaves her hair pinned in place though. Fair enough. Baby steps.

Tells me she lives at the top of Manhattan, up near Fort Tryon Park, so it's tough to get to Astor Place by subway, she explains, especially now that there's so few trains running. So her boss springs for transport.

Or sprung.

Either way, it explains the limo.

And it turns out she hails from Canada. Some city called

Saskatoon. Which she swears is a real place and not something dreamt up by Dr. Seuss.

I signal the bartender and order round two. When it arrives, I tip my glass again.

To Canada.

To Canada.

We drink.

So if you're Canadian, I guess that means you're nicer.

She grins.

Nicer than what?

Nicer than normal.

Really? Is that what you expect?

Round three.

So what brought you in to work today, Nurse? I imagine your boss would be okay with you taking some time off, given the circumstances.

You mean because he's no longer with us?

For starters.

I just came in to gather my things. Plus there's paperwork to be dealt with, whenever a client—when a relationship ends.

You ever had this happen to a client before?

She quiets.

Yes, I have.

I'm sorry.

She sips.

Peril of the profession.

Were you two close?

Me and Langland? If we were close, do you think I'd be here talking to you?

Has anyone else come asking around about him?

Langland's rich enough to get the royal treatment from the

city, which means, you know, an actual ambulance showed up. Plus a few beat cops, and some long-faced detective. The detective asked a few questions, scribbled a few details, but no one seemed too alarmed that an old man had died in his sleep.

And no one else came around?

No. Until you. Why?

Man like Langland, seems like he checks out, people notice.

She shoots me a cockeyed grin over the lip of her shot glass.

Trust me. Langland checked out long ago.

Then she explains to me that Langland, with all his money, had more or less retired to round-the-clock bed-rest. Her job was basically to keep him dry and keep him fed. That's how she puts it anyway. Punctuated with a hollow laugh. I ask her.

Did you find him?

Not really. I mean, I was there the whole time. Monitors just flat-lined. Sometime late Saturday. He slipped away. It can happen.

You were working the night shift?

Covering for the night nurse. She had something personal to attend to. Just my luck, right? I have to cover for her the one night things go haywire.

Bartender tops off our glasses. Nurse digs her handheld from her purse and starts to type. Glances up at me.

I'm just texting Frank. Telling him to take the night off.

I check the clock. It's well past eight. I take this as a good sign.

She stows her handheld.

Now I should ask you, Mr Spademan, just exactly who are you in all of this?

Just an interested third party, like I said.

And what does that make me?

I raise my refreshed glass.

A person of interest.

She raises hers.

To people of interest.

Clink.

Round four.

She reaches for her white bag that's resting on the bar. Starts to rummage. Then mutters.

Now where did I leave my lipstick?

Looks up at me.

Thought I could use a touch-up. I've left too much of my current lipstick on the lips of these shot glasses.

You look good to me.

She smiles. Keeps rummaging. Purse topples. Contents spill. A beat-up paperback slides out onto the bar, like a special delivery, just arrived. *Complete Poems of Emily Dickinson.* Diligently dog-eared.

Nurse points to the cover.

You know her?

Not really. Maybe read it once in high school. *Spark Notes,* most likely.

She's really good. Profound, even.

To be honest, the only thing I remember about her poems is that they sounded like urgent telegrams.

She laughs.

I like that. That's not a bad critique.

She cracks the paperback. Flips pages. Finds the dog-ear she's hunting.

Here's one I think you'll like.

Reads it aloud.

A Death Blow is a Life blow to Some
Who till they died, did not alive become—
Who had they lived, had died but when
They died, Vitality begun.

—————

Closes the book. Looks back at me.

Good, right?

Sure. I like it.

She stows the book.

Yeah, to me it's like scripture.

Raises her glass again. Needs a refill. But first, another toast.

Here's to Death Blows.

To Death Blows.

Her eyes catch mine while the glasses connect.

By now we're on round five, with another round waiting patiently in front of us. We forgo Langland and come back around to her, then to me some more, in limited doses, like two cautious boxers, circling, considering a clinch. What few other customers there were have long since cleared out. Bartender keeps her distance too, making busy work, having seen this brand of courtship play out plenty of times before. And to be honest, five rounds down, I'm no longer at the peak of my investigative powers. I think we both know by now it's time to either call it a night or move to another venue.

Alone or together.

I'm still sussing that out.

So is she, apparently.

She grabs her handbag, while saying.

Well, I live all the way up near Fort Tryon Park and I already gave my limo driver the night off. And, as you know, the subway's not safe at this hour for a lady of my attractive qualities. So unless you can loan me two hundred for a cab, I'm open to suggestions.

Well, I'm in Hoboken.

She laughs.

You mean, like, New Jersey?

Is there another Hoboken?

She slumps.

Just my luck.

You don't like Jersey?

I don't like commuting.

Then I float Nurse a suggestion. One I've been sitting on all night.

What about your boss's place? I've never seen a penthouse view.

Nurse seems surprised, but just a little. And I can tell from her look that this is exactly the kind of bad idea she can get behind.

She thinks about it for a moment.

Downs number five.

Fuck it.

And I motion to the barkeep for the check.

13.

The doorman is not happy.

The doorman is not buying any of this.

Past midnight. Tipsy nurse. Weirdo companion lurking over her shoulder.

Nurse sways slightly. Then says.

I'm pretty sure I left my lipstick upstairs.

Doorman frowns.

I'll send someone up.

But I don't know exactly where I left it. Have to look around.

She leans in. Strains her uniform.

And it's my favorite lipstick.

Doorman frowns deeper.

Okay, but then your friend stays down here.

But what if I need another pair of eyes—

Nurse stifles a giggle.

—another pair of hands?

Doorman, still stone-faced.

I'm sorry, ma'am—

She cuts him off. Calls him closer with a crooked finger. Tips up on tiptoe. Leans in close.

Whispers something.

I don't expect she said Open Sesame, but it has the same magical effect.

————

Elevator to the penthouse.

Doors open straight into the apartment. Penthouse is dark, save for the city view, which is panoramic, painted in pointillist light.

Yes, despite what Persephone thinks, I do sometimes make it out to a museum. Tag along behind a tour group. Pick up a phrase or two.

Pointillist, for example.

Nurse and I step inside. I live in a pretty nice loft in Hoboken, a luxury place that was abandoned by hotshot finance types who fled, and Langland's place makes mine look like the servant's quarters.

Elevator doors slide shut behind us. Nurse turns and locks the place up with a code on a keypad.

Then turns back to me. Fingers to her lips. Says in a shushed voice.

So we won't be disturbed.

In the center of the room sits a high-end bed, now empty. Looks like a leather cocoon that's recently been shed. Shreds of yellow police caution tape hang from the bed halfheartedly, like banners from an election campaign that's already left town. I'm guessing the investigation was brief and the cops closed the case quickly. Old man dead in the night. Not exactly a whodunit. Not at first glance, anyway.

Nurse motions toward the bedroom, then swipes her hand over a wall plate. Doors whisper open. She giggles and quiets me again with that raised finger to her lips, even though we're the only ones here. Then she grabs my wrist and tugs me toward the bed, like we're two teens who've been listening for her parents to pull out of the driveway, and only now just heard them drive away.

———

King-size bed. Bigger, maybe. Emperor-size, if that's a size.

Looks out over another knockout view.

Nurse climbs aboard. Bounces on the mattress. Then beckons.

I pause.

She sours.

What's wrong?

I shrug.

Seems a waste. Such a huge bed. Barely even got used.

She lies back. Makes a snow-angel shape on the ivory-colored bedspread. Giggles. Then leans up on her elbows.

Pats the mattress.

Mr Spademan, I couldn't agree with you more.

The next problem that presents itself is the location of the zipper.

Nurse's whites. Sized to fit tightly.

Oddly sexy, in the right light.

Doorman told us he'd give us twenty minutes, tops.

We take forty.

Then forty more.

Then we kind of leave it open-ended.

First fast. Then more deliberate. No rush, but with some urgency. As for me, it's been a while. Not sure about her, though she's definitely not out of practice. And, for a Canadian, she's certainly not polite.

Wonder if the doorman's even noticing the time. Don't know what she promised him to let us come up here, but at this rate, she may have to deliver it twice.

And suddenly I decide that I don't much like that doorman.

May have to have a word with him.

Renegotiate.

Afterward, we lie awhile. Watch the city flicker on the far side of the darkened glass. From up here, the city doesn't look so sick, which I guess is the whole point of living up here.

Then I check the clock. Three thirty. Tell Nurse.

I don't think you're going to make it back to Fort Tryon tonight.

She nuzzles her head into my chest.

Don't worry, I doubt my boss will complain if I'm tardy today.

Her boss. Her job. The banker. That's right. Langland.

To be honest, for a long rare happy moment, I'd forgotten that's the reason why I'm here.

14.

Next morning. Sun comes knocking.

Check the clock again. Six a.m.

I sit up. Bed's empty. Nurse is dressing in the doorway. Tugs her crepe-soled shoe on, over white stockings.

Morning, Spademan. You hungry?

I find my shirt. Tell Nurse.

I am. I know a place. You like waffles?

She gives me a funny look.

Who doesn't like waffles?

I have to admit, I'm really starting to warm up to this Nurse.

We dodge the morning doorman and duck out of the condo lobby and head east. Nurse clings to my arm like we're a longtime couple going window shopping on a lazy weekend afternoon.

Don't mind. Kind of like it.

There's not much action around in the East Village at six in the morning, but we pass a pair of elderly women handing out paper tracts. Dressed like they're maybe heading to church later, except it's Monday, so they've got a long wait.

One woman hands me a pamphlet, which I accept out of politeness.

Crumple it up once we pass out of earshot.

Nurse stops me. Uncrumples the brochure. One word, printed in block letters, across the top.

AWAKE!

Nurse holds it out to me and asks.

What's this? Some kind of religion?

Not exactly. They're Wakers. Wackos, really. Anti-limn movement that started once the beds took off. They're committed to wakefulness, so they say. You've never seen them before?

Nurse shrugs.

Sure. I see them all the time on my way to work. I've just never taken the brochure.

She opens the pamphlet. Scans it.

I don't know. Sounds kind of appealing, Spademan. I mean, look at Langland. All the riches in the world, best life money can buy, but it wasn't good enough. He needed something more. Tried to find it in the limn. Which only took him further away from anything that really matters.

Trust me, Nurse. You're preaching to the choir.

I point to the tract.

If you're interested, looks like there's a Wakers meeting this weekend up around where you live. In that old Cloisters museum in Fort Tryon Park.

She pockets the tract.

Maybe I'll check it out.

You want an escort? You know, to make sure you don't get brainwashed?

She squeezes my arm.

Let's see how the waffles go first.

The place is called the Waffle Hole, which is a terrible name, and it's tucked out of sight below street level, down a half flight of dingy stairs and through a door where you have to stoop to get inside. Only four tables in the place, but we're the only customers anyway. Chef's name is Horace, and he's also the owner, the waiter, and the maître d', which means he stands over a sizzling griddle in the back and points you toward an empty table with his dripping spatula. You seat yourself then yell out your order, which is not a problem, because the menu's easy to remember.

Waffles.

I wave to Horace, order two of the usual, then Nurse and I take our seats. She looks around.

Nice spot. So there are still hidden gems left in New York.

If they ever close this place, I'll be happy to let the whole city sink into the Hudson, and stay on my side of the river for good.

Nurse laughs.

They don't have waffles in Hoboken?

I nod toward Horace, who's approaching with two plates.

Not like these.

Nurse digs in. Chews slowly. Remarks with her mouth full.

Well, you did not lie.

There's a question I really want to ask Nurse, but I know I shouldn't. You really shouldn't, Spademan. You really shouldn't. You—

I ask Nurse.

So what did you promise that doorman last night? To get him to let us up?

Why? Jealous?

Interested.

I didn't promise him anything. I just told him if he didn't let us up I might have to mention to building management about the time I walked in on him in the Media Room. He was—how shall I put it—entertaining himself.

You don't say.

To be fair, no one ever uses the Media Room anymore.

And what were you planning to do in there, Nurse?

Entertain myself.

I'm pretty sure she's joking. I like her a lot, either way.

She swipes the last bite in a tide pool of syrup.

Spademan, I was thinking about what you asked me last night, about the night that Langland died.

Okay.

You asked if I saw anything unusual. It was nagging at me, so this morning, when you were still asleep, I double-checked the monitor logs. We monitor brain function for every client who's tapped in, mostly just to look for reception patterns, maybe something that will ensure a smoother tap next time. But on second inspection, I did spot something weird. Something small. Very small. But weird.

Which was—?

I don't know—some glitch. In his functioning.

Like his brain was acting up in the limn?

More like the limn was acting up in his brain. Like it was sending something more than stimuli. Just for a second, though. Just a blip. I don't—

Phone in my pocket rings. I pause Nurse.

Excuse me—

Pat my pockets and pull the phone free. Nurse sees it and laughs.

You use a flip phone?

What? They're disposable.

And you don't mind that?

I prefer it.

I flip open the phone and answer it. It's Mark Ray and I can hardly hear him. Cellular service is no one's top priority anymore, especially not in New York. Plus he's calling from upstate, so I'm surprised he could even get a signal.

Hey Spademan—

Crackle crackle.

—it's Mark, just calling to check in. I think I'm going to head back to the city later today.

Okay.

And I wanted to make sure you remembered to return the minivan.

Shit. But I don't say that to Mark, of course. What I say is.

Sure.

Then hope the minivan's still parked where I left it in Chinatown.

Great. I also wanted to let you know that the A/C you ordered is finally here. I'll stay and help Persephone set it up this morning before I go, but then I'm heading back to the city.

I say sure. Of course. The A/C. The one I ordered for Persephone. The one they put on back-order at the store where they wanted her address for delivery. Which I never gave them.

I ask Mark.

Wait. Tell me again. Who's there?

The A/C guys. They're just pulling up.

I tell Mark.

Get her out of there now.

15.

Later, Persephone tells me what happened.

Her version. Right before she stops speaking to me.

Mark Ray never gets a chance to tell me his version of what happened.

Because, by that point, he can't speak to anyone anymore.

Persephone's version:

Pickup truck inched forward, pitching slightly, rocking over the rutted road, then pulled to a stop behind the cabin.

Engine stills.

Two men in the front seat. One riding in the pickup bed in back.

Woods silent.

Both doors swing open. Two men in the front disembark. Both burly. But one's burlier. Wear matching gray coveralls and work boots. With gloves on. Despite the heat.

Number three, same outfit, hops out of the truck's bed and joins them.

They don't speak.

Just get to work.

Work boots crackle over last fall's dead leaves as the second man circles at a jog around the back of the cabin. Not being particularly stealthy. No real need to be.

The third man heads for a window on the side of the cabin. Cups his gloved hands on the glass to peer inside.

Cabin's dark. Looks empty.

The first man, the burly one, walks straight up the porch to the front door and knocks.

No answer.

Knocks again.

Still nothing.

So he tries the knob.

Door gives.

And in he goes.

Mark's waiting in the dark, revealed now in a broad square of bright sun as the door swings wide, and he steadies himself, grips the shovel handle tighter, takes a breath, then unleashes his best home-run swing.

Burly guy parries with a forearm easily.

Wrests the shovel free.

One punch.

Mark's out.

Second man's already circled round back of the cabin and slipped through the rear screen door into the kitchen. Scans the room.

Empty.

Emerges into the livingroom. Signals all-clear to the first man, who's standing over Mark.

Third man joins them and takes his post, on watch at the front door while the other two sweep the house. Only one floor, so this won't take long. First the guest room. Then the bedroom. Then the bathroom.

Find nothing.

The first man, the burly one, stops and pulls his gloves off. Rolls his sleeves up. Absentmindedly rubs his forearm, where he took the shovel hit.

Takes a moment to think.

No way they could have missed her. Maybe she slipped out the back door into the woods.

Running. With a kid.

Won't get far.

Then the second man whistles. Waves the burly one over. Leads him back into the kitchen.

Points to a cupboard. Recently repositioned.

All the plates and mugs jostled.

Together they silently lift the cupboard and place it gingerly to one side.

Then take a look at the wall behind where the cupboard was.

Find what was hidden there.

Cellar door.

Second man swings the cellar door open and heads without hesitation straight down into the darkness, taking the steps two at a time.

The first man, the burly one, hustles quickly back out through the livingroom past the third man and out the cabin's front door. To cover any exits. Figures there might be a storm door leading up from the cellar around back.

Trots lightly down the porch steps, very nimble for a big man.

Then looks up and sees the headlights, bright even in daylight.

Highbeams.

Squints.

The pickup truck's running.

Puts a hand up to shade his eyes.

Could swear he sees a woman at the wheel.

Persephone.

Foot.

Pedal.

Floor.

The airbag erupts in a cloud of white powder as her head ricochets and the truck slams the burly man hard enough to vault
him bodily backward through the front window of the cabin,
like an Old West outlaw thrown through a window in a barroom
brawl, but played in reverse. The window's gone now, as is half
the cabin wall. Just shattered glass and splintered woodframe.
Persephone's foot still slamming the gas, so the pickup truck
keeps climbing the porch with a gravelly roar, monster-truck
tires spinning, belching black smoke, before the engine finally
stalls and abruptly quiets.

And the truck's horn, like an abandoned baby, starts to wail.

They left the keys to the truck in the ignition, for a quick get-
away.

Lucky, she thought, when she found the keys there.

So very, very lucky.

Horn still wailing.

Persephone comes to with her head resting on the airbag like
a throw pillow, like she just woke up from a catnap.

Airbag powder dusts her face like flour. Tastes sour in her
mouth. Metallic. Like blood.

No, wait. That's blood.

She lifts her head. Checks her face in the spider-cracked
rearview. Forehead and cheeks smeared white and red. Nose
bleeding. She blinks.

Sees stars.

Shakes her head to chase them off.

Thinks of Hannah.

She hated to leave Hannah inside but no way she'd trust a

lap belt. Not in this situation. So she left her. Just for a moment.

Hid her. In her playpen.

In the cellar.

Where she thought she'd be safe.

Persephone pauses. Finds her bearings.

Remembers.

There were three of them.

Three men.

Still two.

Goes to unlatch her seat belt.

Won't unbuckle.

Horn still wailing.

She yanks at the buckle again.

Oh no oh no oh no oh no.

Two more men. And Hannah still hidden in the cellar.

She and Mark moved the cupboard to hide the cellar door.

And there's two more men inside. Searching.

Persephone's crying now. Feeling more frantic. More than frantic.

Clawing at that buckle.

Spies a third man also laid out in the living room, through the hole where the window once was.

Laid prone by the collision.

But stirring.

She didn't want to leave Hannah inside but what choice did she have?

Claws at the belt.

Come on Persephone come on Persephone come on Persephone come on and pull yourself together.

Don't scream her name.

Don't scream her name.

Don't scream her name.

She screams her name.

Palindrome echoes mournfully through the woods.

Seat belt gives.

Unbuckles.

She lets the belt zip smartly back and jumps out of the truck.

Stumbles. Woozy.

Wonders why the ground keeps lurching.

Hikes across the porch and through the new hole in the cabin wall.

Arms leaden. Legs jelly.

Reminds herself to stop and puke when she has a spare moment.

Spots Mark. Laid prone. Out cold.

And the first man, the burly one, the one she hit with the truck, is maybe dead and definitely sprawled out awkwardly, legs bent at angles that suggest they won't be any use to him anytime soon.

Steps over him.

Eyes on that third man now.

Still stirring.

Now standing.

Between her and the cellar.

Her and Hannah.

The man shakes his head. Straightens up.

She moves sideways, slowly, cautiously, like someone who's come home and stumbled in on a feral animal.

Circles toward the dining table. Trying to put the table between her and him. He mimics her movements, also circling, mirroring her. And he sneers when he realizes she thinks the table will be enough to hold him back.

He feints left and she spooks.

He feints right.

She doesn't spook.

So they circle the table some more, like in some silly silent movie.

Just the table between them.

He inches forward. Figuring he might as well just go right over the top of the table. Only thing between her and him is some old-fashioned lamp. Easy to sweep aside.

Still no sign of the second man. The one who went down into the cellar.

Third man inches closer to the table. Just about ready to hurdle it. Probably figures he needs to move in just. Another. Inch.

He moves in another inch.

Close enough.

Persephone grabs the lace tablecloth with two fists and yanks it hard while also tugging it upward.

Kerosene lamp in the center of the tablecloth flips skyward.

Full somersault.

Then shatters. Splashes.

Kerosene everywhere.

And the third man looks down, stunned by the sudden stink of oil that's sprayed all over his chest and arms, and he doesn't even notice when Persephone pulls out the silver Zippo from her pocket and clumsily snaps her thumb across the wheel to get it to catch, once, twice, again, come on, again, before it finally sparks, and then she tosses it awkwardly, like some insect she's shooing away from herself, and the lighter tumbles, flame fluttering, toward the man in the suddenly soaked coveralls.

Tablecloth goes up.

Table too.

Man too.

She leaves all three to burn.

Staggers off toward the cellar door.

There were three men.

Then two.

Now one.

Still one.

As she limps toward the kitchen she looks left and right for something sharp.

A shard, maybe.

But nothing presents itself.

Except the cellar door, which is waiting, wide-open.

She stops and lingers for a long terrible second at the mouth of the stairs, hoping to hear something from below.

Too scared even to call out her name.

Just listens. For some sign from Hannah. Something. Anything.

Nothing.

Persephone descends.

Feels the urge to puke again.

Persephone has her own sickening history with cellar stairs.

Heads downward. Lurching slightly.

Too dark to see where the bottom of the stairs is but then she feels her foot hit the cold cement floor and she stops.

Palms the wall for the light switch.

Please God just this once. Please God I'll do anything. Please God take me instead. Please God.

And if Hannah's not here then just take me then too. Take me too. Take us all.

Because I can't God. If she's not here. I can't. If she's not here. Or worse.

Finally finds the switch with her fingers.

Please God.

Click.

She'd left Hannah in her playpen, hastily. Kissed her forehead. Then set her down in the dark.

Told her to be quiet.

Be a good girl.

Mama will be back soon.

Then sobbed while she and Mark shoved that cupboard in the kitchen into place.

Bare bulb brightens.

Takes a second for her eyes to adjust.

She knows this may well be the last moment of her life. Accepts it almost calmly. Feels weirdly resigned to it.

Because she won't go on. Not without her. She just won't.

Not without Hannah.

Her eyes adjust.

And for the rest of her life, Persephone will never be able to quite find the words to describe this moment, even alone, even to herself. She feels at the same time completely empty and completely full, as if something forceful is rushing into her chest while something equally forceful rushes out.

Because Hannah's here.

And she's safe.

Sitting patiently in the middle of the concrete floor, all by herself.

Being quiet. In the dark.

A good girl.

And Persephone understands that there are no words yet invented for how this feeling feels.

———

Scoops her up.

Sweeps Hannah's curls aside, to keep them clear of the blood and tears and snot that all now trickle freely down Persephone's face.

Kisses every part of Hannah's head.

Don't let anything touch you. Don't let anything. Ever.

Hugs her closer. Whispers.

Mama's here.

Then promises. Aloud. To her baby. To herself.

I will never let that happen again.

She's so overcome that she almost forgets.

Almost turns out the light again and hikes back up the stairs before she remembers she never found that other man.

Or the playpen she left Hannah in.

So she turns back. Holding Hannah.

Checks the darkened corners.

Finds both.

Third man's slumped in the playpen, like he's enjoying a siesta.

Head droops at a gruesome angle. Choked and his neck's broken. Arms tied behind his back with plastic riot cuffs.

Persephone stands alone, holding Hannah. Trying to make sense of what she sees.

She looks around. Still clutching Hannah.

Hannah seems happy. Giggling. And babbling.

Just nonsense.

Until she says one word.

———

Persephone nearly misses it.

Hannah speaks so rarely that every word comes as a surprise.

But this one's especially surprising.

Persephone leans in and listens hard in the dark to make sure she heard it right.

Whispers.

What's that, sweet girl? What did you say?

Hannah says it again.

She heard it right.

A single word. That makes no sense.

Hannah says it again.

Dada.

16.

Simon.

In my home in Hoboken. Sitting on my sofa. Smiling.

Simon the Magician.

Hannah's dada.

Ta-da.

The last time I saw Simon the Magician was at my social club in Hoboken. We were shaking hands.

Deal with the devil.

Regret it ever since.

Simon agreed to betray his old boss, Harrow, in order to take over Harrow's empire.

Apparently, that isn't working out so well for him.

So now he's here. On my sofa.

Holding Hannah.

Hello Spademan.

Everyone's back in Hoboken now.

My broken, makeshift family. Safe and sound. That's what counts.

Or so I keep telling myself.

Persephone's sitting on a windowsill, smoking, still angry, still shaken, and not really speaking to me. Waves the smoke out the open window like she's bidding it good-bye.

Mark's sitting at the dining table, nursing a broken jaw,

which was wired shut at the local ER, paid for in cash, to skip all the questions. Ugly bruise the size and shade of an eggplant now spreading over his cheeks. He's destined for a diet of milk-shakes and mumbling, probably for a good six weeks at least.

Hannah's happy. Hannah's sitting on her daddy's lap. Smiling.

Simon's beaming too. Having played the role of the cavalry. Swept in. Saved his daughter.

And then there's me.

After I hung up with Mark at the waffle place, Nurse took a rain check, understandably. And not knowing what else to do, I came here to Hoboken. To stew. To feel useless. Wait for word.

All the while thinking.

I should have been there. I should have stayed. It should have been me who saved them.

I should have camped out in a rocking chair on the front porch with my box-cutter in my fist.

Instead I came back here to the city so I could chase down some renegade hopper. Eat oyster bisque with a bureaucrat. Spend the night in a rich man's bed.

I left.

And Simon saved them.

I should have stayed. But I didn't.

I left them.

That's what I did.

Now here we are.

Hello Spademan.

Hello Simon.

He scratches at his curly black beard. A little bushier than when I last saw him. Hair's bushier too. Like a man who's been on the road awhile. Let his grooming lapse.

Simon says.

I left her in your protection, Spademan.

I say nothing back. Because I've got no good answer for him.

From the windowsill, Persephone speaks up, sharply.

We don't need you to protect us, Simon.

Simon laughs.

Whatever you say. Either way, it's just nice to have the family back together.

Turns to me.

Assuming you don't mind me crashing for a while.

I thought you were busy down South taking over Harrow's empire, Simon.

Yes, well, I had some issues with the flock. They weren't quite ready for my brand of leadership.

You don't say.

My plan hit a snag. Three snags actually.

Persephone pipes up.

Who?

Your sisters.

Persephone, perplexed.

Which ones?

Simon scowls.

All three.

Turns back to me.

Any case, I thought it was an ideal time to regroup. Reconnect with family. Keep an eye on things. Good thing I showed up when I did.

Well, you can't stay here.

Persephone barks at me from the window.

Of course he can stay. Or we all leave. All three of us.

I look to Mark. He shrugs. Says nothing. Seems happy to have his jaw wired shut.

Simon says.

Don't worry, Spademan. I'm not staying too long. Just long enough to figure out who tried to kill my family.

They were nutjobs.

Simon frowns.

I don't think so.

Why not?

These guys had training. Moved in tandem. There's also this.

Simon pulls out a swatch of gray fabric. Ripped from a coverall. Shows it to me. One word, written in stitched script.

Pushbroom.

Simon asks.

Mean anything to you?

Not really.

Though even as I say that, I remember the card I plucked from Lesser's doorjamb. Which also said Pushbroom. Don't mention that to Simon.

Simon stows the swatch. Says to me.

Pushbroom is a security company. Hired sweepers. Work mostly in the limn. But they'll do work out here, for a price.

And who do they work for?

Whoever pays them.

So who paid them to do this?

Simon smiles.

That's what I'm going to find out.

He hoists Hannah. Speaks to her in baby talk.

Because no one fucks with my family, right?

Looks back at me.

Don't worry, Spademan. I didn't travel all this way to hang out with you.

Tickles Hannah.

Did I, girl?

———

Doorbell rings.

I'm not expecting guests. Head to the window and pull back the curtain to take a look outside. Street's empty save for a single cop car parked just down the block.

Not Jersey cops, though.

NYPD.

Head downstairs to the building's lobby and find Officer Puchs at my front door.

Tips his cap.

Evening, Spademan.

What the hell are you doing here, Puchs?

Lieutenant Boonce heard about what happened upstate. Wanted us to swing by and check in on you. I'm sure you're all shaken. But we're going to stick around, keep an eye on things. We'll be right out here. Just wanted to let you know.

I glance over at the cop car. Luckner, his partner, sits in the passenger seat. No smile or wave. Just watching.

Turn back to Puchs.

You know we're in Jersey, right? You two even have jurisdiction out here?

We have a reciprocal agreement with the local authorities. Besides, if push comes to shove—

Puchs smiles.

—we can worry about jurisdiction later.

I glance back at Luckner. Then back at Puchs.

Fine. Thank you. I appreciate it.

He tips his cap again.

Let us know if you need anything. And do send Lieutenant Boonce word when and if you hear anything from Lesser.

Then Puchs turns, looks both ways, and crosses the street back to his car.

———————

I head back upstairs to my apartment. Decide I've had enough of being useless in Hoboken. So I'm happy when my phone buzzes and I get Hy's text. Her message is just a single number.

8.

Figure she's dug up something on Langland. It's seven now, which barely gives me time to get to Williamsburg, even by boat.

I step back inside and interrupt the family reunion. Announce to the room.

I have to go out. There are two cops outside keeping watch. You can trust them.

Simon's wary.

You sure?

I pull a gun from a drawer in the side table by the sofa. Standard-issue cop's sidearm. I rented it once from a Jersey patrolman and never did give it back. Long story.

Offer the gun to Simon. He waves it off.

That's okay. I brought my own.

So I offer it to Mark, who grunts from under his jaw wire. Holds his hands up as if to say, Not me.

So I hand the pistol to Persephone. She slips it in her waistband, behind her back, like a pro. Must have picked that up somewhere.

Then she asks.

And just where are you heading off to?

To run an errand.

Okay. Pick up some diaper wipes while you're out.

Diaper what?

Diaper wipes. We're almost out.

I make a mental note.

Diaper wipes. Got it.

Say to Simon.

Keep them safe.

Next part's harder. Don't want to say it. But I say it.

And thank you.

He grins.

Don't worry, Spademan. You can always count on me.

17.

Hy hangs out in an abandoned warehouse on an empty street in Williamsburg, which supposedly used to be a brewery once. Street's dark and the building doesn't have a name, or a sign, or an official membership policy, but it's open at all hours and is always occupied. Basically it's just a huge room with a wide floor covered with sawdust and a bunch of scavenged couches scattered around. And wires. Lots of wires. Thick black wires lying looped over each other like in a snake pit. And there's so many lit screens everywhere, of all sizes, that it casts everyone inside in a deathly glow. Including me, as I stand in the doorway, eyes adjusting to the darkness.

Building definitely must have been a brewery once. Place still smells like hops. Inside it looks more like an illegal chop shop, though, except not one for cars. For information. All these Netniks, working away with their sleeves rolled up.

Poking around under the hood of the Internet.

It's not hard to spot Hy, what with the pinstriped zootsuit, which practically glows in the dark. She's on a couch near the back, with her wingtips up on a milk crate, fiddling with a handheld that's plugged into a laptop that's plugged into an old hijacked Internet street terminal, the kind that looks like a screen on top of a steel cactus. Someone must have ripped it out of the sidewalk and dragged it here, just for kicks, like college kids stealing a parking meter for their dorm room.

On the couch beside her, some dude in a backward ballcap is

lost in his headphones and tapping on a laptop so old it's the size of a suitcase. That's how Netniks like it, apparently.

Vintage.

The more primitive, the better. Computer equivalent of a refurbished jalopy. Proves you're a better mechanic.

I flag Hy and she motions me over. I sink into the musty couch between her and Headphones. She nods to the laptop screen, which seems to be running something, but nothing I can make any sense of. When I log on to the old Internet, which is not often, I see it like anyone sees it. Just text, a virtual scrolling bazaar for illicit trading, underground bulletins, and chat rooms full of inchoate howling. But what's scrolling across Hy's screen right now isn't English. Looks more like music, except made of numbers.

While she scrolls she asks.

You ever follow up on that motorman?

I got waylaid. It's on the back burner now.

That info was good shit, Spademan. And not easy to unearth.

I've got other things to worry about, Hy.

She points to her screen.

I'm guessing you mean your man Langland. Well, friend, I promise you're not going to be disappointed at what I found.

Hy does her best to translate the number music, tracing the screen with her finger, while I do my best to pretend like I'm following along.

So this Piers Langland. Big banker. Big money—

That much I know, Hy.

Also DOA last weekend. Dead in his bed.

I know that too.

Big political muckety-muck also. Before his passing, he dropped a lot of cash on this year's mayoral race. A lot of cash. Want to guess which candidate?

Bellarmine.

Bingo.

Hy likes to do it this way. Parcel the info out slowly. Draw out the drama. She has a showman's streak. She starts back in.

Here's another fun fact about your mysterious Mr Langland. He ran a foundation for disadvantaged kids. Also bankrolls a school called the Langland Academy. Posh private school upstate stuck in the woods somewhere south of Albany. Special home for wayward whiz kids. You know, troubled youths with gifts who could use a leg up.

Hy gestures to the assembled Netniks.

This crowd, basically. You want to guess at his prize pupil, Spademan?

This time I have no idea. So I ask her.

Who?

Your missing person. Jonathan Lesser.

At the mention of his name, a few pairs of eyes drift up from their screens to watch us. Lesser's legendary, apparently. Among the riff-raff anyway.

So wait—Langland knew Lesser?

He more than knew him, Spademan. He was his fucking benefactor. Brought him to Langland Academy on a full scholarship.

Poor kid made good.

Sure, except Lesser never graduated.

Dropped out?

Not exactly.

Hy taps a few times on her touch screen. Numbers dance. She's hunting for something. While she searches she says.

Remember how, once upon a time, you wanted to find out something on someone, the best place to start was the dumpsters out back of an insurance company or a law firm? You know, where people dumped all the records they were supposed to destroy?

Sure.

Hy chews a thumbnail that's peeling purple polish. Color matches her bangs. Scans her screen. While I wait I wonder how Hy knows any of that stuff about law firms or dumpsters, since she's a little young for paper shredders. Or paper. Must have seen it in a movie once. Though she's a little young for movies too.

She sits up straighter. Squints at her handheld. Then continues.

Well, sometimes the old Internet's like that too. It's like the dumpster full of unshredded documents, except for the entire world. Most of it's encrypted, sure, but you know who they usually hire to encrypt shit like this, before they bury it?

Who, Hy?

She gestures to the room.

Miscreants like us. And we usually make sure to do a job that's just good enough to get paid, but not so good that we can't undo it easily in the future. Just takes patience.

Looks at me.

And genius, of course. Patience and genius. A recipe for conquering the world.

Then she's back to her screen. Still chewing. Still searching. Starts humming. Kind of feels like I've been put on hold. So while she rummages, I ponder. Lesser knew Langland, which he failed to mention to me. And Lesser liked to peep on his former benefactor, which he also failed to mention. Which means—what? It might put Langland at the top of the list of suspects in Lesser's disappearance, except for the inconvenient fact that Langland's dead.

Hy makes one last dramatic tap on the handheld. Then leans back. Looks triumphant. Points screenward.

Voilà!

Not sure what she's voilà-ing. Screen looks like gibberish to me.

What am I looking at, Hy?

Your boy Lesser never graduated because he got recruited out of Langland. For some hush-hush mission. By the cops.

How do you know that?

For starters, his school records stop, right here.

She points at gibberish.

But he never officially left Langland. His scholarship was suspended while he went on some sort of hiatus, which I can promise you did not involve backpacking through Europe. And this timeline coincides roughly with Bellarmine's arrival at the NYPD, post–Times Square, which I'm sure you remember, since it was all pomp and circumstance and hail our new mighty protector.

She jabs the screen with a purple-polished finger.

And check this: That year's police budget? Included a line-item requisition for funding that was never specified. And never delivered. Not officially.

Seems sketchy.

Oh, I'm not done.

Scrolls through more gibberish.

Here's a full security work-up on Lesser, pre-something. Requested by—

NYPD.

Bingo redux. They were vetting him.

For what?

Some kind of work. But wait—what's this, behind door number two?

Taps her screen again.

Personal emails from Langland to Lesser. Congratulating him on being selected. So I went digging through the old NYPD internal memos, found a trove of dumped info outlining some new initiative, some antiterror squad, focusing on the limn.

They left their secret plans online?

Not their plans. This is peripheral shit. Memos and requisitions. You know, like orders put in for new letterhead.

Hy looks at me.

Like I said, no one ever thinks to shred this shit.

So what's the connection to Lesser?

Looks like there was a big push by Bellarmine after he came in, to assemble some kind of limnosphere task force. Involving outside contractors. Unnamed. My guess? Bellarmine went to Langland looking for his best and brightest geeks. Lesser was definitely one of them. So the cops took him on.

She looks around. Then looks at me.

You know, this shit isn't even part of the official Legend of Jonathan Lesser. This shit is dug up fresh, especially for you.

I appreciate it, Hy.

Do you, though?

Then Hy gets serious.

Lesser's well loved around here. Kind of revered. You know that, right?

And why's that?

Because he's one of us, Spademan.

Hy nods to the room.

You know. Weirdo. Misfit. Special kid. Made good.

Just because he figured out how to peep on people's fantasies?

Because he cracked it, Spademan. He found a glitch. And rode it. Around here, that makes you a hero.

She gestures to all the couches. Sofas stuffed with kids, side by side, silent and stooped over and lost in their screens. Only sound the tip-tap of typing. Most aren't older than teens. Some aren't old enough to be teens.

Hy says in a whisper.

That's all anyone's trying to do here, Spademan. Find a glitch. Then ride it.

Why?

'Cause it's like winning the lottery. Or outsmarting the lottery, which is even better.

She turns back to her screen.

So Langland forks over Lesser, who works a year or so on this secret project.

And what's the project?

That I don't know. Because it's secret. Then after a year or so, Lesser bolts.

Why?

Who knows? Ask him. If you can find him.

Maybe he figured something out.

Now Hy's curious.

Like what?

Like maybe how to kill someone through the limn.

Hy looks puzzled.

I doubt that, Spademan. Can't kill someone through the limn. First rule. You know that.

Sure. Unless you outsmart the lottery.

I point to the screen. Still filled with number music. Prod Hy.

You find any sign of Lesser? You know, in there?

She laughs.

In my computer?

No, you know. Out there. In the limn or wherever.

Hey, what I do is find info on the Internet. Personally, I hate the fucking la-la land limn. I'm straight-up straight-edge. Never tap in. Man, I'm practically a Waker, yo.

Then she turns to her screen and taps a few more times on her handheld.

You ready for the grand finale?

Hy taps her handheld once. Leans back.

So this project, the one they recruited Lesser for? Internally, they called it Near Enemy. Got closed down pretty quick too, and apparently never officially existed, as these things usually don't. But because I am a once-in-a-lifetime prodigy, guess what?

What?

She leans back in. Screen lights her face. She smiles.

I found a trail.

And what's at the end of your trail?

More trail, mostly. But I did find a name. Some Bellarmine flunky who ran the day-to-day operations at Near Enemy. You track down this guy, Spademan, and he just might know something about Lesser.

Which is when I get a sick feeling, because I know what she's going to say. Don't know how I know but I know. And I'm about to say the name, but I stop, then she just goes ahead and says it for me. Because to her it means nothing. It's just a name.

Hy presents it with a flourish. Like a punch line. Which it kind of is.

Joseph Boonce. That name mean anything to you?

Luckily in the screen-lit dark of the old brewery, Hy can't see the sick look on my face.

I thank her for the tutorial and pull out my money roll. She waves it off.

Come on, Spademan. You know this shit's pro bono.

Hy, you gotta eat.

You don't know much about the Internet and bank accounts, do you? Don't worry. I do okay.

She gnaws her nail. Scans the screen again. While she scans, she pulls out a pouch of tobacco and rolls a cigarette. Lost in thought. Then she says.

It's funny.

What's that?

Your boy Bellarmine—any chance that he's a Buddhist?

Why?

Near Enemy—it's a Buddhist concept.

Enlighten me, Hy.

See, in Buddhism, they have four virtues, and each virtue has an opposite. For example, one is compassion, and its opposite is cruelty. But each virtue has a near enemy too.

Meaning?

The near enemy of a virtue is an emotion that resembles the virtue, but it's, like, the corrupted version. The near enemy of compassion, for example, is pity. Pity is like compassion, but tainted. Like a bad copy.

Once Hy's done rolling the cigarette, she unrolls it. Dumps the tobacco back into the pouch. Sees me looking. Says to me.

Old habit. I don't miss smoking them. I just miss rolling them.

Dusts her hands off and puts the pouch away.

Okay, Spademan—so what's my next assignment?

I pull a card from my pocket. The one I found in Lesser's door. Hand it to Hy.

You know anything about this?

She reads the card.

Pushbroom? Just that they're nasty. Especially the Partners.

What do they do?

They're sweepers. Very expensive. Top-shelf, for those with a taste for overkill. Pushbroom will find your problem and make your problem hurt in a memorable way. The Partners are the three dudes who run it.

She lowers her voice. Looks around. Too many heads in headphones to worry about eavesdroppers. Still, she's cautious.

The three Partners are very secretive. In the limn, they call themselves Do-Good, Do-Better, and Do-Best. Keep their identities out here a real mystery. Mostly use henchmen for their work in the nuts and bolts. Burly dudes in coveralls who run around and settle accounts. In the limn, though, it's the Partners who bring the pain.

Weird names.

Hey, it's the limn.

And who do these Partners work for?

Whoever pays. They're not committed to any particular ideological struggle. Been known to sell their services to both sides on occasion.

Both sides of what?

Whatever.

I take the card back.

Thanks for the help, Hy.

No sweat. So what's next?

Find out whatever you can on Near Enemy. And Joseph Boonce.

You mean the top-secret antiterrorism initiative that never officially existed? And the cop who's off the books? Sure. Gimme a day.

Just whatever you can find, Hy. And thanks—

But she's already lost in her screen.

I head back into the night air of Williamsburg.

Street's empty. Night's silent. Over the black water, the bridge is lit up nice. Draped in dazzling lights from end to end. No cars. But lots of lights. Another example of the mayor's newfound interest in window dressing. Looking to fend off Bellarmine's charge.

I find my phone and dig another card out of my pocket. The one with Boonce's number on it. The one he gave me. Called it his Batphone. Day or night.

Figure it's time for me and Boonce to have another conversation.

Punch the numbers.

Think about Lesser while I listen to it ring.

18.

Lesser.

Special kid.

So everyone keeps telling me.

When I was a kid, I went to normal school. Normal teachers. Normal classes. Normal rules.

Nothing special.

As for me, I didn't have any particular interests. Girls. Fights. Was in a school play once.

Otherwise, I was just a student. Sat in the back of the class with the bad kids. Tried to stay out of trouble. Mostly failed. Nothing serious. A few scraps, but only fists. In my school, that practically made you a pacifist.

As for schoolwork, I did enough to pass. Then graduated barely and followed my father into his line of work, which was the life plan all along.

Garbageman.

The real kind. With garbage.

My father loved being a garbageman.

Never minded the jokes. Even told a few himself.

Knock-knock.

Who's there?

The garbageman.

Yeah, I know. I could smell you coming from down the block.

Ha-ha-ha.

———

But there was one day I remember, freshman year, I was maybe fourteen, when I got called out of homeroom. By name.

Vice principal beckoned me from the classroom's doorway. Just me.

I figured it was because I'd slammed Terry Terrio's fingers in his locker.

Don't worry. Not hard. Nothing broken. And he deserved it.

Anyway, VP called me out with a bunch of other kids from other homerooms and corralled us all into the cafeteria. Real crowd of misfits. And each misfit no doubt thinking he was the one misfit who didn't belong. Because the kids assembled there were the bottom of the pecking order. The snifflers, the stutterers, the creepy silent kids, the kids who played games with dragons and dice in the corner of the cafeteria every lunch hour, that one hyperactive doofus who could never keep his mouth shut or sit still.

Special kids, in other words.

And then me.

Just a garbageman's son.

And they lined us all up and told us, from now on, we'd have special teachers. Special classes. Special rules.

The crowd moaned. Snifflers sagged. Stutterers stuttered. But-but-but. The silent creeps clutched their books even closer. Stayed silent.

And everyone looked around. Bug-eyed. Distressed.

Must be some mistake.

I don't belong here. Not me.

That's what everyone thought.

Especially me.

In any case, I'm not really sure what exactly they had in mind for us.

The special kids.

Since I cut class every day for the rest of the week.

Monday, first thing, my father barged into the principal's office. No appointment. Trailing curses.

Knock-knock.

Who's there?

My father cornered the principal.

Told him, you better put my son back in the normal class.

Told him a few other things too. I'm not sure what exactly. But my father was known to change a mind or two. Spent a long time as a union man and a fair amount of time in bars. So he was not the type to back down from a difference in opinions. And people usually came around to his way of thinking. Eventually.

Whatever he said to the principal, next day, I was back at my old desk. Old homeroom. Old teacher. Back row. Terry Terrio's bruised fingers still wrapped up in bandages. Terry eyeing me. Plotting a cycle of revenge he'd eventually come to regret.

And me, back to slouching. Keeping my eyes low. Stayed that way for the rest of my time, right through high school, just like a person in prison. Kept out of trouble just enough to keep out of trouble.

And whenever I thought about that day in the cafeteria, I felt glad that my dad got me plucked out from the special kids.

Figured I was extra-lucky.

Dodged a bullet.

I'd always thought that special class they'd pulled me out for was some sort of class for dummies.

Only learned later it was a special class for smart kids.

Special kids.

So they said.

My mother only told me the whole story after my dad died.

I was long out of high school by then. Married to my Stella, who I'd met while doing that school play. I was living in Brooklyn. Riding a garbage route. Following the life plan. Wearing my dad's hand-me-down gloves, the ones he gave me on my first day of work, presenting them proudly to me with a ribbon tied around them.

Kept that ribbon balled up in my back pocket too.

They'd fought a lot about it, my mother told me. I never knew, of course. To me, their fighting just sounded like fighting. Same muted white-noise soundtrack of household unhappiness that I'd long since learned to block out.

My father was stubborn.

No special class for my kid. Don't want him singled out as different. You do that, and he's marked for life, my father said.

My mother felt the opposite.

That this was my one chance to be singled out.

Either way, didn't much matter. Not in the end.

After all, my father died. So did my mother, not long after.

So did my Stella.

So did New York.

Now here we are.

My mother told me, though, that I had this one teacher who'd championed me. English teacher. She was the one who'd put my name in the mix for the special class.

My champion.

Turns out this teacher thought I had an aptitude for language.

Aptitude. Not a word my father ever would have used. Didn't like ten-dollar words. Not crazy about two-dollar words, for that matter.

That's probably why the principal had been so easy to convince. I'd barely squeaked through in the first place.

Only had one champion.

Made me an easy veto.

Either way, a couple weeks after my father yanked me out of that program, that teacher, my champion, asked me to stay for a minute after class.

Class cleared out. Left her and me.

She looked up from marking papers.

I heard your father had you pulled from the special section.

Nod.

Do you know why?

Shrug.

Everything okay at home?

Nod.

You keeping up with your homework?

Shrug.

Then she pulled a thick paperback from her desk drawer. Had a whale and a boat on the front. She put the book aside and asked me if I wanted to meet her on Saturdays for special tutoring. We could meet at a coffee shop. I could tell my father whatever I liked. She had books and she thought I should read them. Thought I'd like them. We could read them and talk about them together.

You mean like detention?

No. Not detention. It's not punishment.

Sounds like detention.

We can start with something fun.

Like what?

She held the thick paperback up.

Moby-Dick.

I scoffed.

No, thanks.

Why not?

Don't like animal books.

She laughed.

Have you read it?

Sounds boring.

How do you know it's boring?

Shrugged. Muttered something.

I'm sorry, what did you say?

I said, does anyone get killed in it?

Yes. Lots of characters get killed in it.

Really? How?

Lots of ways. Whales, for one.

Scoffed again.

Sounds stupid.

Okay.

She put the book away.

Then let's start with something a little more—exciting. Something pulpy. You read pulp?

Shrug.

How about *The Maltese Falcon*?

Like I said. I don't like animal books.

She smiled.

You'll like this one.

She pulled open the drawer again. Pulled out a different paperback. Battered cover. Weather-beaten. Held it out to me. Statue of a bird on the cover. Not promising. Author's name sounded like a ballet dancer. Also not promising.

I shrugged.

She flipped open the front cover. Showed me some scribble. Showed me a year written under the scribble. From a long time back.

See that? That's *my* high school English teacher. He gave this book to me. Asked me to read it. Forced me, really. I was like you. Thought I didn't like animal books.

She held the paperback out to me. I took it. Stuffed it in my back pocket. She winced.

Careful with that copy, please. That's got a lot of sentimental value.

Sure.

You read that, then meet me on Saturday at noon at the coffee shop, and we'll discuss it.

This Saturday?

Yes.

This whole book?

Yes.

By Saturday?

Yes.

This Saturday?

Trust me, you won't want it to end.

Then she turned back to marking papers. Big stack of essays, all marked in red pen. A, C+, A-, B, B+, D, B, and so on. A whole alphabet, on an endless loop. I noticed she'd pulled my essay out of the pile, though. Set it aside. Circled a few words in red pen.

She kept marking. I didn't budge. She looked up.

Yes?

And then I asked her the obvious question.

Why me?

Why you what?

Why me—?

Didn't finish the question. Wasn't even sure what I wanted to ask. She put down the red marker anyway.

Potential. I just hate to see it wasted.

Picked up the pen again.

See you Saturday.

———————

Don't know how that book turned out.

Never finished it.

Never started.

Dropped it down a sewer grate on the street outside the school.

Couldn't be seen carrying around an animal book by a ballet dancer.

What would Terry Terrio think?

And I still remember to this day how the paperback fit so perfectly between the gaps in the grate before I let it drop, like I was delivering it through a mail slot, and the fluttering sound it made as it fell and then vanished, and how it landed in the sewer below with a splash, and how, once I'd let it go, I wished more than anything I could reach down into the darkness and pull it back.

Not sure what we would have talked about at the coffee shop on Saturday.

Never showed.

And next time in class, she didn't mention it.

Never said a word about it to me, actually.

Just stuck my essay back in the middle of that endless pile.

Sometimes, many times, many years later, I'd think about that teacher.

Picture her, sitting in that coffee shop, waiting at a table for two, next to an empty chair. Waiting as the clock clicked toward noon.

Waiting for me to return with the treasured copy her own teacher gave her once, so we could discuss it, like they once did.

Waiting, as noon came and went.

Coffee cooling.

Until it became clear.

I looked her up, by the way, years later. That teacher. After my mother told me the whole story.

The story of my champion.

Hoped to pay her a visit. Say thank you. Say sorry.

Knock-knock.

Remember me?

In any case.

Didn't matter.

Turned out she's dead too.

Tracked her down to a tombstone in Jersey.

Peaceful cemetery. Well-kept plot. Withering bouquet.

Said sorry to a headstone instead.

And I bought that book eventually. The animal book by the ballet dancer. And I read it. And liked it. A lot.

She was right.

Told her that too, when I left my copy at her grave.

Speaking of.

Special kid.

Lesser.

Pervy hopper. Dirty fatso. Total weirdo.

But doesn't deserve whatever's happening to him.

Poor Lesser.

Deserves better.

Figure maybe he could use a champion.

II.

19

Near Enemy.

What's that?

You tell me.

Boonce laughs.

Look at you, Sherlock Garbageman. Congratulations. You figured one thing out.

Don't fuck with me, Boonce. Just tell me.

He doesn't tell me. Instead he leans on the railing of the rotten wooden deck overlooking the dirty Hudson River and chuckles.

In the background, quick-moving clouds of seagulls circle garbage barges on the river and shriek. Dive-bomb garbage. Drown us both out. Then Boonce announces, still watching the river, voice raised against the shrieking.

You know what's the most dangerous thing in the world, Spademan?

What's that?

Now he turns to me. Not chuckling anymore.

A man armed with a box-cutter and one fucking fact.

We're standing on the upper deck of the South Street Seaport, down by the waterfront, at the tip of Manhattan's south end. The deck's railing is warped and the plankway is missing planks, victims of too many bad storms that hit too hard and too few city repair crews that still show up for their shifts.

Behind us, shifty merchants with makeshift wares sprawled

out on ratty blankets stand haggling with clients, most of them tappers aching for another hour in the limn. South Street Seaport used to be an actual seaport once, two hundred years ago or thereabouts, big magnet for commerce, bustling fish market, the whole shebang, until all that got shut down. After that, seaport turned into a shopping mall. Discount t-shirts sold from stalls that once housed fresh-caught sturgeon. Then the tourists left too, and the city went to hell, and now the seaport's more of an all-purpose open-air bazaar, with an open-door policy when it comes to merchants. Which is to say, most of these merchants opened someone's door, took whatever they could carry, laid it out here on a tattered blanket, and now they want to sell to you.

And just as pawn shops used to reliably pop up in neighborhoods where robberies happen, there are a half dozen by-the-hour flop-shops within stumbling distance of the seaport. People sell stolen shit here to raise enough cash to buy an hour in a bed. Some flops even offer ten-minute increments, though it's hard to imagine what kind of off-body fantasy you can cram into ten minutes.

Actually, it's not that hard to imagine.

Either way, the old seaport is an especially seedy corner of the city, even in a city full of seedy corners.

So, naturally, Boonce chose this place for our meeting.

I guess he only closes down Grand Central for you once.

I'd hoped for his office, tucked away in some police tower somewhere, but then, I keep forgetting.

He's off the books.

Boonce leans his weight, arms locked, on the rotting railing and winces. I'm impatient, so I press.

I don't like being lied to, Boonce.

No one likes being lied to, Spademan. And yet it happens every day.

He turns to me. Fidgets with that chunky watchband.

Speaking of which, how's your nurse doing?

What nurse?

Boonce chuckles.

I like that. Play dumb. Look, I can see why she's useful to your investigation, Spademan, given she's the last person to see Langland alive. Oh, and thanks for keeping that piece of information from me, about Langland being dead and all. Good thing you're not the only person on my payroll.

You never told me about Near Enemy, Boonce. Or that Lesser and Langland knew each other. Or that they both knew you.

Boonce sighs, like a husband caught cheating, but one who doesn't really care if the marriage ends.

Look, Near Enemy was Bellarmine's idea. But just the broad strokes. An initiative to protect the limn. You know, get some genius dorks to find all the holes in the limn and plug them.

Boonce gestures to the skyline.

Because that's where the next one's coming, you know. No one's trying to blow up any of this shit out here anymore. The bad guys want to get in there. In the limn. Given what Lesser saw, maybe they already have.

And what about Lesser?

What about him? He was just some brilliant geek that Langland dug up and handed over to me. Some prodigy wasting away at a public high school, totally bored, parents completely useless, had no idea what they had on their hands, and Langland plucked him. Just like most of the kids at Langland Academy. It wasn't a school so much as a salvage operation for brains. Lesser's was the biggest, by the way.

Boonce thinks a moment.

Well, maybe second biggest.

Checks that watch again.

Tell me, Spademan, while you were off poking around in my

dirty laundry, did you ever happen to follow up on the one actual lead I gave you? That Egyptian kid, Salem Shaban?

No.

Well, he's the one you have to worry about.

Why?

Because he's the biggest brain of all.

Boonce rubs his forehead, like a guy with a migraine. Or a decision to make. He makes it, then says.

Here's a little more backstory, since you're so eager for the big picture. I told you Shaban moved here after the States took out his dad, right? In Egypt? When he was a teen? Do you want to know who brought him here?

I'm guessing it's Langland.

Good guess. Shaban was another one of Langland's reclamation projects. Notorious whiz kid. Langland plucked Shaban from Egypt and had him shipped stateside. State Department threw a hissy, of course, but Langland had pull to spare. Then Langland brought Shaban to me, to work on the Near Enemy project. Along with Lesser. The two of them. Top of the class.

So Shaban knows Lesser too.

Knows him? Spademan, they were fucking bunkmates at Langland. And the banker handed them both over to Bellarmine because Bellarmine was Langland's stooge. He'd nurtured Bellarmine since the day he graduated the police academy. Saw a big future for him. Got him all the way to top cop. Hoped to get him to mayor. May yet, I guess. After all, his money's not dead.

Boonce leans down and grabs a briefcase that's leaning on the railing at his feet. Pauses. Asks me.

You see today's *Post*?

I don't—

That's right. I forgot.

Props the attaché on the railing, pops it open, and pulls out today's *Post*. Banner headline.

TOP COP TERROR SCARE: BELLARMINE POISED TO DROP BIG
DEBATE BOMBSHELL.

Boonce points to the headline.

The first mayor's debate is this week. Open-air, just like Lin-
coln and Douglas, down in Battery Park City. And Bellarmine's
been teasing some big revelation all week. Ever since last Saturday night. Coincidentally.

So what?

So maybe his bombshell comes wrapped in a burqa, Spademan.

You think Bellarmine knows about what happened to Langland?

Boonce stows the paper. Buckles the briefcase.

I think he more than knows.

Boonce puts the attaché down and leans on the railing again.
Clasps his hands. Wrings them. Seems actually worried.

Think about it, Spademan. What's Bellarmine's whole platform in the election?

Sleep Tight.

That's right. So who do you think stands to benefit if every
rich fuck in this city suddenly panics because supposed terrorists found a way to crack the limn and blow you up for real?
Which strongman's arms are they going to run in to?

Wait, Boonce. I thought Bellarmine's your boss.

Boonce shrugs.

He is. Which is why we're not having this conversation at my
office.

Boonce watches the garbage barges pass.

Way of the world, right, Spademan? Start out as an idealist,
end up as an underling.

You should have told me all this in the first place, Boonce.

He looks around. Says quietly.

That's the whole point, Spademan. I didn't know all this

before. I'm just piecing it together, just like you. And as you can imagine, with this particular situation, there's not too many people I can turn to.

Then he leans in.

Look, there's one more thing you should know, and then I won't blame you if you bail right now. But I owe you the whole story. Bellarmine started Near Enemy, yes. Appointed me to run it. But his notion was a special division to protect the limn.

Okay.

Well, I was more ambitious. I took it in a slightly different direction. Lesser was working on something for me. A hack, for the limn. Like hopping. But worse.

Boonce kneads his knuckles again. Looks like a doctor who diagnosed himself and got the worst possible news.

Lesser was working on a way to weaponize the limn, Spademan. That's what Near Enemy was really all about. Targeted assassinations in the limn, like drone strikes, but even better, because there's no collateral damage, no near misses. Can you imagine the applications? If you could find someone in the limn and take them out? From any bed, anywhere in the world?

Sure, Boonce. Sounds great. Except it's not possible.

Boonce worries his cuff links, tiny polished cop shields, like he's recalling something. Or regretting it.

All the things in this world that we think are rules, Spademan? Or laws? They're not. They're just problems to be solved.

And Lesser—?

Lesser thought he'd solved the problem.

Did he?

I don't know. Because he bolted. Quit Near Enemy and went back to bed-hopping full-time. Living in squalor. Which is where you found him, right before I found you, and he disappeared.

So why didn't you just arrest him in the first place?

For what? Having an idea? Truth is, that's why I was watching him. To see exactly what he knew. And who he might sell it to. Maybe that was a mistake. Maybe I should have taken care of him the moment he bolted. But, you know, I felt protective of him. Like maybe I could win him back. That was my mistake.

Looks at me. Eyes pleading now.

That's why I need to find him, Spademan. I need to know what he knows, and what he did with it, and who he gave it to. Because I unleashed this. This is on me. All of this. And I need your help to stop it.

I listen. Think a second. Mostly about how easy it would be to walk away. Surprise myself when I say instead.

I'll help you, Boonce. On two conditions.

Just name them.

You hide Persephone. Like we agreed.

Absolutely. Where?

Wherever she wants to go.

She's not safe at your apartment?

I'm not worried about where she is. I'm worried about who she's with.

Simon.

I need to give her a better alternative.

Done. Safe passage. I can do that. What's the other condition?

When we find Lesser, you don't hurt him. He can face whatever he has to face for whatever it is he's done, but he doesn't just disappear.

Boonce laughs.

Look at you, Spademan, getting all sentimental. Unless I'm wrong, this time last week, you had very different intentions for Lesser.

This isn't last week.

All right. I don't touch Lesser. Look, I don't need to. I just need to know what he knows. And who else knows it.

Fair enough.

Which means you need to talk to Shaban, Spademan. Shaban and I have a history. Not a good one. And if it turns out he's in any way mixed up with Bellarmine? Well, obviously, I can't follow that road any further. You can.

Just talk?

Just talk. For now. You won't have trouble finding him. He's set up shop on Atlantic Avenue.

Boonce picks up his briefcase. Offers me his hand. No wink this time. Just a hand.

We shake.

He smiles. Says to me.

A garbageman and an underling. City's last, best hope. Imagine that.

He turns to leave. Then I think of one more question.

Hey, Boonce, you're not a Buddhist, are you?

Why? You in the market for a new faith?

Just wondering about the name Near Enemy.

It's a tactical term. Geopolitical. People divvy up the world into far enemies and near enemies.

What's the difference?

The far enemy is the one you hate, the one you're sworn to fight against. The near enemy is the one you're close to, who you trust, but you shouldn't. Radical Islamists, for example. They think of Muslim nations that don't follow jihad as the near enemy.

And who's the far enemy?

He gestures to the city.

Watch rattles.

We are.

20.

Meanwhile in Hoboken.

Persephone's changing a diaper.

Still waiting on those diaper wipes.

Hannah's lying on her back on the changing pad with her legs up, giggling. Persephone wipes Hannah, once, twice, again. With a Kleenex.

Correction. What's left of a Kleenex.

Chucks the remnants of the dirty tissue into the mouth of the diaper genie she lugged down from upstate.

Laughs to herself. Despite herself.

Diaper genie. Funny name.

Diaper genie, if I rub my baby's ass, will you come forth and grant me my one wish?

And what is Persephone's wish?

To be elsewhere. Anywhere.

Her and Hannah.

Somewhere safe.

And maybe a little nice. Just a little. Just for once.

Because a little over a year ago Persephone was eighteen and living in a tent in the camps in Central Park, sleeping on a borrowed yoga mat and warding off boys with hungry hands.

Warding off worse.

A year before that, she thinks, she was still a kid, really, still worrying about dumb shit like senior prom. Still living in South Carolina, on her father's fabled estate, all paid for by Crystal Corral Ministries, on a property so large that the help would pick her up at the front door of the main house just to drive her to the carport in a golf cart.

Where she had her pick of cars.

Had her pick of everything, really.

Grace Chastity and her three sisters.

Grace Charity, Grace Constance, and Grace Honor.

The four Graces.

She's the eldest.

Now in exile.

Excommunicated, basically.

All four of them named for her grandmother, Harrow's mother, a godly woman. Though Persephone barely knew her. Only from photos. But still revered her.

Still reveres her, actually.

Back then, back when she was taking chauffeured golf-cart rides over rolling grounds toward jam-packed carports, back when she'd routinely order clothes online without even bothering to look at the price, then just give whatever didn't fit or she didn't like to the help, back when her family had a private jet at their disposal, just idling on the tarmac, back when her father had the president's ear and she was known simply as Grace, because she was the eldest of the four Graces, back then she even traveled with her own personal security detail.

Even had an affair with her own personal security detail.

Simon.

Calls himself Simon the Magician.

Who's suddenly reappeared in her life.

Ta-da.

Best she knows, Simon is out in the livingroom right now, playing cards with silent Mark Ray.

Go Fish.

Meanwhile, here she is, stuck in Hoboken, trapped with a baby, unable to even go near the windows, the curtains drawn all day. This after spending nearly a year in a cabin in the woods with no cable, no wifi, no handheld, no nothing.

Not much of a life for the eldest of Graces.

And now she hears from Simon that her three little sisters, the leftover Graces, as she used to call them, are not only all thriving on that estate in South Carolina, but are actually angling to take control of her father's church. Still have their pick of cars in the carport, probably. Still siphoning off her father's fortune, no doubt, even though her father's now gone.

At her hand.

But Crystal Corral is still going strong, even after settling all those lawsuits. And if her father's gone, his fortune isn't. It's not exhausted, apparently.

Not like she is.

Wipes Hannah again.

Once.

Twice.

Discards.

Fucking flimsy Kleenex.

Hannah coughs, then smiles, and Persephone recalls how when Hannah was a newborn, still red-faced and fussy, every sound she made absolutely petrified Persephone. Every coo, burp, gurgle, cough, snort, and hiccup made her heart seize. Because Persephone was convinced every time Hannah made a noise that it was some sort of cry for help. Or a last breath.

A death rattle.

So she'd constantly stare at this alarming new creature, terrified. Unsure just how to keep her alive. Wondering, How do people do this? But over time, she figured out something that reassured her.

Her baby wants to live.

Her baby has no other job than to live.

Her baby is basically a machine for staying alive.

And so she determined, in that moment, to simply follow her baby's example.

To become a machine for staying alive.

Makes her think of that old disco song, in fact. She looks down at Hannah. Tweaks her nose.

Sings it to her.

Ah, ah, ah, ah. Staying alive. Staying alive.

Hannah giggles.

Here we are, together, staying alive, Persephone thinks. Not much of a life, maybe. But we're alive.

Then says to Hannah, One last wipe.

All done!

Wipes her down with the last of the Kleenex, which she tugs from the now-empty box. Balls the soggy tissue and takes her best shot. Buzzer beater. For the win—

Wad bounces weakly off the lip of the diaper genie and falls to the carpet.

Crowd groans.

Persephone frowns.

Used to play a little basketball back in private school. Lost her shooting touch, apparently.

Stoops to retrieve the fallen wad. Looks up to find Simon, leaning in the doorway, arms crossed, watching her.

He gives her a slow-clap ovation.

Nice shot.

She gives him the finger.

Simon smirks. He wears a white turtleneck, despite the summer heat. Always did look good in a turtleneck, she thinks.

But she says nothing. So Simon breaks the ice.

She's a beautiful baby. Takes after her mother.

Really? That's the best you can do?

He smiles.

How so?

I just remember you as being a bit more of a charmer. But, you know. I was young. Impressionable. Vulnerable.

Maybe I'm rusty. Need to get back into practice. Just like you, with your jump shot.

What do you want, Simon?

He straightens up. Uncrosses his arms.

How long are you planning on staying here?

I was going to ask you the same thing.

He inches into the room. Shuts the door softly behind him.

I'll stay here as long as you need me. To make sure you're okay. You're both okay.

Persephone scoffs.

I can take care of myself. Of both of us. I've proved that.

Simon holds his hands up, as if in surrender.

Hell, you'll get no argument from me.

And besides, I've got those cops outside, watching us. We'll be okay. If you need to leave.

I'm not leaving.

Either way.

I wouldn't count on those cops.

Why not?

I generally counsel against counting on anyone. You need to know how to protect yourself. That's why I taught you how to handle that bowie knife, way back when.

And Persephone, despite herself, recalls those long summer afternoons, alone with Simon, out in the barn on her father's estate. Sun slicing through the wood slats in bright dusty shards, through the overwhelming smell of hay and horses. Simon standing behind her in the heat, holding her arms, working them like the limbs of a marionette. Teaching her just how to kill a hay bale. Jab, feint, thrust. Stab, stab, good, again. Showing her where to aim the blade. Honing her knife technique. Then acting as her target. Pointing toward his midsection.

Daring her. Go ahead, you won't hurt me. You won't even touch me. And it was true, she could never touch him, he was too nimble, too swift, always where you thought he wouldn't be. Dodging, dancing, daily. Sweating together in the stifling shadows of the barn. Jab. Thrust. Again. Better. Thrust. Good. Again.

Simon scratches at his bushy beard. Uncharacteristically unkempt. He looks, she thinks, standing here in this apartment in Hoboken, like some kind of mountain man, some haggard hermit returned from the wilderness.

He asks her.

You still have that knife?

Persephone fastens Hannah's diaper.

Sure. Somewhere. What about you, Simon? What are your plans?

I'm going back South. To take my church back.

Your church?

Our church.

Nods to Hannah.

Her church.

Well, good luck.

I could use some help.

I'm sure you could.

Persephone hoists Hannah. Hugs her baby to her hip. Hannah's gotten so heavy now, and she's only getting heavier. Truth be told, Persephone rarely thinks about their future. Because when she does, she can't even begin to imagine what to think.

Great to see you again, Simon. Feel free to swing back by in another year or so.

I don't want to go back alone.

He edges closer. Clasps her elbows now. Firm, like how he used to.

Come with me. I need you. That's the only reason I came back here.

She twists away. Breaks his hold.

Careful, Simon. The last guy who got this close to me ended up on fire.

He grins. Nods. Backs away with his palms up. Holds her gaze though.

We should do this together, Grace. It's ours. It belongs to us. To the three of us.

You had your chance to stick around.

But I'm here now.

I don't need you here now.

Well, I'm here.

That's true. And as long as you're here, why don't you make yourself useful?

Just name it.

Run to the corner and get me some diaper wipes.

Simon's about to speak when he's interrupted by a knock at the bedroom door.

Persephone nods toward the door.

You want to get that?

Simon opens it.

Mark, standing in the doorway. Jaw still wired shut. Mumbles something. Sounds like *Mrmrmr*.

Simon shrugs, annoyed.

What?

Mrmrmr.

Another shrug.

Mark angles a handheld, a cheap one bought for just this purpose, and scrawls something on its screen with his fingertip. Holds the handheld up, like a flash card.

SOMEONE AT THE DOOR.

Simon says.

So?

Mark scrawls again.

ANSWER IT?

Simon scowls. Persephone brushes past Simon. Says to Mark.

I'll get it.

Says to Simon.

I think since the cabin, Mark's a little door-shy.

Simon stops her.

No. I'll get it. You two stay here.

Simon doesn't talk about his past much, not to Persephone, not to anyone, not about all those years he spent before Harrow found him and hired him. Rescued him, really. Rechristened him Simon the Magician. Harrow had faith in him, that much was true. Taught him life lessons. New ones. Better lessons, about how to have a better life. That's what Harrow always promised him.

But Harrow also understood that the old lessons, the ones Simon had already learned, as a kid and as a teen and in his twenties, on battlefields here and abroad, all those formal and informal lessons, so brutal and bloody—those lessons had their usefulness too.

Once you've learned them. Can't unlearn them.

Harrow liked that. Counted on it.

What Simon had already learned.

Harrow liked to have it at his disposal. Liked to have Simon on the end of a leash. Teaching other people lessons. That was Simon's job.

Simon still relishes the look on Harrow's face, on that day back in the limn, at the moment when Harrow realized the leash had finally snapped.

One of those lessons, the dirty ones, that Simon learned during his two tours overseas, before he was discharged for exhibiting a certain brand of overzealousness that could no longer be channeled constructively, was this: It's better to kill someone who wants to shake your hand than it is to shake someone's hand who wants to kill you.

Important lesson.

Simon's put it into practice, more than once.

Sounds harsh, yes, but then, survival's harsh.

Yet another lesson, Simon thinks.

Then Simon answers the front door.

Encounters two young men in matching gray coveralls.

Simon wonders what the fuck they're doing here. So he asks them.

What the fuck are you doing here?

Clean-cut men. Well built. Stand with their hands clasped behind their backs. Legs spread. Loose military stances. Both have a single word, *Pushbroom,* stitched in script on the breast of their uniforms.

First man speaks.

Sir, I wonder if we might have a moment of your time?

Simon smiles.

Perfect timing. Come on in.

21.

From the South Street Seaport, it doesn't take long for me to cross the river and get to Atlantic Avenue in Brooklyn. I head straight for the strip of the avenue that, before Times Square, was a thriving Arab neighborhood. Full of markets, scent shops, religious bookstores, you name it. You could hear the call to prayer on loudspeakers all day. Mosques filling up with the faithful.

That's all gone now. The mosques, the markets, the bookstores. Along with pretty much everything else.

Atlantic Avenue is also where a half dozen men hatched the plot against Times Square. Five men in a backroom under a bare bulb, with a sixth man, arrested later, funneling funds from overseas. Who knows how exactly they planned it. I never sought out the stories afterward. Never cared too much about the who, what, and why of it.

Especially the why.

By then, I'd pretty much lost my faith in why.

So I never learned the exact address of the building that housed the meeting that hatched the plot to explode a dirty bomb in Times Square.

Didn't care. Not about that, or much of anything else.

And the mobs that visited Atlantic Avenue in the days after Times Square didn't care too much about details either. Or exact addresses.

Just burned out every storefront. Just to be sure.

Local crowds gathered to cheer.

Local cops gathered to watch.

Didn't lift a finger.

Let mayhem rule.

Then came in and mopped up afterward.

Then, a few weeks later, after Bellarmine was hired, the cops unleashed some mayhem of their own.

On the night of the Atlantic Avenue sweep.

Cops came after midnight.

Special ops. Special cops. The lethal kind, who never bothered to memorize Miranda rights.

Clad in black. Move in tandem.

Red laser dots dancing over locked doorways.

Hand signals. Gloved hands. Give the go-ahead.

Boots unleashed on doors. Doors caved in with a clatter. Suspects scrambling as they're yanked from their beds, still tangled up in the sheets. Some half-dressed, some half-cursing, dragged into hallways under sweeping flashlight beams, wrists zipped up in plastic cuffs, then shoved down the staircase. Some more than shoved.

A few unfortunate escape attempts shot down as they fought back. Or at least that's how it got written up in the reports.

Half the block rounded up. The other half getting the message.

And who could be blamed if, in all the commotion, in an apartment or two, or in a shop or two, or in a mosque or two, the occasional candle got knocked over, or a jar of scented oil somehow shattered on the floor, starting an unfortunate fire?

Burned half the block down?

Who could be blamed?

Bellarmine beamed at the next day's press briefing.

Framed by flags. A soundtrack of shutter clicks as he detailed the department's greatest success yet.

And no one protested, not really, not afterward, except those being rounded up and locked away, but it was hard to hear their objections over the sound of sirens and camera shutters and cheers.

Post crowed the loudest, of course.

ISLAM-DUNK! TOP COP TOPPLES TERROR MOSQUES.

Maybe there were a few hand-wringing editorials in the more liberal-leaning papers, a few outraged callers to the public-radio shows, but for the most part, everyone else in the city just sat on their hands, at least those who weren't busy applauding.

Can't say I sat home and cried about it either. What news of it trickled back to me.

I wasn't paying much attention to the news at that point.

I was plenty busy. For one, I had a wife to bury.

Just kidding.

They'd already buried her for me.

In any case, Atlantic Avenue emptied out.

And all the immigrants who lived there disappeared.

Between the cops and the sweeps and the roving gangs that came afterward, picking through the ruins, anyone who looked even vaguely Middle Eastern couldn't move out fast enough. Some to Michigan. Some to elsewhere. Most to anywhere but here. Some headed back home, overseas, so I heard. Didn't have any trouble getting on flights, just as long as the flights were one-way, and pointed away from New York.

And for a while, you could skateboard down the center of Atlantic Avenue and you wouldn't see a single person. Just plywood and graffiti. Old angry flyers stapled to telephone poles or blown by the wind and stuck under the melted tires of burned-out cars.

THE MUSLIM MENACE.

Hand-drawn. Hook-nosed. Scowling sheikhs with scimitars, looming over a New York skyline.

So much for the melting pot. Melting pot had a meltdown.

And the brownstone neighborhoods in the blocks nearby quickly emptied out. Too many nights of riots. Too many cars flipped over and torched. Too many visiting mobs with Molotov cocktails, tossed by masked men with indiscriminate aim.

Love thy neighbor, until thy neighbor gets firebombed.

Then fuck thy neighbor.

And fuck this neighborhood.

But now.

Lo and behold.

Signs of life.

A headscarf.

A hijab.

Lone woman in a burqa, trailed by chattering kids.

Two men in skullcaps and sandals arguing out front of a cleaned-up storefront.

Cop car slowly creeps the wrong way down the street. A whoop-whoop tells the two men to keep it moving.

They comply. Disappear behind a doorway.

Cops move on.

Still.

Signs of life.

These days, most storefronts on Atlantic are long since abandoned.

Most storefronts.

But not all.

And not this one.

———

It's a brand-new scent-and-oils shop, the Grand Opening banner hanging proudly across the windowpane like a pageant contestant's sash. Step inside and the store still smells of fresh paint, and the bright white walls are lined with shelves of glass bottles, arranged by shade—rows of yellow, green, and blue bottled oils, imported scents and rare essences, so the signs say. Boxes of incense sticks spill open along the walls, and slippers and skullcaps are stacked in wicker baskets, offered for sale. Beside them, paperback Qurans are piled up and offered for free.

When I enter, I interrupt two clerks, wearing vests and long robes that graze the floor. The first one wears a skullcap and a healthy beard, while the other has a skullcap, a healthy beard, and a double-barreled shotgun slung on a strap over his shoulder.

Have to admit. Scene looks like a setup to a joke.

A garbageman walks into a perfume shop—

All of us stand silent. Waiting for the punch line.

Then I grab a bottle of yellow scented oil with a knock-off name from a nearby shelf and inspect it. Ask the clerk how much.

Before he can answer, a voice from the back corner of the shop instructs the clerk in some foreign tongue.

Arab-sounding. Though it's not like I'm an expert.

Voice then says to me in English.

Consider it a gift.

The kid stands in the doorway at the back of the shop, half-draped in a beaded curtain. I only call him a kid because he looks so young, even younger in person than in Boonce's photos, looks maybe fifteen, sixteen, tops. Short and slight. Rimless round glasses. Baggy tweed three-piece that hangs off bony shoulders. Ugly burn the size of a palm print flares across one cheek, wrapping down around his throat and disappearing under the open collar of his white dress shirt. Burn must affect his throat, since when he speaks his voice is soft and sounds like sandpaper. Salted with a slight English accent, the posh kind. And unlike the clerks, who are both heavily bearded, the kid's cheeks are completely hairless. Not a whisker visible.

Doorway behind him leads to a staircase.

I ask the obvious.

You Salem Shaban?

I am. This is my shop. And who are you, if I may ask?

My name is Spademan. Friend of Jonathan Lesser. Wondered if I might have a word.

I'm afraid I haven't seen Jonathan Lesser in years.

Yeah, well, no one's seen him in about a week.

It's just that I'm not sure I can help you, Mr Spademan.

I won't take up too much of your time.

Shaban says something to the clerks in that other language. Then says to me.

Certainly. Let's retire to my office upstairs.

He's heading back through the beaded curtain when I ask him about his name, as an icebreaker, mostly.

Salem? That means peace, right?

He looks over his shoulder.

Yes. Though in English it's often spelled Salaam. However, I chose to spell my name in English with an E. You know, like the witch-hunt.

Then he nods toward the staircase.

Shall we?

His office above the store looks like it's out of some old movie. Huge wooden desk covered with a weathered leather deskpad, with a vintage pen-and-pencil set stuck like antennae in a small round paperweight. Wooden swivel chair, wooden blinds, tilted just-so. Cast thin bars of light, like a jail-cell window, across the surface of the desk. Everything's antique, all older than Shaban by a century or so. Same goes for the large dusty globe that sits on a round wooden stand by the desk. I inspect it while Shaban takes his seat. The globe must be plenty old because so much of the world is left blank.

I spin the globe. Stop it with my finger. Land on a continent labeled Terra Incognita. Sounds like a good place to take my next vacation.

Shaban settles into the chair behind the desk and offers me a hardback chair facing him. Hundreds of hand-addressed letters, piled in collapsing stacks, are splayed out messily over the surface of his desk. More stacks are lined up on top of his filing cabinets. More stacks along the floorboards too. His desktop's a mess of letters and loose stamps and long lists of handwritten addresses. Names on the lists are all Muslim names from the looks of it, all el-this and al-that. Office looks like a political campaign in the final frantic days before the vote.

You mailing out your Christmas cards, Shaban?

He smiles.

Just spreading the word.

Seems pretty inefficient. Using the Pony Express, I mean.

You pick your targets. Then wait. Word gets around.

He points to the biggest pile on his desk.

Funny, isn't it? Hand-addressed mail is the most secure way to send out a message these days. They listen to your phone calls, read your email, collect your texts, tail you in the limn, watch you dream, record every thought you've ever had. Yet no one can be arsed enough to steam open an old-fashioned letter. So tell me, what can I help you with, Mr Spademan?

You knew Jonathan Lesser?

Of course. You know that, or you wouldn't be here. You say he's gone missing?

Yes. Since last weekend.

I'm sorry to hear that. Not so easy to do in our modern world. So many eyes watching us all the time.

Well, he managed to slip away. Or be slipped away. By someone.

Jonathan's smart. And slippery. And he runs with a bad crowd. I know, because I used to be part of it.

Then you discovered religion.

Rediscovered, but yes.

Shaban opens a desk drawer. Pulls out a Ziploc stuffed full of something. Looks like twigs and leaves.

These days, I haven't even touched a keyboard in years. Feels good. To be free of all that.

Shaban opens the Ziploc. Takes a pinch. Holds it out to me.

Do you indulge?

In twigs? No, thanks.

I figured as much. But it's rude not to offer.

Salem sticks the plug into his cheek, then zips the baggie closed. Holds it up for me to see.

Khat. Very bad habit. I picked it up in Yemen but never really got hooked until I moved here. During the long hours of coding, with Lesser, actually. It's supposed to help with your concentration, but I could never get Lesser to try it. Hopping was always a sufficient high for him.

Salem sticks the baggie back in the drawer. Slides it shut.

You were asking about Jonathan.

Before he died, he saw something. While he was hopping. Peeping on your old headmaster, Langland.

And what's that?

Woman in a burqa. Suicide bomber. In the limn.

Well, that's certainly a strange fantasy for someone to be indulging. Even Langland.

It wasn't a fantasy. It was an incursion. An attack.

And that's why you're here talking to me? I assume it's not because you consider me a general expert on the topic of Islam.

I heard about your newfound interest in politics. From another old friend of yours. Joseph Boonce.

Shaban laughs.

I should have known that name would come up eventually. How is Mr Boonce? We didn't part on good terms, exactly.

So he tells me. He says you gave up government work to take up political agitation.

Agitation? Is that what they're calling it now? If you mean encouraging people to come back and live on Atlantic Avenue, then yes, he's correct. Of course, I'm sure he knows exactly what I'm up to.

Shaban gestures to the walls. Then stage-whispers.

Eyes everywhere.

So what you're doing isn't political?

I certainly don't think of it as agitation, Mr Spademan. More like urban renewal. This city could use some of that, don't you think?

Sure. But tell me this. Who fucked up this city in the first place?

I don't know, Mr Spademan. Seems to me the city's been on shaky ground for a long time.

How about your dad? What did he think about agitation?

My father's dead, as I'm sure you know. He was a passionate, dangerous man. And he was killed many years back in an American drone strike in Egypt. Which is when I came here, to New York. Have you ever been to Egypt, Mr Spademan?

No. I hear it's not doing too well.

Leave not a stone standing on a stone, is how the biblical imperative puts it. We all seem to be intent on following it to the letter.

To be honest, Shaban, I'm not too torn up about what's happening in some faraway desert.

Shaban smiles wearily.

People never are.

Shaban looks bored, like he's had this argument many times before, and knows it well. Too bad. He's going to have it again. I didn't expect to get into it with Shaban. But now that we're here, we're getting into it.

You don't think you people started this?

You people?

Your people.

Shaban absentmindedly traces his fingertips over the contours of his burn. Gnarled skin that never healed right. Says to me in his sandpaper croak.

Extremists. Drones. Attacks. Counterattacks. Your god. My god. At the end of it all, you're just left with rubble. To my mind, there's not much point in sifting through it afterward, trying to find fingerprints so you can figure out who is responsible. It's still just rubble.

He turns to the window shade. Parts two blinds with his fingers.

Look out there, Mr Spademan. You want to fight with me over these streets? These blocks are poisonous. Toxic. We're all just squabbling over rubble.

Lets the blinds close. Faces me again.

But that's the whole story of history, isn't it?

There's no rubble in the world that's worse than what you people unleashed here.

Isn't there?

I'm sorry, but did we nuke your country?

He traces that burn again.

Nuke? No. Not if we're being technical. But we're all responsible for our fair share of rubble in the world.

Maybe so. Maybe not. One crucial difference, though, Shaban. My wife is buried under your rubble.

I'm very sorry to hear that, Mr Spademan.

So maybe you can understand why I'm personally not too excited about your plans for urban renewal.

I don't say this in any way to minimize your loss, but we've all lost loved ones.

Like your sister?

Yes. Like my sister. For starters.

That's funny, because they say you murdered her.

Shaban eyes me for a moment. Stills his tongue. Then speaks.

Who says that? Joseph Boonce?

An honor killing—that's what you call it? You killed her and then you tracked down the men who raped her and killed them too. For starters.

Whoever told you that is wrong. My sister died in the same drone strike as my father and mother did. You can look it up.

Yet somehow you escaped.

Yes. You sound disappointed.

Just trying to straighten out the details.

Shaban shifts in his chair. Adjusts the baggy tweed suit jacket. No way to make it fit right. Says to me.

Mr Langland brought me here to America. People used to be able to do that, you know. Come here freely. To America. Even Egyptians. Shocking, I know.

Well, money like Langland's will clear a lot of red tape.

Yes, it will. At times I worry that's all we have left now, really.

What's that?

Money and rubble. And the will to fight endlessly over both.

Well, Langland's done fighting. He's dead, by the way. That attack on him in the limn? Looks like it worked.

Shaban looks surprised, or very good at pretending.

Really?

Yes.

Salem pauses. Thinks for a moment.

In the limn? But that's not possible.

Isn't it? Isn't that what you and Lesser were working on for Boonce?

He stays silent. Ponders his options. Then says.

Near Enemy was a total failure. And completely in opposition to my sense of ethics. Once I realized that, I left. Boonce knows all this—

You do any hopping these days, Shaban? Because I hear you were very talented.

I don't indulge in the limn, Mr Spademan. If you'd asked me that straightaway, I could have saved us both a lot of time.

But I heard you were some hotshot hopper. Could really bend the limn to your will.

I was. A real slick motherfucker, as we used to like to say back at Langland's school. But then I rededicated myself to my faith. The day I reopened my Quran, I closed down my bed, and I never went back. Do you know what the Prophet said, Mr Spademan? Angels of mercy do not enter a house wherein there are pictures. I've interpreted that to mean that I am forbidden to go into the limn. Which is, after all, nothing more than a house of pictures. An illusion, which you can live inside. That's how most devout Muslims interpret it, truthfully. So if you're worried about Islamic extremists ruining your escapist fantasies, I can assure you, your limn is likely very safe from them.

Pulls the khat from his cheek and drops the wad in the trash.

As I said, Mr Spademan. This is my only indulgence now.

Then he hesitates. Seems like he's deciding whether to say whatever it is he's about to say. He takes his rimless glasses off and pulls a cloth from his pocket to polish them. Without his glasses, Shaban looks even younger. Even less threatening. He looks at me and says.

Before you go, Mr Spademan, there is one thing—

What's that?

I know Jonathan Lesser, perhaps better than anyone. So wherever he is, whatever he's doing, whoever's got him, you need to find him.

I'll be sure to pass along your concern.

No, I—what I mean is, Lesser is brilliant. He was the smartest of all of us, and that's no small thing for me to admit. There's no limit to what he's capable of, do you understand?

So I've heard.

Mr Spademan, the things in this world that we believe are not possible are not rules. They're not laws. They're only problems to be solved.

Funny. Your old boss Boonce was just telling me the same thing.

It was kind of our mantra back at Near Enemy.

So what's your solution these days, Shaban?

I send out invitations to a slightly better world. See who accepts.

He wipes the lenses of his glasses, then puts the glasses back on, looping the wire arms around each ear in turn. One ear, his right, is barely a remnant, eroded away by burns. Like the ear of a sand-blasted statue left for eons in the desert.

I just mean that you need to find Lesser, Mr Spademan. Find out what he knows. Before anyone else does. Including Mr Boonce.

I'm sure you'd love to know what Lesser knows, right, Shaban?

Mr Spademan, you mistake my tone. I'm not curious. I'm frightened. You should be too.

Of what? Of you?

He smiles politely.

It was a pleasure to meet you and to have this conversation. Now if you don't mind—

He gestures to a toppled pile of envelopes waiting for addresses.

I have many more invitations to send out before I'm done.

Part of me wants to invite Shaban somewhere private to continue our conversation. I've never been one for debate-club banter, but his manner got under my skin, more than it should. Something about the cool confidence of someone who's had the same argument a million times, and has never once come close to changing his mind.

Maybe I could change his mind.

Given time.

Instead I leave him to his twigs and leaves and head back out to Atlantic Avenue.

On the street outside, my pocket buzzes. I pull my phone out, though I'm almost too worked up to answer. But it could be Persephone. Or Boonce.

I flip it open.

It's neither.

Call from:

Lesser.

Interesting.

So I answer.

Turns out it's not Lesser calling, it's Moore. The skinny kid. Using Lesser's phone. At first I don't recognize his name even when he tells me. So he repeats it.

You know—Moore. Lesser's pal? From Stuyvesant Town? We met last Saturday. I bought you that sandwich from the deli.

Wait. I bought that sandwich.

I needed to get in touch with you, Spademan. I found your number in Lesser's phone. I'm at Lesser's apartment right now and I need to see you.

Why?

Because I found Lesser.

Really? Where is he?

I don't know.

I thought you said you found him.

More like he found me. Come here and I'll explain everything.

Okay. Give me half an hour.

I'll be here. And Spademan, there's one more thing you should know.

What's that, Moore?

It happened again.

22

When I get to Lesser's apartment, front door's still hanging limp off busted hinges. Inside, Moore's waiting, curled up on that same bare mattress, with his knees pulled up to his chest. Looks spooked and somehow skinnier. Draped in that same Army coat.

Otherwise, apartment's vacant.

Okay, Moore. Where's Lesser?

He's not here.

So I noticed.

But I heard from him.

Okay. Where is he?

He didn't say.

Right about now, I'm losing patience with Moore.

Well, what did he tell you?

He didn't tell me anything. He couldn't. All I got was a ping.

Moore holds up his handheld, like this will mean something to me. Then he says.

Every hopper has a ping. In case things go really bad. In case the sweepers get you and you can't get free. They've got you tapped in and you can't tap out, and you can't communicate to anyone out here, so you send a ping. Just a personalized signal that will bounce around the limn. A little ripple in the code. Hope someone notices. Only other hoppers even know to look for it. It's kind of a last resort. A distress call.

And you got one from Lesser.

Yes.

When?

About an hour ago.

So he's still alive?

Somewhere. And someone's got him. In there.

Who's got him?

Moore croaks the answer.

Sweepers. Must be.

But Moore, he's out here somewhere too, right? I mean, his actual body is out here, tapped into a bed somewhere.

Moore's eyes empty.

Sure. He's somewhere. That's why they snatched him up. So they could take him somewhere, dope him up, and tap him in so he can't tap back out again. That way they can make it last.

What last?

The punishment.

And where do you think they took him in the limn, Moore?

Moore's face drains. Voice cracks.

A black room.

I was worried Moore was going to say that. Like everyone, I've heard rumors of so-called black rooms, hidden in the shadowed corners of the limn. Secure sites out here, where they tap you in, and secure constructs in there, nearly impossible to crash. Black rooms. One way in. No way out. Poor Lesser. By this point, he probably wishes he was only dead.

Moore croaks another request.

You have to get him out, Spademan. I know Lesser's done some bad shit but he doesn't deserve this. Whatever you had in mind for him? Last Saturday night? I promise you. Black room's worse.

Moore's right. And now I've officially gone from killing Lesser to finding Lesser to saving Lesser in less than a week.

Strange week.

Okay, Moore. Tell me about that other thing.

He looks up with those empty eyes again.

What other thing?

You said it happened again.

Promise me you'll save him, Spademan? He's a special kid—

I'll do my best. Now tell me, Moore. What happened again?

Moore hugs his bony knees closer, like a kid at a campfire on a cold night who can't get warm. Collects himself. Takes a breath.

Unspools the tale.

Moore explains there's a bed-hopper, calls herself Bad Penny, who likes to peep on twisted pervs in the limn. She uses the info she gathers to shame them out here in the nuts-and-bolts world. Fashions herself a kind of citizen crusader. Plasters pervs' names across every chat room, hacks their contacts and mass-messages everyone they know. In this case, she'd targeted an East Village scumbag by the name of Loeb. Greasy mouth breather who runs a candy shop in real life, likes to invite local kids into the backroom to sample his special stash of rare sweets. Takes Polaroids of all the kids. Posts their photos on his Wall of Fame.

Nothing twisted.

Not out here, at least.

But he uses the photos to create likenesses in the limn.

Crude likenesses.

But then, Loeb's a crude guy.

So apparently last night he's tapped in and this hopper, Bad Penny, decides to peep in on his antics, catch him in the act.

Moore whispers.

But it went wrong.

Let me guess.

Moore spills the rest. Loeb got a visit from a woman in a black burqa. Then a bear hug. Then boom.

Apparently, Bad Penny barely escaped in front of the final fireball. Screams still ringing in her ears long after she tapped out, only some of which were her own.

Moore wraps up the tale. Shaken. Understandably. Says to me. This happened maybe an hour ago. It's all over hopper chatter. This Loeb, do you know where he taps in?

Sure. Bad Penny already posted his address, photo, construct coordinates, everything. He taps in from his apartment in Alphabet City, on Avenue D, above his candy shop.

And this hopper, Penny, you think she was involved in this somehow? Given her grudge against Loeb?

You kidding? She's wrapped up in a blanket right now, sipping soup and muttering. One of her hopper friends posted the story online, as a warning to other hoppers. Now all the hoppers are talking about it. It's all over the old Internet.

What are they saying?

Stay out of the limn. Some don't believe it, of course. Claim what she saw was just a prank. But a lot of people do believe it. And they're spooked.

What do you believe, Moore?

I believe it. After Lesser? I believe it.

Okay, Moore. Give me that address.

Outside Stuyvesant, in the abandoned playground, I pull out my phone and punch that same number again.

Boonce answers.

What is it, Spademan?

He's in a black room, Boonce.

Long silence. Then he asks.

Who's got him?

I don't know. Sweepers, maybe. Pushbroom, probably.

No, a black room is way bigger than sweepers, even Pushbroom. Black rooms don't even officially exist. Best I know, there's only one operational black room in New York. It was supposed to be shut down. I can check into it and get back to you.

By the way, Boonce, it happened again.

What happened?

Our friend in the burqa.

When?

About an hour ago. Different hopper witnessed it. It's all over hopper chatter. Matter of time before it becomes a bigger deal.

Spademan, I made some inquiries, and I was right—this is Bellarmine's big bombshell. This news about the limn. The one he's going to drop at the debate.

When's the debate?

In two days.

So that gives us two days to find Lesser. Which means I have to get going.

Where are you headed?

To find out if this guy Loeb is still alive.

Takes me twenty minutes to get to Avenue D. The downstairs door to Loeb's building is unlocked, so I head inside and up a flight of stairs to the walk-up and knock twice.

No answer. But it's ajar. So I enter.

Spot Loeb in his bed, still tapped in.

Apartment's dark and smells about as good as you'd imagine. Still, I've seen enough dead bodies, especially ones lying in beds, to know, even from across the room, that Loeb is never getting back up again.

Walk closer to the corpse in the cot.

No marks on him. Looks like he passed away peacefully.

Either way, I know the world won't mourn the passing of a lowlife like Loeb.

Not until they find out how and why he really died.

Figure I'll leave him for the neighbors to discover. Three days, bad smell, call the landlord to investigate, always seemed like a quiet guy, etcetera. Tell reporters the usual tale, the kind that gets buried in the back pages of the *Post*. Which this tale will, until someone pieces it all together. The hoppers' panicked chatter, and now Loeb's fresh corpse. And Langland, before that. Someone will add it all up. Tell the world. Seed panic. Probably Bellarmine, unless someone beats him to it.

Stay out of the limn.

They've found a way in.

And they can kill you in there now.

For Bellarmine, the timing couldn't be better. Whole city hits the panic button a week before the polls? Voters will stampede straight into his waiting embrace.

Elect the strongman with the soothing promise.

Sleep Tight.

Unless I can find Lesser first.

When I came in, I locked the apartment door behind me to keep out nosy neighbors, so when the key turns in the lock, I hear it turning.

Whoever's coming in does it noisily, like they're not expecting company.

Door swings open and I'm already waiting.

But it's my turn to be surprised.

She just stands in the doorway, hand on the key that's in the lock.

Maybe takes her a second to place me.

Or to figure out what the hell I'm doing here.

So I fill the silence.

Hello, Nurse.

23.

Nurse pulls the key from the door and pockets it, slipping it in the front of her crisp white uniform.

Straightens her hat.

Spademan. So is this my rain check?

I'm actually here to see your friend Loeb.

He's not my friend. He's my boss. As of yesterday.

I turn and nod toward the stiffening corpse.

You might want to update your résumé.

She closes the door quietly behind her, then gestures to Loeb's dingy flat and laughs drily.

How the mighty have fallen, huh?

I'm eager to catch up, Nurse, but first, let's talk about the dead guy.

Sure. This happened about an hour ago. I just stepped out to call 911.

It took you an hour to decide to make a phone call?

To be honest, I didn't know what to do. And, to be honest, I never made the call.

Having stowed the key, she sets down her white leather handbag, then strides across the room until she's only inches from me. Close enough to put her hand flat on my chest. Close enough to remind us both how much closer we were just a few nights ago.

Says in a quiet voice. Not pleading. Just explaining.

Spademan, we both know, I call this in, it's done for me. I'd say I'd lose my license, but let's be honest, after Langland, it's already lost. I mean, look around. This is the only job I could get after losing Langland, and this one I had to find on the Internet, no reference checks, no questions, all cash.

Gestures to Loeb.

Too bad today was payday, huh?

So what happened?

I don't know, Spademan. I've never lost anyone before, I swear. With Langland, I just chalked it up to the fact that he was ancient. I mean, they warn you this can happen, but—

Now the tears come. They tumble. And despite myself, I hug her. Don't quite believe her. But I hug her. Then hear another voice at the door.

Hello?

I look up to see a man, hovering in the doorway. Long man, long trenchcoat, long patterned tie, long face. Long hair too, but balding, so he's got it swept up in a messy comb-over. Best described as balding hippie. Which is the worst kind of hippie.

Plus, he's wearing Birkenstocks.

Trenchcoat and Birkenstocks.

He gives a cheery wave. Then flashes a badge.

You all mind if I come in?

The long man stows the shield and makes his introductions. Offers me a handshake that feels like a wet paper bag full of tongue depressors. Announces cheerfully.

Detective Dandy. James Dandy. NYPD.

It takes me a minute.

Jim Dandy?

His eye twitches.

I prefer James.

Fishes a notebook from his pocket. Old-fashioned spiral-bound. Pinches a tiny pencil. Licks its tip. Looks up at us.

So I hear we have a body. I'm guessing it's not either of you two.

Points his pencil stub at Loeb.

Oh. This fat fuck.

Walks over and pokes Loeb in his bed, then scribbles something in the notebook. Turns back to us.

Well, in my considered professional opinion, he's dead. Either of you want to fill in the details?

I'm not sure what to say, and Nurse just stands there, defiant, and Dandy waits, fiddling with his tie knot, until he points his pencil toward Nurse's red-cross hat.

I take it you're the nurse.

She smiles.

Excellent deduction.

Dandy hesitates. Wags the pencil at Nurse again.

Don't I know you from somewhere?

You tell me.

Because you look awfully familiar.

I look like a nurse. We all look the same.

No, no, we've met before. On another dead-in-a-bed. That's right. Just the other night. At Astor Place.

Nurse answers with a tight grin.

Yes, that's right.

Dandy chuckles.

Rough week, huh?

Pencil stub swivels toward me.

And you are?

I shrug.

Nurse's aide.

Dandy chuckles again. Shakes his head. Nods toward the corpse.

See, I wouldn't expect a shitbag pederast like Loeb to have a nurse, let alone a staff.

Nurse speaks up.

I answered an ad on the Internet. I just started yesterday.

Sure. Newly looking for work after Astor Place. Mr Langland was his name, if I recall correctly.

That's right.

Dandy gestures to the body.

You want to walk me through this one?

Nurse stalls. So I interject.

She doesn't know. She wasn't here.

No?

She was with me.

Really? Where?

Down the block.

Doing what?

Killing time.

Dandy shuts his notebook. Says sarcastically.

Well, I guess that settles it then.

I'm serious. We've been out for hours. Just got here ourselves. You can ask the neighbors.

And your name is?

Name's Spademan.

Dandy smiles.

Well, that's certainly memorable. Mr Spade Man. Don't even need to write that down.

Let me ask you something, Detective Dandy.

Shoot.

They let you wear sandals on the job?

He looks down at his Birkenstocks. Wiggles his toes. Toes crack. Looks back at me.

I got foot issues. Fallen arches. Occupational hazard.

Okay. Here's my other question. How'd you even know to come up here to look around?

I'm a detective, Mr Spademan. That's my job. I detect.

Because I figured Loeb here would have festered for weeks if we hadn't found him. Recluse like him.

Dandy scratches at a wild eyebrow with the pencil stub's eraser. Almost loses his pencil in the thicket. His eyebrows look like two birds taking flight. Notices me noticing. Gestures to his brows, then points to his balding head.

God's idea of a joke, right? Never where you want it to be.

Pockets the pencil.

Anyhow, we got an anonymous call about a body an hour ago. I happened to be in the neighborhood, so I said I'd drop by.

And you know Loeb?

Oh, sure, I know him. Local diddler. Every neighborhood needs one.

But you never took him in?

Oh, I'd have loved to. But he's never diddled anyone out here, best we know. And what people do in there—

Dandy shrugs.

—is what they do in there.

I find I'm developing a fondness for Dandy, despite myself. Figure I'll prod him a little. See if he's got any more information that might come in handy. Who knows?

Handy Dandy.

Detective Dandy, that's two dead tappers turning up in less than a week. That's not suspicious?

Nurse shoots me a look. I shoot one back. Call it a draw.

Meanwhile, Dandy stashes his notebook and starts rummaging through his trenchcoat pockets. Looks distracted while he answers me.

Hey, it happens. Friend, to tell you the truth, I don't concern myself too much with the electric wonderland. I work out here. With the real bodies.

Finally finds what he's hunting for, which turns out to be a pack of cigarettes. Taps one out. Protruding butt looks like a chimney on a factory. Offers it to both of us in turn and we both decline. Dandy shrugs and sticks the butt in his mouth, stows the smokes and starts another pocket excavation. While he talks, his cigarette bounces like a conductor's wand, counting the orchestra in.

And see, because I'm out here with the real bodies, that means that, unfortunately, even when a fetid ball-hair like Loeb expires, I have to make inquiries. You know? Especially when we get an anonymous tip to check it out.

Still rummaging. Seems frustrated. Looks up. Cigarette bobs.

I don't suppose for some reason either of you carries a lighter?

I pull out my Zippo. Spark it. Dandy looks pleasantly surprised. Dips his cigarette, then takes a deep inhale. I ask him one last question.

You ever work with a cop named Joseph Boonce?

Long exhale.

Boonce? Never heard of him.

How about Robert Bellarmine?

Dandy chortles.

Bellarmine? Of course. Never met him personally. I'm way too low on the totem pole for that. But I know him, sure. Everyone does. That cop's going to be our next mayor.

Dandy must have decided he's gotten as much as he's going to get from us, up to and including the light from my Zippo, because in the end he doesn't even stick around long enough to finish that smoke.

Butts it out on Loeb's belly. Looses an acrid stink. Dandy looks at us conspiratorially. Bounces those Groucho brows.

The guys from forensics are not going to like that. At. All.

Then he scribbles something and rips the page from his notebook. Holds it out to Nurse.

Like I said, on the department totem pole, I'm so low that

I'm basically underground. But I do like to solve mysteries. So if you hear anything else about suspicious deaths among the tapped-in, give me a call.

Dandy's about to leave when he remembers one last thing. Snaps his fingers. Goes back to pocket-fishing. Pulls a card out. Hands it over.

I found this on the doormat outside. Must have fallen down from the jamb when you opened the door. Mean anything to you?

I take it. Read it.

PUSHBROOM.

I shrug.

Nope.

He winks.

Well, keep it. As a souvenir.

Then he salutes and says he'll see us around, and disappears back down the stairwell.

I pocket the card. Nurse pockets the slip. Then says to me.

Well, I suddenly find myself free tonight. How about you, Spademan? You got any pressing plans? Or should we find a way to kill some time together?

24.

Puzzle it out. Assemble an inventory of what I know so far for sure.

In short, not much.

Someone grabbed Lesser and dragged him to a black room. Someone found a way to kill people through the limn. And someone apparently hired Pushbroom, the cutthroat sweeper agency, to track down and murder all the people in the nuts-and-bolts world that I actually care about.

Might be the same someone, in all three cases.

Either way, I'm still stuck wondering what exactly I'll find when I rip open the envelope at the end of this game.

Because so far?

No clue.

Though I am starting to wonder if I won't find Nurse's name in there somehow.

Either that, or she's turned out to be the world's unluckiest nurse.

In the meantime, the Pushbroom calling card stuck in the door-jamb at Loeb's apartment is troubling me, so I tell Nurse I'll spring for a cab to take her home. Just to be safe.

She protests. A little.

Less about the cab than about going home alone.

You remember I live up near Fort Tryon Park, right? That's a two-hundred-dollar fare, easy. Two fifty with tip. And I never did get paid by Loeb.

I pull out my money roll. Count what's left, which isn't much.

Not enough to cover the whole ride, but maybe enough to start a conversation.

So we flag a cab. Open negotiations.

Cab pulls up a half hour later to the gates of Fort Tryon Park, a patch of tree-choked wilderness nestled high on the rocky northern tip of Manhattan. It's late now, long past midnight, and Nurse gets out, alone, and thanks the driver, then stoops to snatch her white leather handbag from the backseat. She stands upright, straightens her skirt, her white uniform bright as a flare on the darkened block. Closes the back door and turns to walk home. Cab's taillights pulse red, then the cab pulls away, down into the further darkness of the avenue, shrouded under a canopy of drooping branches.

And Nurse heads off alone, clutching her bag, toward the black iron entrance gate to the park.

It's pretty safe to assume she doesn't notice the Town Car with its headlights off, half a block back, that's been following the cab since midtown and is now rolling to a stop.

Safe to assume, too, she doesn't notice the two men inside the Town Car. Both in gray coveralls. *Pushbroom* in script stitched over their hearts.

Safe to assume she doesn't notice them get out of their car together.

Or notice that they follow her into the darkness of the park.

Nurse's cab pulled away already. Disappeared up the street.

Then stopped.

Now sits idling.

Cabbie having already killed the lights.

Cabbie sits in the driver's seat and watches in the rearview as the two men in the coveralls get out of their Town Car and trail Nurse.

Then the cabbie turns the ignition off. Gets out of the cab. Tosses his tweed cap into the backseat.

White knight in a yellow cab.

Okay. I confess.

I'm the cabbie.

The Pushbroom card was troubling me, and I wanted to keep an eye on Nurse, so I convinced the real cabbie to grab coffee for an hour and rent his cab to me. Let me drive Nurse home. Just to be safe.

Put down a hefty deposit, too, and promised him double on my return. Cabbie wasn't hard to convince. Seemed eager for the coffee break.

Even threw in the tweed cap for free.

Nurse told me she lived near Fort Tryon Park, but I didn't expect she lived *in* Fort Tryon Park. Because best I know, there's nothing in Fort Tryon Park save for trees, the Cloisters, and bushes reliably bursting with cutthroats and pervs.

I quicken my step to catch up to Nurse and her two pursuers. By the time I pass through the gates of the park, Nurse has twenty paces on the men behind her and I'm a good twenty paces behind them.

But closing.

The four of us, now in a loose caravan, wind through the wrought-iron entrance gate.

Black mouth of the park, in a permanent gape.

Swallows us all.

The first man in coveralls hustles to close the gap on Nurse on the lamplit path.

Few working lamps in the park anymore. No one wants to pay to keep them lit. So there's no pools of light, just pools of darkness, surrounded by pools of deeper darkness.

Second man in coveralls lags behind lazily, just a backup, really, keeping an eye on things, though there's nothing much out here to keep an eye on.

Second man no doubt starts to wonder if he even needs to be here, given it's just one woman. Which is right about the moment when I close the gap on him.

Gloved hand clamps over his mouth.

Traps the scream in.

Hand's gloved, so he won't try to bite.

Like I said, some things in the universe feel simple.

Cause and consequence.

Take our second man, for example.

The one who's now stashed in the bushes, hands clutching feebly at a throat wound that's not going to get a chance to heal.

That's the consequence.

Some might say the cause is a long life of bad choices and regrettable inclinations. All of which led him here, to a dark park, following an innocent woman up an empty path, within reach of my gloved hand.

I don't see it like that, though. To me, it's much simpler.

The cause is hidden in my hand, blade still half-extended.

With plenty more consequence to come.

First man doesn't notice the commotion on the path behind him. Too busy closing the gap on Nurse.

She must sense him now because she starts to stride more quickly, though she isn't running. Or screaming. Not yet.

Instead, the first man hustles and watches as she hunts around in her handbag for something. Probably searching for a handheld, he assumes.

Or maybe a whistle.

Go ahead, the first man thinks.

Let her whistle.

I figure there's now enough ground opened up between me and the first man that my only chance is to catch him at a dead run. Second man didn't put up much of a struggle, but I did lose a stride or two.

And the first man's now close enough to reach out and tap Nurse on the shoulder from behind.

Her striding. Him reaching.

Finally, he reaches her.

Taps.

She spins.

He expects her to scream now, but she doesn't.

Just smiles.

Smiles and jabs.

Turns out it's not a whistle she was fishing for.

It's a syringe.

That's now buried needle-deep in the first man's face.

Nurse thumbs the plunger calmly.

Who knows what's in the needle, but whatever it's full of, so is the first man now.

Some kind of wobble juice.

Man wobbles.

Drops.

The heavy kind of drop, with no effort to catch himself, so his head bounces hard on the pavement, like someone trying to crack a stubborn egg on the edge of a porcelain bowl.

Egg cracks.

Spills.

Meanwhile, I play catch-up.

When I get there, Nurse is standing over him, looking down.

Then she looks at me. At my face. Then down at my box-cutter. Doesn't seem too alarmed by either.

Nods to the box-cutter.

Don't worry, you can put that away. What I pumped him full of? He's not getting back up.

She looks down again at the first man, dropped in a heap, foam now edging his lips. He gives one last startling spasm, then stills. I say to her.

Nice job.

Thanks.

I take it whatever was in that needle is not as subtle as what you used on Langland and Loeb.

She looks me over again.

Smiles.

Well, look at you. You figured one thing out.

Actually, that's two things I've figured out so far, if anyone's keeping count.

25.

Nurse prods the dead man with her crepe-soled shoe.

Says to me.

Should look like natural causes. At first glance, anyway.

Nods back toward the bushes.

What about yours?

I wince.

Doesn't look too natural.

She tosses her syringe into the underbrush. Wipes her hands down on her skirt.

Don't worry. A couple bodies in these bushes won't raise anybody's eyebrows. We take care of a lot of trespassers that way.

We?

She hikes her handbag strap back up on her shoulder.

Come on. Let me take you home to meet the sisters.

The Cloisters sits like a low-slung stone fortress on a hilltop at the highest point of Fort Tryon Park. It's got views on all sides, of the city to the south, the Bronx to the north, and the Hudson River to the west, and on the other side of the river, unspoiled New Jersey.

Unspoiled New Jersey. Sounds like an oxymoron, I know.

But the millionaire who built the Cloisters way back when also bought up all the land in Jersey on the other side of the river so no one could build anything that might sully the view.

Remains unsullied, to this day.

Might be the last thing in this city you can say that about.

———

As we walk toward the Cloisters, Nurse tells me the story.

Not her story. That comes later.

The story of the Cloisters.

The Cloisters, she says, used to be a museum, assembled from different medieval missions found all over Europe. All the stones were shipped over here, to America, at the behest of a millionaire. Then he bought all this land in virgin Manhattan and reassembled the monument here, at the park's highest point, then gave the whole thing to the city as a gift. After the millionaire died, the city ran the Cloisters as a museum, stuffing it full of artifacts and knickknacks. When hard times hit, the city stripped out all the art and put the building on the market. Real estate wasn't exactly booming, but this was an easy sale: good bones, prime location, river views. A few overseas investors sniffed around, but eventually got outbid by an anonymous consortium. Snatched up the Cloisters for a fortune, then closed it to the public. Refurbished it. Restored it. Then reopened it as a private home. Part sanctuary, part commune, part refuge, part retreat. And who was the money behind this private consortium?

I barely believe Nurse when she tells me.

Wakers.

Apparently, Wakers have money.

As Nurse is finishing the tale, I interrupt to ask her.

You mean, like those two old ladies we saw in the East Village? Who handed us that brochure?

Yes. More or less. Though those two were a little—

She hesitates, choosing her words.

—old guard.

I think of the brochure. What it said across the top. Bold letters. And how I should have paid closer attention.

AWAKE!

Say to Nurse.

You told me you'd never heard of Wakers.

She shrugs.

It seemed a little early in our relationship to discuss religion.

And those Wakers live here? In the Cloisters?

Yes.

But who would want to do that?

She smiles.

Me, for one.

We enter through a pair of enormous oaken doors under an arched stone doorway, and inside it's cavernous and dimly lit. No more art, no more tapestries, just bare rooms and bare walls and spiral stone stairwells. Vaulted ceilings that disappear into darkness. Stained-glass windows, perfectly preserved. The only light comes from guttering candles, flickering in sconces.

And there's nurses.

Nurses everywhere.

All women, of all ages, some look ancient, some look like girls. Some dressed in nurse uniforms, some in simple bed-clothes. A woman in a white nightgown passes with a nod, then disappears behind privacy curtains, which are draped from the ceiling like long gauzy bandages to divide up the makeshift rooms. All the furnishings are modest. Wooden stools and low-slung cots. Iron candle holders. Candles lit up everywhere.

Behind the curtains, silhouettes stir.

We pass through a great hall, our footsteps echoing.

Mine, anyway. She's on crepe soles. I'm in steel-toe boots.

In the center of the great hall hangs a weird medieval chande-lier, a giant iron wheel dangling heavy from the ceiling, ringed in candles. The candles look like little white monks, bowed in prayer, robed in wax, their heads aglow.

I ask Nurse. In a whisper.

What is this? A hospital?

Sort of.

So who are the patients?

We are.

How long have you been living here?

Since not long after I moved to New York. I was having a hard time. They found me. And helped me.

And what do you all do here?

We're awake.

She puts her hand on my back and guides me down another hallway. Down a stairwell, into an alcove. Parts a curtain. Says to me.

This is my room.

It's a tiny space set off from the main hall and down two or three stone steps. A towering stained-glass window lets the only light in. These must be the last stained-glass windows in New York that haven't been busted up or broken by vandals or looters. Makes you wonder how these peaceful Wakers ward off all the ruffians.

Then I remember what Nurse said, back in the park. About the bushes full of bodies.

Nurse shows me where she sleeps. Just a cot in a cubbyhole. Side table holds a candlestick. A book lies facedown, spread-eagle like a suspect, on the bed.

Nurse picks up the book and flips through it. I've seen this book somewhere before. *Complete Poems of Emily Dickinson.* Diligently dog-eared.

Do you remember that poem I read to you? Back at the Plowman that night?

Sure. The one that sounded like an urgent telegram.

She nods. Finds the page.

Reads it again aloud.

A Death Blow is a Life blow to Some
Who till they died, did not alive become—
Who had they lived, had died but when
They died, Vitality begun.

Shuts the book.

I tell Nurse.

I still like that one.

She smiles.

I thought you would.

Sets the book aside. Points to the curtain.

Close it.

So I close it.

Then I sit down next to her on the cot. Cot groans under my weight. She leans forward. Grabs my collar. Insofar as a t-shirt has a collar.

She reels me in. Kisses me hard. Like I said.

An urgent telegram.

I pull back.

Nurse, I promised I'd get you back home. You're back home. Now tell me what the fuck is going on.

She grins.

Promises, promises.

You didn't find Loeb, did you? Or Langland. At least, not dead.

I found them both. After a long search. They turned out to be perfect choices.

Why?

Because hoppers like to watch them.

But what do you need with hoppers?

Nurse unpins her hat. Sets it carefully on the side table. Pulls more pins out so her hair starts to tumble. Loose strands unfurl. She helps them with a shake.

It's not hoppers we need. It's witnesses. People to tell the world.

Tell them what?

That the limn's no longer safe. No longer worth the risk.

And meanwhile you're out here sticking dreamers with needles and making sure they don't wake up again.

That's right.

Then let the world put two and two together. Let them think someone's found a way to kill people in the limn.

That's right. Just like you did.

But why?

To wake people up. People who are wasting away in the limn. There's a beautiful world out here, if you're awake enough to see it. Are you awake, Spademan?

Trust me. I'm plenty awake.

She grins.

That's what everyone thinks. Until they wake up.

I stand.

And here I thought that Wakers were just a bunch of old women hanging out on street corners, handing out pamphlets.

Nurse gives her hair one last shake.

There's been a change in leadership. Change in strategy. A younger faction that believes we need to adopt more proactive tactics.

But Nurse, if you're out here, sticking people full of sedatives, who's that in the limn? In the burqa?

She sighs. Stands. Takes my hand. Steps up on tiptoe. Lips inches from my ear.

Follow me.

26.

An indoor courtyard, under a stained-glass skylight, nestled deep in the center of the Cloisters.

Outside, it's nearly dawn. Sun's just rising, but it already feels like high noon. Morning air rolls in and licks the wilted city.

Heat wave's coming.

Inside the courtyard, embedded in the stained-glass dome, angels and heralds hover.

Send dusty beams of colored light down to the floor.

In the beams, a single bed.

In the bed.

Me.

Nurse sits by the bed, tweaking settings. Adhering sensors to my skin. Carefully, lovingly, like she's applying bandages to a wounded soldier sent back broken from the front.

She pauses, hand poised over my vein. Thumb on the plunger of yet another needle. Ready to slip it in. Asks me first.

You trust me?

I nod.

You sure?

I nod.

She asks why.

I give the only answer I can think of.

Why not?

She smiles. Slips the needle in.

Okay, Spademan. See you soon.

———

I wake up.

In a white room.

No walls.

No ceiling.

No floor.

Well, there must be a floor, because something's holding me up.

Can't see any floor, though. Just white. In all directions.

And in the middle of the white room.

Me.

Just me.

Just a garbageman.

Then.

Very far off.

In the distance.

A black pinprick.

A black dot.

A black speck.

A black spot.

Coming closer.

A black blot.

An ink spill.

Against white.

A black smear.

A black flicker.

A black flame.

Closer still.

A black ghost.

A black mirage.

A black dream.

————

A black burqa.

A woman in a black burqa.
  A woman in a black burqa, standing in front of me.
  Peer past the veiled screen of the burqa.
  Black eyes.

Lift the veil.
  Of course.

I ask Nurse.
  Why so violent?
  People need to be scared out of the limn.
  But why a burqa? Why a bomber?
  It's what people are most scared of right now.
  You couldn't conjure up some other kind of nightmare?
  Given what already goes on in there, who would ever know the difference between that and a regular dream? This is the one fear no one ever conjures in the limn. No one dares.
  But if you're out there, sticking needles in people, who's in here?
  One of the other nurses. We swap. Take turns.
  And why pick on hoppers?
  Because we knew they would come back and tell the world, Spademan. Spread the word. Seed fear. Hoppers gossip, after all.
  And how could you be sure they'd tell people what they'd seen?
  They told you, didn't they?

Nurse stands before me in the white room in a black burqa with the veil lifted.

I look closer. Notice something. Tell her.

Your eyes are black in here.

They're black everywhere.

I could have sworn they were green.

Look again.

Then Nurse explains the rest of it to me.

Tells me how a younger faction of Wakers decided they needed to do something radical. That the pamphlets weren't cutting it. They needed to make a real impression.

So they decided to stop trying to argue people out of the limn, and start trying to find a way to scare them out for good. And one by one was too slow. They knew they had to start a panic. But they had few ideas and no real expertise.

Then a woman arrived one day at the Cloisters.

Knocked on the oaken door. A nurse answered.

The woman wore a black burqa, Nurse explains.

Then she tells me the rest of the story.

We never saw her face or knew her name. This was maybe a month ago. She just arrived, knocked on the door, and we welcomed her in, as we do. Everyone's welcome here. We brewed her tea. Sat and talked. She told us she had something that we Wakers would want.

What's that? we asked her.

An idea, she said.

She explained to us that she could teach us to break into people's dreams, in the limn, to scare them. Explained to us how to do it. We said sure. But how do we really instigate change? There's nothing we can do that will stop people from tapping in.

It would only take a few bodies, she said. A few people who never wake up. After that, people will start to believe the limn is no longer safe. Let hoppers spread the panic, she said. Then she laid out the rest of the plan for us. The sedatives part we already understood, of course, and we already had easy access to tappers because so many of us are nurses. I volunteered for the first one, because I believed the most.

Before she left, her teacup drained, she said, Make sure you target the hoppers. Choose people that hoppers spy on. We asked her why. Because hoppers gossip, she said. And gossip is the lethal virus, the one you need to unleash.

But how do we scare the hoppers? we asked her.

Show them what they're most afraid of, she said.

Then she pointed to herself.

A suicide bomber. In a burqa. One who slips into your most secret dreams. Who wraps her arms around you and in her arms brings death. If it's panic you want to instill, that's what you'll show them, she said.

We were hesitant at first. It seemed reckless, irresponsible, given the recent history of this city. But she convinced us. Told us, You must do what you must do. Don't worry about the dreamers. They need to be woken up. The limn is nothing but a house of pictures, is what she said.

I ask Nurse.

Those were her exact words? House of pictures?

Nurse shrugs.

Yes. A house of pictures. Why?

A man said the same thing to me recently. What about her voice? Was there anything strange about it?

Nurse thinks.

Now that you mention it, her voice was slightly garbled. Rough like sandpaper. Why?

———

I ask Nurse to tap me out.

When I come to, Nurse is already there as well, back in the Cloisters, leaning over me, guiding me out. Skillfully. Smiling.

She whispers.

Wake up.

I sit up in the bed. Take a second to get my bearings. Tubes still dangle. She puts a calming hand on my back.

Take your time.

No, I have to go. I have to find Lesser.

Why?

I turn to Nurse and ask her.

Lesser was the first one, right? Your first witness?

Yes. With Langland. A test case, really. And then Loeb. That's it. Just those two.

But why did you choose Lesser?

I knew about him because I worked for Langland. Langland was obsessed with Lesser, with the fact that he'd failed him somehow, betrayed him, and now Lesser was haunting him in the limn, like his personal ghost. Once I learned all that, Lesser seemed like the perfect witness for our purposes. We could show him Langland dying in the limn and he'd spread the word out here. Wake everyone up. But he never told anyone, except you.

He never got the chance, Nurse. He disappeared the next day.

Well, when we didn't hear anything, that's when we went after Loeb.

How many did you plan to kill?

As many as it took. No one's mourning either of those two men, Spademan. A few will sleep, but we'll wake up so many.

Spoken like a true fanatic, Nurse.

She smiles.

A fanatic is just someone you don't agree with yet. Besides, when did you become so delicate, Spademan?

I pull the last of my tubes out, not gently. Tell Nurse.

A lot of people think that Lesser knows something. That he discovered something about the limn. And the reason they think that is because of your stunt.

We had nothing to do with Lesser's disappearance. We just wanted him as a witness.

Well, the people who have him now? They think it was him who killed Langland, or at least that he figured out how to kill someone through the limn.

What people?

I don't know yet. Bellarmine, maybe.

And where is Lesser now?

In a bad place.

So what are you going to do?

Get him out.

But why you, Spademan?

Turns out he's kind of a special kid. Figure he deserves a second chance, at least.

And you're the one to save him?

I shrug. Tell Nurse.

Who else?

27.

We stand outside the Cloisters. Say good-bye. She asks first.

So what's next?

I find Lesser. Hopefully rescue him.

No, I mean what's next for you and me? Are you going to turn us in?

To who?

The proper authorities.

I have no idea who that is anymore.

Nurse's changed into nightclothes. Swapped her uniform for something long and loose and white. Hair's up now in a hasty ponytail, the bobby pins all banished. Stands in the grass in her bare feet. Looks like a different woman. Swipes a strand back from her face.

I'm sorry I lied to you, Spademan.

Don't worry. It happens every day.

It seemed necessary.

I'll take it as a lesson. Never trust a person from Saskatoon.

We're not all bad.

No. Just you.

She smiles. Tips up on tiptoe toward my ear. Whispers.

Admit it. We're a good team.

I don't even know your name, Nurse.

She leans closer. Tells me. Softly, in my ear. It's a nice name.

She stands flatfooted again.

You sure you can't stay, Spademan? Kill an hour or two before you go?

I've got to get home. I've got people waiting for me.

She sighs.

People. They ruin everything.

Then she leans in. Grabs my collar again. Kisses me again. I don't resist, but this is becoming habitual.

I'd say bad habit, but that's a terrible joke to make outside a cloister.

Find my purloined taxi still parked on the street, and I decide to drive it to Hoboken.

I know I've left a cabbie fuming in a coffee shop, but I tell myself I'll make it up to him. Quadruple the rental price.

As I drive, phone on the passenger seat lights up and starts to jitterbug.

Check the caller ID.

Unknown caller.

Which is a good enough reason not to answer, but against my better judgment, I answer.

Hello? Is this Mr Spade Man?

Yes, it's Spademan. Who's this?

Detective Dandy. James Dandy. NYPD. We met last night.

How'd you get this number?

I'm a detective, Mr Spademan. I detect.

So you said. What do you want, Dandy?

You asked me about a cop, named Joseph Boonce? I told you I hadn't heard of him. Well, I got curious. Decided to look him up. His record was a little hard to access. Seems like he's—

Off the books?

—something like that. Deep into some cloak-and-dagger intrigue, in any case, that's way above my station. Joined the force about a year before Times Square. Got passed over for Bellarmine's gig. Then thrown into some other project.

Near Enemy.

That's right.

And he joined the force after Times Square. That's what he told me.

Either way, he seems clean, Spademan, or at least very good at covering his tracks. Just thought you'd like to know.

Thanks, Dandy.

Not all of us are dirty, Spademan. There's a few good cops left. Just have to find them. I'm still running down a few things on those two cops that Boonce keeps close, Puchs and Luckner. I can't vouch for them personally, but I'll see what I can dig up. And as for Bellarmine—

Phone buzzes again. Another call coming in. Check the caller ID.

Speak of the devil.

Joseph Boonce.

Dandy, I have to go.

Okay, I'll be in touch. Spademan, you be care—

I hang up. No time for niceties.

Answer Boonce's call.

Spademan, I found him.

Lesser?

Yes. Or at least, I found the black room. It's here, in the city. And it's Bellarmine who's running it.

You sure?

There's only one black room in Manhattan, and there's only one person with access. I know because we originally set it up for Near Enemy. It was supposed to be shut down, along with the project, and as far as I knew, it was. But Bellarmine's got it up and running. Has to be where they're keeping Lesser.

The whole thing's a mistake, Boonce. A misunderstanding.

What do you mean?

Lesser doesn't know what they think he knows.

And how do you know that?

Just trust me. Can you do that?

I trust you, Spademan.

Good. Now can you get me into this black room? In the limn?

I can do that too. It won't be easy, but I can. You tell me who your tech is and I'll make sure they get whatever they need for access. I had full security clearance for that room. But who's going to go in there and get Lesser, Spademan? You?

No. I'll find Lesser out here.

Then who?

I have friends.

The kind of friends who can handle this?

I hope so. Where's the black room site out here?

Now this you're going to love.

Where, Boonce?

If you had to hide a black room in a city like this one, where would you hide it?

I'm not in the mood for riddles.

Humor me, Spademan. Think about it. Where would you hide a room in New York that you never wanted anyone to find?

I think about it. Then it hits me. Of course.

Times Square.

Bullseye, Spademan—

Then I lose him as the taxi plunges into the depths of the newly refurbished Holland Tunnel.

Times Square.

Black room.

Plan it out as I drive back to Jersey.

This should be simple, actually.

Not easy. But simple. Hopefully.

I'll find Lesser out here in the black-room site in Times Square and tap him out. And I'll send Mark Ray into the limn to find Lesser in the black-room construct and free him in there, to make sure he's clear to be tapped out. With a black room, you have to do both at once, out here and in there. Time it to the minute. Otherwise, Lesser won't fare too well.

Like I said. Simple.

As I puzzle this out, though, there's still one part that puzzles me.

Nurse and the Wakers are the ones who staged the attacks in the limn, looking to seed panic. Woman in a burqa crashes your dream while hoppers look on, aghast. Meanwhile Nurse, out here, stabs the dreamer full of enough whatever to make sure he never wakes up again. Let the hoppers think they've witnessed a murder in the limn, freak out, gossip, and spread hysteria. The plan was to clear out the limn eventually. Wake this whole city up, whatever it took. Got the idea from an actual woman in a burqa, some kind of computer whiz who showed up on their doorstep with a garbled voice. Sounds like the same woman who called me to kill Lesser in the first place, which is weird, if he was meant to be their witness all along.

Meanwhile, Bellarmine catches wind of the attacks and decides to tell the whole city about it, nominating himself as the strong protector. Then Bellarmine grabs Lesser and stashes him in the city's only black room, looking to wring a secret out of him that Lesser never knew in the first place. Apparently using Pushbroom, the limn's nastiest sweepers, as muscle.

Like I said. Poor Lesser.

But it all adds up, more or less.

Except for one thing.

Shaban.

Shaban and Lesser were best friends, going back to their Langland days. Bunked together. Combed through code side by side at Near Enemy. So Shaban's known Lesser longer, and probably understands him better, than anyone.

And Shaban, for all his cool confidence, seemed the most concerned of anyone that I find Lesser and bring him back.

Find out what Lesser knows.

So what exactly is Shaban so worried about?

28.

I arrive home to Hoboken and park my cab across the street from the patrol car. Knock a knuckle on their window. Wake up Puchs, who's snoring softly.

Rubs his eyes. Rolls his window down.

Morning, Spademan.

Spots my taxi.

You moonlighting now?

Luckner's got her shades on, and she never speaks or smiles anyway, so I have no idea if she's awake or asleep or dead.

Ask Puchs.

Any trouble?

He shrugs. Stretches out his thick muscled arms, the ones with the sleeve tattoos, snakes and flames all the way up to his shirtsleeves, and yawns.

Nope. All quiet.

I say thanks and head up to my apartment.

Shaban.

He's hiding something.

At least one thing.

Either way, I figure there will be plenty of time to ask him what it is. Once I save Lesser.

Wouldn't mind paying Shaban another visit in any case.

Twist his arm a bit.

Just a bit.

But Lesser comes first.

I actually like my simple plan, save for one thing.

The part I don't want to admit.

Which is that Mark, for all his hours on bed-rest and all his tap-in expertise, for all his nifty tricks and angelic swordplay, is currently hobbled, and temporarily gun-shy, and even on his best day he might not be up for this kind of raid, at least not alone.

We're not talking about an overzealous pastor and his passel of farmboy flunkies, as was the case with Harrow.

This is a black room.

And whether it's Bellarmine's men, or Pushbroom muscle, or both who are standing guard over Lesser in there, they're experts, and they're nasty, so sending in Mark alone is a real long shot. And it's not fair to Mark. Not even fair to ask him. And it's likely not going to succeed.

So maybe I don't send him alone.

Truthfully, this is the part I'm not admitting to myself.

That I know someone else who has the skills to get this done.

Someone who's sleeping on my sofa right now.

And all I have to do is ask him for his help.

Nicely.

In some way, that's going to be the hardest part of all.

Head down the hallway toward my apartment and find there's someone waiting for me, casually leaning with his back on my front door.

A man in gray coveralls. Looks to be dozing.

Not dozing, actually.

Dead.

And not leaning, exactly.

Nailed to the door.

Note pinned to his chest by one of the nailheads. Right under the Pushbroom patch. Note obscured by a bloodstain now.

Note reads *Nice try*.

Ink's red, so I'm guessing it's also blood.

Man nailed to my door like a cheerful Christmas wreath.

I knock next to his head. No answer. But it's unlocked.

Tip the door open.

Anybody home?

Simon's in the livingroom, rocking a sleeping baby.

Looks up. Shushes me. Mouths the words.

She's sleeping.

I step inside. Close the door quietly. Mouth the words.

Why is there a man nailed to my front door?

Simon scowls. Says in a whisper.

They paid us a visit. Slipped right past your useless cop friends outside. Could have used your help, actually. Since there were two of them.

Two? Where's the other one?

In the bathtub.

What's he doing in the bathtub?

Draining.

Mark looks up from the dining table. Looks haggard. Scribbles something with his finger on his handheld. Holds it up.

I WASN'T MUCH HELP.

Persephone enters from the bedroom. Smells like smoke. Mouths the words.

Where have you been? You've been out all night.

I whisper.

Running errands.

She wipes a thumb over my cheek. Thumb comes back crimson.

You're covered in lipstick, Spademan.

Okay, I need everyone out right now.

When I say that last part, I forget to whisper.

Sort of forget.

Either way, Hannah wakes up. Looks around. Starts bawling.

Persephone scowls. Same scowl as Simon.

Great. Now look what you've done.

Persephone retreats to the bedroom to soothe the baby and I sit at the dining table and lay out the plan for Mark and Simon. Mark's game, because he's loyal. But Simon balks. Not a shock.

He points to Mark.

So me and this angel cake are going to break into a black room? You ever been in a black room, Spademan?

No. Have you?

Yes.

Working? Or as a guest?

Both. Different occasions.

Simon looks at Mark. Back at me.

Full raid on a black room? Two people aren't going to cut it. Even if one of them is me.

I have someone on the inside who's going to help us get in.

And who's that?

Can't say.

Simon scowls.

Of course not. And what will you be doing out here while we're in there risking our necks for some fat-shit hopper loser I've never even met?

I'll be rescuing that fat-shit hopper loser out here.

Simon scoffs. Leans back. Crosses his arms.

Great. Or here's an alternate plan, Spademan. We leave the fat-shit hopper loser to his fate. He made his bed. Then he peeped on someone else's bed. Either way, I'm not inclined to risk my neck for him. Because if you end up in a black room, there's usually a reason. So what's the reason here?

It's a mistake. A misunderstanding.

Sure. It always is.

Simon, I need your help.

And I don't want to say the next word. Don't want to say it. Don't want to—

I say it.

Please.

Simon guffaws.

Actually guffaws.

Spademan, last time we spoke, I think you said you would kill me if you ever saw me again.

I misspoke.

No, you definitely said you would kill me if you ever saw me again.

This is Simon, twisting the knife. Enjoying it. I ask again.

Simon, please. Just this once.

He looks at Mark again. Looks back at me again.

I appreciate the please, Spademan. I do. But honestly, patching things up with you is not why I came back here.

So why are you here, Simon?

He gestures to the bedroom.

I came to get her. Get them both. My family. Take them home.

And how do they feel about that?

They're warming to the idea.

I doubt that.

Simon smiles.

Ask them.

He lets that last answer linger in the air, because he knows he's right, and I know he's right, and I don't want him to be right, and I don't want them to leave. But they're not prisoners. They're family. Someone's family, anyway.

So I say to Simon.

You do what you want. You can leave right now. And if they follow, that's up to them. But before you go, do this one thing.

Help me. Save this kid. He doesn't deserve what's happening to him.

No one deserves what happens to them, Spademan. That's what makes the world so interesting.

Simon leans back in his chair. Holding all the cards and knows it.

Leans in again.

So where's the physical black room? The one out here?

Times Square.

Finally Mark chimes in. Or scribbles. Holds the handheld up.

SHIT.

I say to both of them.

It's okay. I'll go.

Even Simon's surprised.

You'd do that for Lesser? Go into Times Square?

If it's in Times Square, the security will be light. They won't be expecting visitors. I'll be in and out in an hour. What is it the mayor likes to say? No worse than a visit to the dentist, right?

Simon smirks.

Depends which dentist.

And with that, I can tell that Simon is going to do it. He won't say it. Won't give me the satisfaction. But he'll do it. He asks.

What about Persephone? And the baby?

They stay here.

Under whose watch?

Those cops are still outside.

Those cops are useless. We've already established that.

This will only take a couple of hours, tops. They'll be fine.

You've said that before, and you were wrong before.

I know that, Simon. But we don't have time to find someone to stay here, and I need both of you in there. They'll be fine.

Mark scribbles.

WHO'S TAPPING US IN?

Mark, you remember Mina, right? She's running Rick's old place now in Chinatown. Renamed it the Kakumu Lounge. She'll set you up. Watch the sensors. Make sure you're okay. Like I said, I have an inside man. He's going to feed her the coordinates and access codes. Everything she needs.

Mark scribbles again.

WE NEED A NURSE.

I know.

Mark scribbles.

MARGO?

No. I've got someone else in mind.

Now that everyone's on board, we sit at the table and plot it, ironing out the last few details. As we do this, I think back over my week's to-do list.

Kill Lesser. Find Lesser. Save Lesser.

Like I said. Strange week.

But we're almost home.

I call the meeting to a close. Adjourn Simon, Mark, and me. Tap the table with my knuckle. Knuckle stands in for a gavel.

Tell the two of them, as they rise, to get some rest. Big day tomorrow. With just one last thing to do.

Simple.

Let's get Lesser.

III.

29.

Next day.

Daybreak.

Skyline bakes under the sunrise.

Mercury tickles triple digits.

Sidewalks shimmer. Asphalt bubbles.

Heat wave's here.

Start the day with the same simple thought I went to bed with.

Save Lesser.

Make like a champion.

Then be done with it. All of it.

Boonce, Bellarmine, Shaban, the whole lot of them.

Get back to being who I really am.

Just a bullet.

I collect Simon and Mark, then we all head to the pier and board my boat, and I point the bow toward Manhattan. Boat's nose bobs as we skirt the wake of passing barges. On the other side, I deliver Simon and Mark to Canal Street. Direct them toward Chinatown.

Then rev the outboard again and steer myself north toward Times Square.

Meanwhile in Battery Park City.

On a piazza by the waterfront. A crew sets up a dais. Erects barriers. Hangs bunting. Fits steel bars into steel joints.

Builds a stage.

Big debate today.

Bellarmine versus the mayor.

Race now running neck-and-neck.

Dead heat.

Fresh *Post* screams from nearby newspaper boxes.

TOP COP PROMISE: EXPECT A SURPRISE.

Meanwhile in Chinatown.

Simon and Mark arrive at the Kakumu Lounge.

Mina's been prepped. She opens early. Welcomes Simon and Mark at the door in a black kimono. Hair still shaved to the skull. Looks like a monk. In heavy eyeliner.

Smiles for Mark. No smile for Simon.

And no mention of the cross-shaped scar on her forehead that he left her with.

I'd asked her nicely for this one favor. Promised her she'd never have to see Simon again after today.

So she doesn't ask them many questions, or say much of anything really. Just leads them in and readies their two beds.

Mark settles in. Relieved. It's been nearly a week, which for him is too long. Mina coddles him. Makes sure he's comfortable.

Simon handles his own gear, tubes, needles, settings, gauges. He's done plenty of solo tap-ins. Prefers it, actually. Just hopes this gizmo Mina has all the right codes and coordinates.

And hopes she remembers that one maneuver he asked her beforehand to learn.

Just one.

Just in case.

As for Pushbroom, Simon's not too worried about Pushbroom. He expects they'll run in to the Partners, but he's grappled with Pushbroom plenty in the past, and he's never come out hobbling. He has a particular history with one of the Partners, the one who calls himself Do-Good. The other Partners he's keen to meet. Only knows them by reputation.

Well, Simon thinks, I've got a reputation too.

Slaps two fingers on his forearm.

The nurse steps up to help him find the vein.

Simon looks up.

The nurse smiles.

Let me help you with that.

By this point, she's introduced herself to everyone already. Got it out of the way when they first arrived.

Simon, Mark, Mina—nice to meet you.

When they asked her name, she told them simply.

Nurse. Just Nurse is fine.

Meanwhile in Hoboken.

Persephone and Hannah, holed up again. Awake since five. The single mother. On her own. What else is new?

Persephone's bone weary. Hannah's fussy. Wailed all night. Persephone soothes her now but it still doesn't help, of course.

Bounces her on her hip. Shushes her.

Come on, baby. Come on, now.

That doesn't work either.

So she whispers to Hannah.

Don't worry. We'll go home soon. We'll be home soon. We're going home.

And wonders to herself if she really means it.

Meanwhile on the waterfront.

Me.

Making like a tourist.

And like so many tourists before me.

I'm heading for Times Square.

30.

No subways stop in Times Square anymore, so I dock my boat near Chelsea Piers and walk north.

Chelsea Piers is a series of huge empty soccer fields on a reconverted pier on the river, laid out side by side under hangars and abandoned, so the green rectangles now look like farmers' fields left to fallow, patches of plastic grass that will never fade, dusted in white chalk markings. There's a big golf-ball-driving range up here too, under light towers that don't light up anymore. People used to come here to thwack balls at all hours, with towering nets that rose on each side to catch the errant shots. Supposedly, once upon a time, you could take a trapeze lesson too.

Hit a ball into a net. Run around on plastic grass. Swing on a rope over a sandpit.

That's what people in this city used to do for fun.

Imagine what they did for work back then.

Swap electronic money. Trade electronic gossip. Wrestle over ever-smaller scraps of real estate.

New York City, in its heyday.

Piers are empty now, of course. Long since left to ruin.

You'll have to learn how to trapeze somewhere else.

Used to be art galleries around here once too.

Used to be art.

Among the fancy condo towers.

And an elevated park. Built on an old railway track gone to seed. Then revived.

Big ribbon cutting drew all the politicians.

Wore hard hats. And big smiles.

Anyway, the railway track's gone back to seed again.

Nature's version of its own reclamation project.

Re-reclaimed.

I walk under it.

Head north.

Walk up Ninth Avenue.

Once you hit the Thirties, civilization starts to peel away in earnest. The Dirty Thirties, they call them. Former Hell's Kitchen. Boonce's childhood playground, so he told me. This is where, if I carried a Geiger counter, I'd start to hear the first faint click-click-click.

But I don't need one. Everyone knows the boundaries by now. The risky blocks. Which intersections you don't go beyond.

In the Dirty Thirties, ten blocks south of Times Square, it's only half-toxic, so there's still a few stubborn storefronts open. Still a few dollar stores and Army Navy outlets. One or two last tenacious Irish pubs. Still advertising happy hour, like there are any happy hours left.

But these Hell's Kitchen pubs survived the bad old days. Then the good old days. Then the really bad days.

One bad day in particular.

Heard a bartender once talk about working that day.

Bomb sounded over the din of the place like it had happened far away, like in a whole other city. But the blast was also close enough that it trembled the foam on the freshly poured beers on the bar.

Someone had just bought a round for the house. Pint glasses laid out in a line, like soldiers awaiting inspection.

Bar went quiet. After the explosion.

Someone killed the jukebox.

Dead silence.

A long moment of collective breath-holding.

No one knew what it was. But everyone knew it was bad.

Then everyone in unison, all those seated at the bar, this band of merry regulars, so used to drinking all together, without a word, they each reached out and grabbed a beer, one by one, and drank it down, single gulp.

Bartender too.

Then he poured another round, this one on the house.

Then he turned the jukebox back on and cranked up the music to drown out the wail of the arriving sirens.

Pass that pub on Ninth.

Still open.

I'll admit. I consider it.

But I keep walking north.

Past darkened windows with a neon shamrock, lit up 24/7.

Door propped wide with a waste can stuffed full of spent butts and ashes.

Just a handful of radioactive regulars inside at the bar.

Head east to Eighth Avenue and Fortieth Street.

Walk alongside the big vacant lot where Port Authority once stood.

Spot two or three clickers, with their homemade hazmat suits and Geiger counters and surplus gas masks, lugging bulging garbage bags, like apocalyptic Santas. Still sifting and picking through the debris of Port Authority. Even at this early hour, even at this late date.

Like there's anything left in there to be salvaged. Maybe you'll find a half-melted fridge magnet that says WELCOME TO NYC.

You have to give it to clickers, though. Unlike the rest of us, they never give up hope.

Port Authority. Once a bus station. Now it just looks like a burial ground for concrete blocks. Buses were still busy for maybe a year or so after Times Square, but only the ones headed outbound. Not too many people were arriving by bus, and those who were got rerouted to Grand Central. Port Authority stayed open for maybe another year, limping along, though a lot of workers wouldn't even report to work, being that close to Times Square. Then the authorities claimed they'd caught wind of some alleged bus-bomb plot, some plan to pack a Greyhound with petroleum and dynamite and nails and whatever else and send it hurtling into Port Authority. It was just a bunch of online chatter really, lunatic ramblings overheard, but it gave them the excuse they needed.

Let swing the wrecking ball.

No one mourned. Save maybe bums.

Did seem symbolic, though.

The crumbling of Authority.

Next stop on our tour.

Northeast corner of Fortieth and Eighth.

Across the street from the empty Port Authority lot stands an empty skyscraper.

The old *New York Times* building.

Not the old old *Times* building. It's the new old building, the third one, the fancy skyscraper that looks like a needle stuck inside a ladder. This was the final home to the *New York Times*, at least back when it was still printed on paper, and back when it was still based in New York.

It's no longer available on paper, of course. Just an info feed now, piped into the limn, news of the world, rendered in roving pixels. The *Times* ditched paper long ago, no more newsboys and home delivery. Then the *Times* ditched these offices too, of course. Moved to Boston, I think.

Kept the name though. *Boston Times* just doesn't have the same ring.

The skyscraper's long since been abandoned. Squatters and clickers are the only reason the white Entry Forbidden tape got peeled away from the lobby doors.

Left to flutter. Like a surrender flag.

I'm headed to the *Times* building, by the way.

That's where they're keeping Lesser.

But not this *Times* building. And not the old *Times* building either.

I'm headed to the first one. The original one.

On Forty-Second Street.

The one Times Square was named for in the first place.

31.

Simon and Mark arrive on a runaway subway, train swaying and racing, bullet-speed, through tunnels that flicker like an old silent movie, except the car is anything but silent.

Track noise nearly deafening.

Car jostles. They steady themselves.

Mark Ray's in his usual off-body getup. Shirtless. White raiment wrapped around his nethers. Gold sandals with straps tied up to the knees. Blond curls wild.

Like an angel.

Mark's got a persona he adopts when he taps in. Calls himself Uriel. Name borrowed from an actual angel in the Bible. Name means God Is My Light. Uriel was the angel charged with keeping Adam and Eve out of Eden, once they'd fallen.

Mark finds that inspiring, somehow.

Along with his knuckle tattoos, the ones that spell DAMN and ABLE, Mark has a tattoo spread across his shoulder blades. Reads I RULE in the real-time world. Rearranges to spell URIEL in the limn.

And then there's the wings, of course.

Unfurl as needed.

Right now, they're tucked out of sight.

Mark cracks his knuckles. Clears his throat. Says aloud.

Man, it feels so good to be able to talk again.

He shouts over the subway noise.

Hello! Hello!

Shout swallowed up by voracious track-rattle.

Simon stands next to him, scouting the train car. Simon's not in any particular off-body getup. Simon just looks like Simon. White turtleneck, stretched over the kind of physique that they don't make normal clothes for. Black beard, now neatly trimmed. Facial expression of general disdain.

Only allows himself one sartorial flourish in the limn.

Bandoliers.

Two stained leather gun belts slung across his chest in an X.

He saw them in a movie once. As a kid. On a bandito. Always liked how they looked.

Saves them for special occasions.

And at each hip, holstered, Simon carries a silver handcannon. Repeating revolvers with eight-inch barrels. Two fistfuls of Dirty Harry macho overcompensation.

Also reserved for special occasions.

Normally Simon doesn't work with munitions. Hands are more than plenty.

But then again, this is a black room.

Just like a wedding.

There's no such thing as overdressed.

Simon unholsters a handcannon and holds the barrel to pursed lips. Shushes Mark. Steel wheels clatter over broken old track as the train hurtles forward.

Subway car's empty, save for these two. Simon can't help but note that Mina dropped them in perfectly. It's very tricky to tap someone into one of these moving subway-train constructs.

Car's covered in graffiti too. Like how they all used to look in New York.

Car shakes again. Jostles. Mark nearly stumbles.

Simon steadies him.

Easy now.

Then the lights go out, just like in a murder mystery.

Two passengers on the Disorient Express.

———

Lights come back up.

Simon's mid-explanation, shouting over subway noise.

—so don't worry. This is a common black-room scenario.

A subway?

Yes. Or some kind of train.

Why?

Because the programmers protect the black room from intruders by constantly moving its virtual location, hopping from server to server, all over the world. Train's just a metaphor for that. A moving target.

Lights go out again. More rattling. More jostling. Now in darkness. Tunnel lights flicker past.

Lights come back up.

Simon says.

It's just like any construct. Use your environment. Play to your strengths. Your whole angel-boy bit should come in handy in here.

Sure. But that's the problem.

What's that?

Mark flexes, bare-chested. He's not Simon, but he's muscular.

He grunts.

Bends double.

Sprouts wings.

Stands straight.

Tries to stretch his wings to their full expanse. To take flight.

Can't do it in the subway car.

Says to Simon.

Little cramped in here.

That your only trick?

No. I know a couple more.

Okay then. Surprise me.

Lights go out again. Brakes whine and outside the windows sparks rise from the track like a flock of fleeing birds.

Car rattles loudly. Settles down.

Lights come back up.

Mark and Simon both notice at the same moment.

Far end of the car.

Company.

Man in a cowboy hat. Tipped over to shade his eyes. Feet in cowboy boots, crossed at the ankle. Spurs on boots. Hands rest on twin holsters. Like he's been waiting for them all day.

Leaning back against the door at the far end of the train that connects to the next subway car. The door that's between where Simon and Mark are and where Simon and Mark need to be.

Between Simon and Mark and Lesser.

Hat tips up.

Bone-white toothpick in his mouth.

Toothpick shifts.

Howdy, boys.

Simon frowns.

Do-Good. It's been a while.

Cowboy sneers.

Toothpick shifts.

Too long, I'd say.

Mark pipes up.

Do-Good? That's his name? What is he, some kind of do-gooder?

Simon smirks.

Not exactly.

Then says to Do-Good.

I thought I told you last time I saw you that if—

Do-Good grins but otherwise doesn't bother to answer or even listen to the rest of what Simon's saying, just draws on

Simon, firing off both of his six-shooters, which turn out to be fully automatic. Fills the car with tracer rounds. You can do that in the limn. Normal laws of munitions do not apply.

Revolver chambers smoke and spin like barrels of a Gatling gun.

Strafes the car.

Four or five tracers perforate Mark Ray's wings right away, leaving ragged blood blossoms on white feathers. Mark winces, bends double, ducks, and folds his wings over himself, creating a kind of feathered cocoon. Scurries behind a seat-bench, looking to take cover. Partly to shield himself from Do-Good's gunfire, and partly to shield himself from what he knows is coming next.

The sound of Simon's handcannons.

Which comes.

Car shudders.

Boom boom.

Then another boom-boom as these first shots echo in the confines of the cramped subway car, and after that Mark can only hear ringing.

Then faraway gunshots. Or at least they sound far away.

Okay, now they're getting closer. Or just louder.

Tracers sear the air with a zip-zip-zip.

Followed by the zing-tang-zing of bullets ricocheting inside a metal box.

Mark shuffles sideways to crouch behind the subway seat-bench, which splinters plastic with each fresh hit. Realizes there's nowhere to move in here. And he's not much use to anyone crouched over with his wings folded on top of him.

Taken under his own wing, as it were.

Simon, meanwhile, stands calm in the aisle and just empties the two handcannons.

Boom boom. Boom boom.

Except they won't empty. Despite his best efforts.

Why would they?

It's just a dream.

Boom boom.

Zip-zip-zip-zip-zip.

Zing-tang-zing.

Do-Good opts for a scattershot approach, while Simon focuses on kill shots.

Takes careful aim again.

Boom boom.

Both hit.

Mark can tell because Do-Good's knocked suddenly backward like a punch-drunk boxer on wobbly pins. Behind him, there's a fresh Jackson Pollock painted on the subway car wall.

Large sucking wounds devour Do-Good's midsection.

He doubles over. Looks down. Frowns.

Toothpick shifts.

Well, Simon, now you've gone and done it.

Then Do-Good winces. Grimaces. To be honest, it kind of looks like he's taking a dump.

Large sucking wounds make an entirely different sucking sound.

Close like apertures. Completely.

Do-Good straightens. Adjusts his newly shredded denim cowboy shirt. Looks up at Simon.

Toothpick shifts.

This was my favorite shirt.

Simon stands watching this whole display, handcannon in each hand, leaking gun smoke.

We going to do this all day, Do-Good?

Zip-zip-zip-zip-zip.

Clouds of newly splintered subway seat.

Simon dodges. Sighs.

I guess so.

Takes aim again.

Boom boom.

This time, one hits.

Do-Good staggers again.

Makes his taking-a-dump-face again.

Mark sees an opening.

Makes his move.

Rushes down the center of the subway aisle in a running crouch. Wings still folded over him, like Dracula's cape.

Do-Good looks up. Snorts.

And what are you planning to do, angel man? Flap me to death?

Mark rises. Spreads his wings. Looks like a bat. But white. Presents a sudden blinding expanse of trembling feathers. Distracts Do-Good just long enough that he doesn't see what's held in Mark's hands.

Sword hilt gripped in both fists.

Flaming blade.

Mark's other trick.

The cuts won't kill Do-Good, of course.

After all, you can't die in the limn.

But given that one arm is here, one leg over there, another leg at the far end of the car in four cleanly separated pieces, and his torso is twitching limbless at Mark's sandaled feet, it's going to take a lot of strenuous mental dump-taking for Do-Good to put himself back together again.

Not to mention that Do-Good's head is about forty yards be-hind them on the subway track. And counting. Complete with cowboy hat.

Should buy them ten minutes, at least.

Enough time to get to Lesser.

Simon's impressed. Nods to Mark.

Nifty trick.

Mark wipes his bloody blade on his raiment.

Everyone always conjures the guns. No one respects the sword.

Simon's hand is paused on the handle of the door that leads them to the next car.

Says to Mark.

Well, don't celebrate yet.

Big sticker on the door cautions: DO NOT TRAVEL BETWEEN CARS WHILE TRAIN IS IN MOTION.

Simon asks.

You ready for car number two?

I don't know. Number one wasn't so bad.

Two will be worse.

What's in car number two?

I don't know. But my guess—

What?

Do-Better.

Then Simon turns the knob and slides open the door.

32.

Battery Park City.

Platform's assembled.

Flags draped. Bunting hung.

Security sweeps the plaza. Dark suits, sunglasses, and earpieces. Men mutter into their lapels.

All clear.

Main suit signals.

Okay, you can let the cameras in.

TV trucks inch into the designated parking area. The beep-beep-beep of trucks in reverse.

Reporters and camerapeople disembark. Unload gear.

Talking heads check their hair in the side mirrors of their news vans.

Straighten skirts. Smooth out wrinkles with sweat-dampened palms.

Find their marks.

Test microphones.

Check check check.

Hoboken.

Hannah won't take the bottle.

Persephone gives it one last try.

Coos.

Come on, Hannah.

No dice.

Persephone, perturbed. Decides to nurse her. Would prefer not to, since she's alone. Needs to be vigilant. And nimble.

But then again, the cops are watching.

And Hannah's hungry.

What else can she do?

Forty-Second Street and Broadway.

Picture me.

In Times Square.

Crossroads of the world.

They built the old *Times* building, the original one, at the turn of the nineteenth century, back when the intersection of Forty-Second Street and Broadway was nothing more than a muddy pit that the locals called Longacre Square. The millionaire who owned the paper persuaded the city to put in a subway stop. Then he convinced them to rechristen the muddy pit in honor of his paper.

Times Square.

Paper didn't stay long, not in that first building, at least. A few years later it moved a few blocks over and then, eventually, to that sky needle across from where Port Authority once stood. In the meantime, Times Square got fancy. Then seedy. You've probably seen the old photos. Hookers and XXX. Peep shows and hustlers. Saturated with neon enticements. And it stayed like that for a long while, just filth and rot, before it became something else entirely.

Prettied up and Disneyfied. Reborn as the country's favorite tourist attraction. Crossroads of the world, decked out in brand-new video billboards, neon ads as tall as the buildings, mandated to a minimum wattage. Each sign fighting to outshine the others. Looked like Vegas, but crammed into ten city blocks.

A million people a day, so they said. Population of a good-sized city, passing through Times Square, each and every day.

Why?

Because it's Times Square.

It existed to be looked at, photographed, visited, checked off the bucket list. You went to Times Square to say you'd been to Times Square.

And, once a year, on New Year's Eve, they dropped the ball.

Streets overflowed in all directions. So crammed you could barely stand. Stomp your feet to stave off the cold.

Count it down.

Ten.

Nine.

Eight.

Etcetera.

One.

Happy New Year.

The ball-drop happened each year at the top of One Times Square. This was the same building that was originally built to house the *Times,* way back when. The *Times* left but the building stayed, changed its name to One Times Square, got a facelift and a dozen more floors. Housed a lot of different businesses over the years, but eventually got recast as a prestige address for start-up tech companies. The office space was way too expensive and, frankly, too corny for any legacy business. After all, what local wants to work in tourist-choked Times Square?

But for a start-up firm looking to make a name? Imagine One Times Square on your business card.

Instant credibility.

So these small ventures came, and set up shop, and dreamed big, and mostly failed. The usual story.

Save one.

Small tech firm called Negative Creation.

Plucky start-up. Shilling software. In particular, a special service that let you run a business meeting online, using 3D avatars. Had to strap on clunky goggles, talk through headset mikes and listen through earpieces. And the virtual conference room you visited looked like an architect's 3D rendering of a conference room.

But still.

Kind of cool.

Definitely had potential.

And eventually this company found a way to ditch the goggles and make the experience totally immersive, the conference room suddenly stunningly lifelike, assuming you were the kind of person who'd be stunned by a lifelike conference room. But they got all the details right, the little things, right down to the faint smell of lacquer from the boardroom table, or the springy give of the plush-pile rug under the stiff soles of your avatar's leather business shoes. Or your Tevas, if your avatar was the type to wear Tevas.

Pick any shoe you liked. Any avatar, really.

That was the appeal of it.

And lifelike details like that made all the difference.

Soon the company, expanding, took over the entire building. Filled every available office in One Times Square.

Growing exponentially. Metastasizing. Like a tumor.

And that's the end of the story of Times Square.

First came the tumor.

Then came the radiation.

One Times Square.

Front door's unlocked.

Boonce told me not to expect too much security.

Maybe one or two guards on the way up, but really, who signs up for security duty in an empty building in toxic Times Square?

So there's just one guard at the front desk. Dozing. Don't blame him. It's still early.

Not in a police uniform either. Or Pushbroom coveralls. Just standard tactical black. Must be one of Bellarmine's private guard. Moonlighting. Which makes sense. If this is Bellarmine's secret black room, no need to broadcast its location to the world. And no need to tie it back to the NYPD, which might just lead to awkward questions down the line.

Instead, just leave a burly Teutonic-looking gentleman at the front desk in all-black garb to scare off stray clickers and other random weirdos who happen to wander by. Just make sure your Teutonic security guard isn't prone to catnaps.

Like this one.

His head bobs.

Like he's dreaming about answering a string of boring questions in his sleep.

Poor guy.

I don't bother with subterfuge, no phony hello-howdy-do, no ginned-up flower-delivery story or casual I'm-here-to-see-Mr-X, because no one ever comes to Times Square holding a bouquet or to see anyone. Instead I just walk straight toward him at a healthy clip. He startles, sits up, fumbles at his holster, and while he fumbles I grab his collar, punch him twice in the bridge of the nose, and he's out.

Back to his catnap.

Most security guards, their first instinct, especially if they see you coming straight at them quickly, is to grab for the holster.

And do you know how long it takes you to unlatch a holster and get a service pistol free?

Not very long. Just long enough for me to make sure you won't get a chance to use the pistol.

I rest his head lightly on the counter.

Feel bad.

He's just doing his job.

And it's a shitty job.

Day shift in Times Square.

Bank of elevators behind him.

Still functional.

I hit the Up button.

Head for the top floor.

33

Battery Park City.

Two motorcades.

Bellarmine's is the first to arrive.

Three gleaming Escalades glide into the secure parking area cordoned off behind the dais.

First car's full of security. Third car's full of security.

Second car carries Bellarmine, his driver, and his two personal bodyguards.

Bellarmine in the backseat. Cocooned in black leather. Air-conditioning on high. Tinted windows sealed. Not a sound leaks in.

His brow's furrowed.

Lips moving.

Flipping through the last few flash cards.

Debate prep written on index cards.

Getting ready to drop his bombshell.

His motorcade parked and unloaded, Bellarmine waits in a tent. Flash cards now stashed. Sits on a folding chair with a wisp of white paper tucked into his collar. Makeup woman applies the last few dabs of powder. For the cameras.

Bellarmine's a big man. Not fat, but solid. Bulky. Broad-shouldered. Like an old-school cop.

Black brush cut. Thick mustache.

Chair sags under his weight.

Two muscular cops in shades and dress uniforms, one woman, one man, who don't leave his side, sit on chairs beside him and silently scan the tent.

Outside.

Second motorcade arrives.

Four cars long. Extra car. Just because.

The mayor always likes to know he's got the biggest motorcade.

On the runaway train.

Simon slides open the subway car door that leads to the tiny platform between the two cars.

Tunnel roars.

Simon turns back and tries to speak to Mark over the clamor, but all Mark can hear is clamor.

Door behind them slides shut.

And for a moment the two of them are squeezed together on the small swaying platform where the two cars connect.

Simon mouths the word.

Ready?

Mark nods.

Then Simon opens the second car's door and they tumble inside. Slide that door closed behind them.

This car's empty too.

In the respite from the track noise, Mark asks.

So who's Do-Better?

Simon scowls.

There's three of them. The Partners who run Pushbroom. Named after figures in some medieval parable. In the story, a pilgrim meets three virtuous men on the road. Do-Good. Do-Better. And Do-Best. Each one better than the last.

So what's Do-Better like?

Don't know. I've only ever tangled with Do-Good.

Then they turn and navigate slowly down the aisle of the train toward the door at the car's far end. Walls and windows are splashed with garish spray paint. More subway graffiti, of the usual sort. Tags. Slogans. Bubble letters.

Mark reads it.

Okay.

Not exactly the usual graffiti.

It's a record of something, it turns out. Graffiti reads like a transcription of the last few moments of a torture session. Of the moment right before the person breaks.

Oh God.

I don't know what you want.

Dear God.

Written in spray paint in big bubble letters and left as a warning for whoever comes next.

They inch forward.

Oh God.

Please help me.

Walls signed like a guest book.

Help me.

Postcards from an Inquisition.

There's no mercy.

Mark and Simon inch forward.

Both waiting for the lights in the subway car to blink out. Waiting for the door at the far end to swing wide. Waiting for whoever's waiting for them to finally show his face.

Lights go out.

Lights come up again.

At the far end of the car.

The whoever appears.

But not showing his face.

Showing hers.

———

One Times Square.

I'm in the elevator, going up.

Listening to Loverboy.

Working for the Weekend.

Muzak's just like roaches.

Even a nuke can't kill it off.

So the company that built the platform that hosted the fake conference tables figured out pretty quickly that, as long as you were building fake dream worlds, there's a big market for realities far beyond a conference room.

Problem was, the bandwidth required was enormous. As in, break-the-Internet huge.

So they pulled up stakes.

Left the Internet.

Built their own Internet.

Called it the limnosphere.

As real as real.

The rest you probably know.

You've probably experienced it once or twice yourself. Maybe more than once or twice.

Virtual playground for humanity's dark side.

Though it wasn't like that at first.

At first, all the press releases promised New Life With No Limitations. The lame shall walk. The blind shall see. Every dream now becomes a reality.

The No Limitations part of their pitch was correct, but not in the way that they meant.

Limnosphere.

It's bigger than all of us now.

And this building? This address?

One Times Square?

This is where they flipped the switch to turn it on.

Big ceremony.

Held at midnight.

Broadcast around the world.

Simulcast to the NASDAQ floor. Kept open late just for the occasion.

Shown twenty stories high on the billboards outside. Back when Times Square was still packed with people.

The company's apple-cheeked owner, a boy genius, barely thirty, stood giddy with his hand poised on the big switch.

Not the actual switch. A novelty switch.

Built for the photo op.

Count it down.

Ten.

Nine.

Crowds in Times Square chanting too.

Eight.

Seven.

As well as the brokers on the NASDAQ floor.

Six.

Five.

Apple Cheek's beaming.

Four.

This kid who'd grown up dreaming of changing the world.

Three.

Now he would. Though not exactly. Not change it.

Two.

Just replace it.

One.

Flip the switch.

Happy New World.

Fireworks soaring up over Times Square, bright thudding explosions you could see for miles and miles.

Ding.

Twenty-fifth floor.

My stop.

Another guard in the hallway sitting on a metal folding chair.

This one's not dozing. Not reading. Not texting.

Just sitting.

Like maybe he's expecting me.

Blond brush cut. Similarly Teutonic. Could have come in a matched set with the one in the lobby.

He pops to his feet and kicks the folding chair aside.

Doesn't grab for his sidearm, unfortunately.

Just assumes a fighting posture.

Knees loose. Hands up.

Waits for me.

So much for my walk-straight-toward-him-punch-punch-while-he-fumbles approach.

Too bad. I'm fond of that approach.

His stance suggests training. Krav Maga, I'm guessing. Or maybe something Brazilian. Definitely something expensive. Practiced for years, no doubt, against some poor dummy in a sweaty gym somewhere. All that pent-up childhood rage leaking out through head blows, neck blows, body blows, killing blows.

As for me, I consider the box-cutter.

Still in my pocket.

My fingers find it.

Grip it.

I've found there's no fighting style yet invented that isn't improved by the addition of something sharp.

I approach him. Slowly.

Teuton bounces lightly, waiting. Adjusts his fighting stance.

As for me, I don't assume any kind of stance.

My best advantage is I don't really have a style.

Just a few rules I learned in a Jersey schoolyard.

Rule one: Start hitting.

Rule two: Keep hitting.

I move toward Teuton slowly and look for my opening.

That's the other lesson I learned in the Jersey schoolyard.

No matter what, there's always an opening.

He hikes his tactical trousers, the kind with all the little pockets, which is the wrong move, because he telegraphs exactly what's coming next. And, sure enough, he looses two smooth and elegant roundhouse kicks toward my head, which are very pretty, and very slow.

Both miss.

He readjusts. Assumes his stance again. Gets ready to unleash a third. A move he's practiced a million times in a fancy gym somewhere.

And when he does, I know that, for just a fraction of a second, just the time it takes to loose each kick, he'll be standing on one leg, as stable as a flamingo. One leg in the air, one leg on the ground, and a whole lot of vulnerable in between.

Here's another trick I learned in a Jersey schoolyard. Learned it, in fact, the day after Terry Terrio learned how to do a roundhouse kick in his fancy judo class.

When someone tries to kick you, dodge. Then go for the other leg.

All you need to do is knock it out. Using your arm, leg, broomstick, whatever's handy.

As for me, I use my leg.

He kicks.

I dodge.

Then swipe.

Teuton goes down. Drops like two tons.

And in a fight like this, once you're down, that's bad.

Because then I have a chance to get on top of you.

Which brings us back to rule number one.

Start hitting.

Followed by rule number two.

Keep hitting.

Repeat as necessary.

Teuton's out.

But there's something weird about it. Because he's too big, and too quick, and frankly too skilled to go down that fast.

Not exactly without a fight, but close enough.

Like I said, I can hold my own, but I'm not Bruce Lee.

Either way, this is way too easy.

This is Terry Terrio easy.

Almost like someone told him to look tough, raise his dukes, take a few pokes, then take a fall.

But who would tell him that?

Not Lesser.

Bellarmine?

Or maybe I'm just better at punching people than I remember.

In any case, I leave him napping.

And head toward the door at the end of the hall.

34

Battery Park City.

Mayor's motorcade arrives. Entourage spills out of four shiny limos. Suits, thugs, assistants, factotums.

Factotum. Good word.

Means toady, basically.

Interns on headsets bark orders at other interns. All waiting for the mayor to disembark.

Chauffeur in full regalia holds the limo's rear door open. Chauffeur has more brocade on him than a banana-republic general.

Holds the door. Waits.

Then out comes our mayor.

To a fusillade of flashbulbs.

Gives a wave.

Enjoys an entrance.

Might seem weird that the mayor of a dead city still gets so much pomp and circumstance.

But there's still a lot of money here, if you know which pockets to pilfer.

So what if the center of the city is abandoned and radioactive?

Think of your average banana republic.

Power is often built on the back of ruin.

On the runaway train.

She's maybe six-six. In flat feet.

Bare feet, actually.

Toenails painted black. Fingernails too.

Her head tickles the underside of the roof of the subway car.

She's tall, and she's Asian, maybe Korean. Dressed in a sharp black suit and a crisp white shirt, perfectly pressed, spotless, open at the neck. Neckline looks like it was freshly cut with the sharp end of a brand-new blade.

Black hair, with a shaved head.

No, not shaved.

What do you call it?

Pixie cut.

She smiles.

Hey fellas.

Mark answers.

I don't suppose you'd just let us pass through.

She smiles wider. Great smile.

No can do, unfortunately.

As she says this, she holds up one hand, blunt nails, tar-black polish, with her five fingers spread wide, a chunky silver ring balanced on the middle knuckle of each finger.

Wait. Not rings.

Buzz saws.

Tiny buzz-saw blades about the size of throwing stars.

Mark's impressed.

Nice accessories.

She nods toward him.

Nice wings.

Like they're flirting now.

Then she wiggles her fingers, as if she's waving toodle-oo.

Saws jingle like jewelry.

Simon scowls.

She smiles.

Simon the Magician. Such a pleasure. I've heard so much about you. You going to show me some of your famous tricks?

That depends. What's the plan?

She shrugs.

Well, my plan is to send you both back topside in little chunks. Let your brains try to figure out whether you're still alive or not.

Simon scoffs. Rests his hands on his holstered revolvers.

I just hope you put up a better fight than Do-Good.

Glint off the saw blades as she gives them both a wink.

Says to Simon.

Well, it's not like they call me Do-Same.

Simon draws and fires but she's already dodged sideways while also giving three quick and effortless wrist-flips, sending three spinning saw blades arcing toward Mark.

Like little silver Frisbees, he thinks, in that weird slo-mo moment as he watches them sail toward him. Then he wonders why she uses buzz saws and not traditional throwing stars. Seems like an unnecessary flourish.

Then he dodges left. Presses himself flat against the scratched-up subway window.

Two saws arc wide. Warning shots.

Third saw hits the window with a thunk about two feet away from Mark's face.

Bad aim. Mark smirks.

Then the third saw starts spinning.

Sawing. Spitting glass.

And racing toward his face.

The blade splits a long gash in the spray-painted window as it slices toward him like a quick snake slithering through water.

He jumps back.

It barely misses.

Blade blows him a kiss as it passes by.

Okay, he thinks.

So that's why she uses the buzz saws.

She's in a crouch now and airmailing three more blades quickly thereafter. This time toward Simon.

He fires off each handcannon one more time, two loud booms that do nothing, just shatter seats, then he dives right as the saws slice the air over him.

Do-Better laughs. Impish laugh.

Simon rises and brushes himself off, just in time for the saws to circle back.

Boomerang. After all. Just a dream.

Laws of physics aren't really laws in here. Just suggestions. Just problems to be solved, Simon thinks, as both blades hit him with a stereo thunk-thunk.

Dumb move, Simon thinks. Should have seen that one coming.

Stupid Simon.

Saws sink in.

Blades bite.

Then start to spin.

White turtleneck dyed red.

Simon snarls. Lets his grip slip on a handcannon, which clatters to the subway floor and misfires. Punches a hole the size of a grapefruit in the window.

He holsters the second long revolver and grabs at the wound high in his left arm, just as the buzz saw chews its way through the muscle, then sails clear toward the back of the car.

Simon clamps his right hand over the wound.

Then looks at the back of his right hand.

So that's where the second saw landed.

Simon starts to go into shock. Fights it off.

Saw still spinning.

Chews into his hand.

Through his hand.

Then into the wound he's clutching.

Simon still snarling. Until finally he screams.

One scream. Can't suppress it.

Buzz saw cuts a beeline through his body and sails free out the other side, whipping blood in great arcing swaths like a sprinkler as it spins.

Mark flies.

Or, at least, spreads his wings.

Does his best.

Bounces.

Toward Do-Better.

Aptly named, as it turns out.

Not a drop of sweat on her, not a mark, as both Mark and Simon bleed.

Mark keeps aloft in the cramped car just long enough to dodge two more spinning saw blades. They whiz past him and bury themselves in the subway's ceiling. Chew through. Sail out spinning into the darkness of the tunnel and whatever lies beyond.

Mark gives his wings two muscular flaps and rushes her and conjures, then readies, his sword.

Blade aflame.

And with two tiny gestures, barely perceptible, like she's simply knocking gently on someone's front door, Do-Better sends two more spinning buzz saws straight toward him.

One veers left. One veers right.

Ha-ha, this time you missed me, he thinks. Until he realizes she didn't.

Each saw having snipped blood feathers in his wings.

Clipped a few of his flight feathers too.

The ones you need to fly.

———

Blood sprays.

Stained wings.

Mark plummets.

Wings clipped.

Sword clatters.

Mark's grounded.

Flame out.

Simon sits and leans against a bench, legs splayed, and groans like a Civil War soldier in the middle of having his leg sawn off.

Bite the bullet, Simon thinks.

Bite the bullet.

Unghhhhhhh.

And he sweats and grimaces and aims to stitch his wounds back together. Or, at least, the wounds that prevent him from holding the guns.

These wounds aren't real, he tells himself.

These saws aren't real.

The pain, though.

The pain is real.

Grinds his teeth and wills the tissue to reattach.

Mark's facedown on the dirty subway floor.

Tries hard to rise.

Fails.

Flops.

Wings flutter.

Do-Better steps over him, elegantly, lifting her bare feet with the grace of a dancer. Walks down the car toward Simon, who's still sitting against the bench of seats. Blood-soaked. Sweating. Snarling.

Trying to stitch those grievous wounds.

She stands over him. Lingers. In her black suit, she looks like a funeral director. The most elegant funeral director you've ever seen. Everything about her just-so. The well-cut hair. The well-cut suit.

The saw blades.

Well cut.

A figure of surgical precision.

Simon marvels at her, actually, at the same time as he realizes he's starting to black out. From the exertion of the wound-stitching.

Fuck these wounds, he decides. Let them bleed.

He's suffered worse.

Survived worse.

Grimaces as he thinks this. Edges of his vision fading to black.

Do-Better just stands over him, watching him, head cocked. With great interest.

Like lots of hunters, she likes to come in close to observe the final moments.

Then she holds up one last saw blade.

You won't die, Simon. You know that, right? You of all people should know that.

She spins the lone silver blade on the tip of her finger until it sings like an instrument.

But I can make sure this experience is one you remember for a good long time.

She stills the blade from spinning. Holds it out for him to see. It shines like a lucky coin.

Says with a smile.

Bye-bye, Simon.

Sitting splay-legged, Simon lifts a handcannon, the long revolver looking comically clumsy, like a cartoon gun smithed for

Yosemite Sam. Barrel droops. Do-Better only watches, curious to see what he thinks he's going to do next.

He doesn't even bother trying to aim it in her direction. It's bad enough trying to heft it. Barrel just points off randomly toward the end of the car. Toward nothing. Well, toward Lesser, maybe, in some farther car, some future car, at the far end of the train, the last car, the end of the line, the person they both came here to rescue, the person they were supposed to save.

All of this for some fat-shit hopper, Simon thinks. No, not just that. You have to get back. Back to your family. Back to your church. Take back what's yours. Can't bleed out in a black room.

Thankfully, Simon's got one last trick to try.

One last thing he'd worked out with Mina. Beforehand. Just in case. As a fail-safe.

Hopes Mina remembers.

And hopes she can actually pull it off.

And really hopes she doesn't hold that scar against him.

Simon looks up at Do-Better. His face drawn under his blood-speckled beard. Eyes bloodshot. Rimmed red.

Do-Better smiles.

It's a shame, Simon. Strong brute like you. Handsome too. Different circumstances, we could have been an item.

I don't think so.

Why's that?

I'm a family man now.

And with that, he screams with everything he has left in his lungs. Screams a name.

Mina!

Then pulls the trigger.

Barrel booms.

Fires wide.

Hits nothing.

But it wasn't meant to.

Leaves a gaping hole in a plastic seatback.

Just a distraction. Designed to turn Do-Better's head for a moment. Fluster her. Just for a moment. Which it does.

She looks back to where the shot sailed wide.

Shrugs.

Well, I don't see—

Turns back to him.

Simon's gone.

35.

Two minutes, sir.

Bellarmine nods absentmindedly, without looking up from his handheld, then goes back to the message he's typing.

Fat, clumsy thumbs. Tapping something. Texting someone.

The temporary tent they're all beneath flaps sharply in a strong wind that swirls up off the river. An unsecured flap sounds a loud snap, like a whip crack. Bellarmine looks up again from his handheld. Not startled. Just alert. Then goes back to texting.

Two guards flank him.

One woman, one man.

Both in police dress uniform. Navy-blue coats fastened tight with gold buttons. Gold braiding at the shoulders. Crisp hats. Sunglasses.

The male guard raises his arm to check the time.

Shakes his wrist to free his watch from under his stiff coat sleeve.

Above his wrist, a sliver of skin becomes visible.

Peek of ink.

Tip of a tattoo.

Snakes and flames.

Watch checked, he pulls the sleeve back down, then says.

Ready?

Bellarmine grunts, nods, eyes still on the handheld.

But the guard's not talking to Bellarmine.

———

The first thing Simon does is he vomits. All over himself, all over the bed, all over the wires and tubes and sensors and screens, in great heaving gushers of vomit that far exceed what you'd think one human body could contain.

Then, spent and vomit-soaked, Simon looks up at Mina, his face as gaunt as a cadaver. Still snarling, though. And eager to get back to the action.

Says to her.

Thank you, Mina. And I'm sorry about the scar.

She says nothing. Stays poised.

He shrugs.

I deserve that.

Settles back into the bed. Says to Mina.

Whenever you're ready.

The wake-up call.

It's a sudden searing overwhelming pain that accompanies tapping out and coming out of bed-rest. As all your physical senses suddenly come back online.

It's bad.

Can be very bad.

Depending on how fast you come out.

Even at the best of times, it usually takes several minutes to recover.

Simon came out fast. And he doesn't have several minutes.

Ergo the vomit.

A responsible nurse would never, ever tap someone out, especially rapidly, then tap them back in right away. The shock to your system alone is too much, like hitting all your five senses with maximum wattage, then cutting the power suddenly, then hitting them all again. You'll blow your mental breakers. Short the fuse box. Could cause yourself permanent damage. Definitely cause yourself temporary pain.

For her part, Nurse just stands back with her hand over her mouth. Like she and Mina are grave robbers who just opened up a tomb and found someone still alive inside. Nurse's seen a lot and she's not a squeamish woman. But she's never seen this maneuver done before. And right now she looks ready to faint.

In driving, they call it the bootlegger's turn. Crank the handbrake at highspeed, spin the steering wheel, fishtail the car, then peel out in the opposite direction.

This maneuver is kind of like that, but for your brain.

Simon, sweat-sheened, says sharply now.

Mina! Do it!

Mina hesitates.

Knows she could jerk Simon back and forth like this, in and out, for an hour if she wanted to. For a lifetime. Hit him hard with the wake-up call so many times he'd heave himself dry.

Kind of like Rick did. At Simon's hand.

No, she hasn't forgotten. Thought maybe she'd forgiven, but as it turns out, she hasn't done that either.

Cross-shaped scar on her forehead aches.

But Mark's still in there. And she still likes Mark.

Simon she can settle with later.

Simon barks.

Mina!

And she taps Simon in again.

Nurse hits him with another load of drugs as he goes down.

And just before Simon goes under, his snarl finally dissipates, and he looks at them both like a lost soul dredged up from the shadows of the sea.

Looks about to say something sorrowful.

But then his eyes roll back in his head and he sags back into the bed and he's gone.

Do-Better looks left, right, left again, as if maybe Simon just scrambled off and hid beneath a bench like some mischievous little kid.

Looks for a blood trail.

Mark's trying to rise behind her but she's not too worried about him.

Plenty of time to finish him off.

Not too worried about Simon either, but she's curious, so she wanders down to the end of the car. Toward the door where the two of them entered.

Makes no sense he would retreat backward.

Nothing back there now. The cars behind them have all disappeared.

That's how the black-room train works. Last car vanishes once you leave. Each new car you enter becomes the caboose.

Maybe he managed to get himself tapped out, she thinks. Yank the rip cord. That would be one bumpy ride, though. And pretty cowardly to leave his friend behind. To take the brunt of her frustration.

Which is mounting.

While she's thinking all this, she idly slides the subway car door open and looks out into the retreating tunnel, just out of curiosity, mostly.

As the door slides open, the subway roar doubles.

She leans out and peers out into the darkness, then shrugs.

Oh well, she thinks. If he did somehow sneak out here, there's nothing out here for him but track.

As she thinks this, something rustles behind her.

Not something.

Someone.

Simon's back.

Looks like hell, and he's barely breathing, and he's not even sure he's strong enough to raise his leg and kick her through that door and out into the tunnel.

Nope. He's wrong.

Turns out he's plenty strong enough.

Short scream swallowed by the shrieking of the subway.

Then back to the normal rhythmic rumble as the train rattles on.

Simon hoists Mark to his feet. Says to him hoarsely.

That won't stop her, just delay her. I bought us maybe three minutes, tops.

Mark steadies himself on a pole. Folds his bloodied wings back. Says to Simon.

I'm good.

Then Mark reaches out and grabs the knob to the door that leads to the next car. As they walk through the doorway, Mark's thinking, Three of them. Simon said there were three of them.

Do-Good.

Do-Better.

Do-Best.

Ready?

The female guard in the tent on the waterfront nods, then reaches to her belt and unhooks her handcuffs.

In the half inch of skin that's exposed between her dress-white gloves and her dress-coat sleeve, a sliver of tattoo peeks through.

Same tattoo. Snakes and flames. Matching set with the male guard.

Loyal bodyguards both.

Loyal.

But not to Bellarmine.

She flips open the handcuffs and Bellarmine half looks up from his handheld and then, his attention snagged, shoots her a quizzical look, then starts to speak just as the other guard, the man, takes a quick half step behind him, loops his arms deftly through Bellarmine's arms, yanks them up, and pins him.

Handheld drops to the tent floor.

Nearby factotums note the rustle and rise in surprise. Drop their clipboards with a clatter.

Bellarmine squirms. He's much too strong to be held like this for more than a moment.

But all they need is a moment.

Bellarmine struggles, jerks, sputters, says aloud.

What the fuck—what—you think you're going to arrest *me*—?

The female guard holds the one cuff cocked open, its small pointy catch exposed. Then she swings it, scythe-like, and digs it deep and buries it into the softest part of Bellarmine's neck.

Aiming for the artery.

Cuff cuts deep.

Second guard unpins Bellarmine.

Bellarmine drops to his knees. Shocked.

Cuff still stuck. Neck spurting in rhythmic arterial spasms.

The female guard sidesteps to avoid the halting geyser.

There's a shout. Then a gunshot. Then a second gunshot.

The female guard goes down, like she fainted. Maybe at the sight of all the blood.

But she's down.

More shouts and confusion.

Bellarmine's suited security detail, who'd been busy securing the grounds, now turn on the two guards, drawing, taking aim, firing, advancing, taking aim, firing.

The male guard backs away slowly from Bellarmine, his white gloves, no longer spotless, held high in surrender.

His tattooed arms now half-exposed.

Snakes and flames.

Finally, from elsewhere in the tent, one last gun crack from a crack shot.

Second guard's head jerks sideways from the headshot.

Topples sidewise.

Hits the grass.

But Bellarmine has long since bled out.

Bellarmine's dead.

So it's done.

Mark slides open the door to the next car.

The third car.

Together he and Simon enter.

Mark spots a man at the far end of the car, but it can't be Do-Best, Mark thinks.

This man's in a suit, tied down to a chair, arms behind him, legs splayed wide, just sitting, waiting, in the middle of the aisle, with a white hood covering his head.

Must be Lesser, Mark thinks.

Lesser. Finally.

Simon looks at Mark. Nods. Simon's thinking the same thing. Pats Mark on the back.

Okay. We're almost home.

One Times Square.

The door at the end of the hallway is locked for some reason but two kicks easily splinter the frame. Then I give it a shove with my shoulder to dislodge the deadbolt, which dangles as the door swings free.

I figure I'll probably walk in, find maybe one more Teuton,

maybe a bored-looking nurse flipping through a copy of *People*, probably an elaborate black-room bed obscured by a coil of tubes and monitors and securitized sensors. And in the bed, Lesser. All that's left then is to tap out Lesser, and make sure to time it with Mark and Simon, assuming they've found him in the limn.

That's what I expect to find.

I do not expect what I actually find, once I kick in that door.

An empty office.

Fluorescent lights.

Gray wall-to-wall carpeting.

Floor-to-ceiling windows.

And just one man, in a suit, tied down to a chair, arms behind him, legs splayed wide, just sitting, waiting, in the middle of the floor, with a white hood covering his head.

Sitting.

Waiting.

For me.

Wiggles his shoulders. Wriggles his wrists.

Like Houdini.

The ropes binding him drop to the ground.

Wrists free, he raises his hands.

Reveals a chunky metal watchband.

Then reaches up and pulls off his white hood.

No bed.

No black room.

No bodyguards.

Just Boonce.

Looking up at me.

Says one word.

Boo.

36.

Dumb silence under the buzz of ancient midtown fluorescents.

Until I finally ask.

Where's Lesser?

Lesser's dead.

Since when?

Since about five minutes after you left his apartment in Stuyvesant Town last Saturday night. Since however long it took me to get in there and get him to tell me everything he knew, which he did, under maximum duress. I don't know. Maybe ten minutes? I wasn't timing it.

But what about the black room—

There is no black room, Spademan.

But who—

Me.

Why?

Boonce stands. Adjusts his suit.

Because I wanted what Lesser had. What he developed at Near Enemy and then kept from me and then stole from me. I wanted to know what it was and I wanted to take it from him and I wanted to use it for myself. And I did, and I did, and I will.

But Lesser didn't know anything—

That's not true. He just didn't know what you thought he knew. Or, frankly, what I thought he knew. But he knew something else. Something better.

Boonce shrugs off his suit jacket. Folds it over his arm.

You know, the funny thing is, Spademan, if you'd actually just killed him that first night in Stuyvesant Town, before I could get my hands on him, none of this would have happened. In a weird way, if you had killed him that night, you would have saved him. If you'd just done the one and only thing in this world that you are good at.

Boonce drapes the suit jacket over the chairback.

It would have been terrible timing for me, of course, and I would have been very angry, and I would have tracked you down and dumped you in the river and found that bitch of yours and her baby upstate and left them buried in the woods. But at least you would have kept what Lesser had out of my hands. Which, of course, is what I assume the person who hired you to kill him was hoping to do all along—

Boonce undoes a cuff link.

—hoping to keep what he had from my hands, I mean—

Fingers the tiny NYPD shield.

—and it almost worked. Almost.

Pockets the shield, out of sight.

Do you know who that was, by the way? The woman who hired you to kill Lesser?

No.

Boonce thinks a minute. Fidgets with the other cuff link. Shrugs.

Me neither, to be honest. Though I have a hunch.

Undoes the second cuff link.

That's what I like about your friend Simon, Spademan. Even though he fucked up my plans back in the woods.

Something about my face at that moment makes Boonce pause. Then smile.

Yeah, that was me. I hated to get in bed with Pushbroom, but I figured I needed to set a fire under you. Increase my leverage. Then Simon intervened.

Pockets the second shield.

See, I like Simon because he's like you, Spademan, except he's always willing to do what needs to be done. Without reservation or hesitation. You, not so much.

Boonce starts to fiddle with his watchband. While he does this, I reach into the pocket of my coat. Check for the box-cutter. Still there.

Ask Boonce.

But what about Bellarmine?

There is no more Bellarmine, Spademan, as of about—

Checks his watch. That fucking watch.

—four minutes ago, give or take. Great tragedy. The city's last protector, cut down in his prime, right before his big announcement. Looks like some rogue cops did him in. No doubt he's the victim of some vast terrorist conspiracy. But the city will survive, of course. And our beloved mayor will win yet another term.

So you work for the mayor.

Boonce laughs.

Oh no.

Tugs at the knot of his silk tie.

Are you beginning to understand at all, Spademan? Even a little bit?

Loosens the tie and slides it out from under his stiff white collar.

I have to admit, Spademan, I had no more idea than you did who Lesser saw in there that night, this crazy burqa woman running around and blowing herself up in the limn. And I was definitely curious. I mean, if that had actually been true? Someone had actually cracked that problem? Killing people in the limn? I worked years on it and I couldn't crack it, despite all my best efforts and my whiz-kid protégés. It's too bad it all just turned out to be a hoax perpetrated by some coven of hysterical fanatics, living together in a drafty castle in a park, trying to spook a bunch of hoppers into waking up the world.

Boonce folds the tie. Hangs it over the chair.

That part of the story I only found out thanks to you, Spademan. So all your running around the city wasn't totally for naught. Chasing that nurse like a lovesick kid. I hope she was worth it.

Chest clenches when he says this. I tighten my grip on the box-cutter in my pocket.

You're wrong, Boonce. She's not—

He holds up a hand to cut me off.

Spare me.

Then unbuttons the top button of his white dress shirt at the collar. Works his way slowly down through the buttons, taking his time. Relishing this. Letting the silence linger. I grip the box-cutter and wonder just how much longer I should listen. There's no one up here but the two of us, as far as I can tell. Just us, at the top of One Times Square. And I'm not sure if Boonce's got some new surprise waiting, some further twist, some gang of guards in the wings about to pounce, but I don't really care. Whatever happens, there's not enough space between the two of us now that I can't finish him before I go down. I only need a head start and two or three good swipes at a soft spot.

Last rule of the Jersey schoolyard. Last rule, and the most important one, but the hardest one to learn.

There's no one you can't take down, no matter how big or fast or strong, as long as you yourself don't care about ever getting back up again.

Boonce unbuttons the last button on his shirt.

You took me for a pretty buttoned-up guy, didn't you, Spademan?

I did.

Well, here's your lesson. Your last lesson. Before we part ways.

Boonce shrugs the white shirt off.

Sometimes there's more to people than what you see.

Boonce folds the shirt over the chairback.

Then he straightens up, bare-chested. Inked with tattoos from neck to waist. Every inch of his torso, covered. Down both arms to the wrists too. Looks like a freak in a circus sideshow.

Like the star of the freak show.

Snakes and flames.

Hoboken.

Puchs and Luckner sit in the patrol car, watching.

Puchs yawns. Stretches those tattooed arms again. Scratches them.

Luckner stares straight ahead.

Luckner's phone buzzes.

She looks down.

Checks the phone.

Then stows it.

Says to Puchs.

That's it. Let's go.

Puchs perks up.

What's the order?

Luckner checks the chamber of her automatic.

The whole building.

Everyone?

Everyone.

Puchs nods, smiles to himself, then checks his pistol too.

Then they get out of the car, walk briskly across the street, and head inside into the lobby of the building.

Some hapless neighbor loiters in the lobby, by the mailboxes, shuffling through junk mail. Barely glances up when the two cops enter. Maybe feels a little safer when he sees them, actually.

Luckner raises her pistol toward him and fires twice. Drops the neighbor and dents the mailbox with a double clang.

Then Luckner runs a finger down the intercom directory.

Finds the apartment number.

Buzzes.

Persephone's voice crackles in the speaker box.

Hello?

Luckner leans in.

Ma'am, it's Officer Luckner from downstairs. We've got shots fired in the lobby. Hold tight. We're on our way up.

And Persephone buzzes them in.

Last car.

Train lurches.

Mark and Simon hobble aboard and let the door slide shut behind them.

Head toward Lesser, seated at the far end, in a suit with a white hood over his head.

Lights go out.

Lights come up again.

And now, between them and Lesser, sitting in a seat, or not sitting exactly, but coiled, hunched, is a huge mound of knotted muscle. They can only assume it's a man. It's bald-headed and hairless. The rest of it just looks like a gnarl of scarred flesh. Skin the color of something that's been left out to spoil. Faint foul odor in the car now too. The beast before them wears no clothes, save for some rags wrapped clumsily around its midsection. Some needless nod to modesty.

Turns its bald head, which looks like a thumb bent on top of a clenched fist.

Beast squints.

Spots them.

Grunts.

Begins to stand.

Fold upon fold of muscled flesh unfolding.

Beast rises.

Regards them both.

This hairless creature with pinprick black eyes and a mouthful of splintered teeth.

Looses a kind of strangulated cry.

A wheezing roar.

And around the splintered teeth, something like a foul smile forms.

Then it stretches out its two corded arms and wraps its thick fists around the poles on the opposite sides of the subway car.

Sets its feet.

Gets its grip.

Snarls.

Tugs.

There's the shrill sound of metal buckling.

As the subway car starts to fold in on itself.

The foul smile widens.

Do-Best.

37.

I finger the box-cutter in my pocket again. Grip it. Get ready.

Boonce checks his watch again. You can barely see it now, that big chunky watch, lost against the backdrop of all his fancy tattoos. Now that I look closer, I realize how elaborate the tattoos are. Not just snakes and flames twining up each arm, but a whole panorama of apocalypse etched across his chest, and back, and neck. An ink-black swirl of snakes and flames and horses rearing and pale cloaked riders with skeletal faces shrieking and sinners wailing and lost souls writhing in final agony as the Earth is rent open and damnation is loosed upon the world.

Boonce looks up from his watch.

Admiring my ink?

Nods to his chest, his neck, his arms.

Took years. Painful as fuck, I will say that. To the kids watching at home? Do not get tattoos.

Looks back to his watch.

Okay, so your friends in the limn should be arriving in the last car right about now, assuming they got through Do-Good and Do-Better, which I think is a pretty good bet. To be honest, Do-Good's a bit of a hayseed and Do-Better—well, my money might be on her, she's good, but then, all due respect to Simon and that angel friend of yours. In a different world, I'd like to think that Simon and I could have worked together. Accomplished great things.

Looks up at me.

Ah, well. Regrets.

As Boonce talks, he walks the perimeter of the office, which is floor-to-ceiling windows on all sides. Behind him stretches the backdrop of dead Times Square. Towering neon billboards that haven't been lit for years, sitting blind and dead-screen gray. On other buildings, the signs that no one bothered to turn off still cycle through old ads no one will ever see. Ads for canceled sitcoms, forgotten blockbusters, Broadway spectacles long since closed. There's one ad on repeat in the background, for some kind of newfangled circus. The ad must have played fifteen times while we've been standing here. Some kind of circus starring clowns with long chins and white faces. Acrobats in leopard prints. Panthers leaping through burning hoops. Just playing to a dead square now. To emptiness. To nothing.

Boonce watches it too. Then turns back and says to me.

So let's just assume your friends made it through. As for your lady-friend with the baby back in Hoboken, well, the odds are a little worse for her. I've got my best men on that case. Well, best man and best woman.

Stage whispers.

That Luckner is a beast.

My chest clenches again when he says this, twice as hard as before. Feel Boonce's fist wrapped around my heart. Tightening.

Say to Boonce.

Don't. They're just—leave them out of it.

He smiles. Says nothing.

Boonce, please. Please. Leave them alone.

His smile dissipates.

No, Spademan, you leave them alone. Again and again and again. You left them alone in the woods and you left them alone in Hoboken. That's what you do, apparently.

You don't need to hurt them to hurt me.

He cuts me off again.

Sorry, but it's done. My people tend to be pretty quick, if that's any consolation.

Checks his watch. Waiting. Still. For something. So I ask him.

Why, Boonce?

He looks up at me. Impatient now.

Do you know what I've learned in my time in law enforcement?

What?

There are fingers on triggers in this country, Spademan, and all they need is an excuse to pull. That's what they're born to do, that's what they're trained to do, and it's what they live to do. That's all they are—fingers. And without triggers, these fingers have no meaning. Triggers, and a reason to pull.

Boonce checks his watch again.

So these fingers, Spademan, they lie in wait. For a reason. A story, really. A story to tell you, to tell me, to tell themselves.

Boonce gestures to the city.

To tell them.

Checks the watch again. Not yet time. So he continues.

That's what I do, Spademan. I'm a storyteller. I write stories.

Looks back out over the skyline.

More specifically, I write endings.

Boonce slips his hands in his suit-pant pockets.

Here's my latest story, Spademan. Tell me what you think. It's the tale of an Arab exile who comes to a fallen city and works to recruit others to join him. Let's say he's a brilliant prodigy with a tragic past, with a reason to hate America, and now he's found a way to tear into the one last refuge that's left to any of us. The magical limnosphere. Our beloved last hiding place. Those of us who matter, anyway. Good so far, right?

I don't answer. Just let Boonce prattle. He waits a second, gets no answer. Prattles on.

Now let's say our dangerous terrorist hatches a plot to murder the very millionaire who brought him here. I have to admit, that was a twist even I didn't see coming, but sure, I can work with it. And then let's say our terrorist goes even further and murders a mayoral candidate—the one man he fears might be strong enough to stop him. What then would we all be willing to do to bring down a man like that? If we heard that story? What would be justified then?

There's a faint hum rising in the room now and the windows seem to start to thrum. We're high enough up that at first I think it's maybe just a high wind. Boonce notices it too. Smiles. Continues.

Do you know what I'd be willing to do if I heard a story like that, Spademan?

What's that?

Pull all the triggers. Every last one.

But that story's not true, Boonce. Not any of it.

True or not, it doesn't matter, once the first shots have been fired. Wars aren't fought over ideas, Spademan, or beliefs—you must know that. They're fought over stories. You tell your story, I tell my story, then we fight. The winner gets to write the ending. That's how history works.

So what, Boonce? You're going to—kill Bellarmine? Kill Shaban? Burn this whole city down?

He smiles.

For starters.

His smile lingers, like the afterimage on a TV that's just been turned off. It's not the smile of someone who knows he'll win. It's the smile of someone who's already won and feels sad that the game is over, and was won so easily.

The smile fades. Then he shrugs. Lost in some private thought. Checks his watch again.

What are you so anxious for, Boonce?

He looks out the window. Over the stilled city.

I'm just waiting for my triggers to arrive.

As he stares at the skyline, I put my thumb on the slide of the blade in the box-cutter in my pocket. Slide the blade forward. Find a good length. Ready it. Run my thumb along its edge. Figure I pull it out, then it's four good steps to Boonce, if I take him at a dead run. He's close enough to the window now that I can tackle him and maybe send us both straight out through the glass and into the sky. I wonder how strong these windows are. What kind of impact they can take. What it would take to shatter them and send us both out over the square in a shimmering cloud of shards, sprinkling down around us as we fall.

From this height, it's three, four seconds before we hit the pavement of Times Square.

Long enough to get some cutting in. Work on his throat on the way down.

While we drop.

Just like the New Year's ball.

Three.

Two—

Tempting thought. And I'm almost ready. First, though, I have to ask.

What was it, Boonce? What had Lesser figured out? What was worth all this?

Boonce looks back at me, and he's about to speak—then his eyes flutter. He looks left, right, left again, winces, as though he's recalling something painful.

Then he looks at me.

Says nothing now.

Just flexes his hands.

Breathes deeply.

Exhales.

Now he speaks.

Something so much better, Spademan. So much better. You can be my witness.

Witness to what?

To this.

Boonce closes his eyes slowly. Exhales again. Deeply. Coughs up a guttural growl.

Then opens his eyes wide.

His eyes completely white now.

If you'll excuse me for just a moment, your friends have finally arrived.

38.

Simon and Mark are so distracted by this heaving mound of seething muscle and the subway car collapsing that they don't notice the white-hooded figure in the chair at the end of the subway car suddenly tremor, spasm, settle calmly, then rise slowly to his feet.

Then reach a hand up to pull off the white hood.

A red hand.

Pulls the hood off.

Revealing his face.

A red face.

Boonce.

But Boonce stained red.

From head to hands and every inch of exposed skin in between, Boonce's flesh is colored crimson. White-blond hair cropped close to the skull.

Hair white.

Eyes white.

Smile white.

Flesh red.

Bright red.

Blood-red.

He's got Mark and Simon's attention by now.

Boonce stands in his suit, straightens his tie, and in one swift movement strips off the jacket and shirt, tears them away and discards them, leaving him bare-chested.

No elaborate tattoos on his torso in the limn.

Just one tattoo. Inked across his chest.

In Gothic script.

NOCEBO.

Boonce looks down at his chest. Then up at Mark and Simon. Asks them both.

How's your Latin?

Mark and Simon say nothing.

Boonce smiles.

Rough translation? I will harm.

Then Boonce walks calmly toward Do-Best, who's still snarling like a beast on a chain, and Boonce pets him gently, then places his palm on Do-Best's forehead like a faith healer.

Do-Best seizes. Then drops.

Just slumps without a sound to the subway floor. Shivers. Then stills.

Boonce looks down at him almost sadly, like Do-Best's a dog he had to put down.

Then he looks back up at Mark and Simon.

Be thankful. You guys would never have got past him.

One Times Square.

Boonce is still standing there, in front of me, eyes closed, motionless, calm, his arms loose at his sides, breathing steadily, like he's meditating.

And me with my box-cutter. Thinking.

This is it.

This is the moment.

The box-cutter's ready.

More than ready.

I'm ready.

Do it now.

Do it now.

Do it now.

But I don't.

Because there's one more thing I need to know.

Hoboken.

Puchs knocks three times on the apartment door with a knuckle, his other hand gripped around the gun.

Doesn't even flinch at the sight of the dead Pushbroom guy nailed to the front door with the note.

Just knocks.

No answer.

Tries the knob.

Door's unlocked.

So he half turns the knob quietly, then signals to Luckner.

Signal tells her, Cover me. I'm going in.

She nods, though she's not happy. Leave something for me, she thinks, as Puchs turns the knob slowly the rest of the way.

Door opens with a click.

Puchs cracks open the door and peeks into the apartment.

Thinks of calling out Persephone's name but doesn't want to spook her and besides, what does it matter? This won't take long.

Just a woman and a baby.

Won't take but a moment.

Puchs slips inside.

One Times Square.

Boonce's eyes slide open again.

He looks at me. Seems almost surprised I'm still here.

This is harder than I thought, but it's a trip, Spademan. Such a trip. Too bad you'll never experience it. I'll have to leave you in a moment. Leave you here, in Times Square, where it all began. It's fitting, though, isn't it? To leave you here. Where you were born.

I was born in New Jersey, Boonce.

He smiles.

Someone was born in New Jersey, maybe. Spademan was born in Times Square.

And that's when I ask him. The obvious question. The same question I asked him the first time that I met him, back at Grand Central Terminal.

Why me?

He shrugs.

The motorman.

Not the answer I expected. So I say to Boonce.

What about the motorman?

He's the last piece, Spademan. The last loose end. And I thought, stupidly, because I have a sentimental streak, that it would be okay to let him live out his life in peace up in Beacon, what few years he has left. Just let him live out his days in exile. And I figured no one knew. No one left alive, anyway. But then Harrow and his little henchman, what was his name?

Milgram.

Yes, that's right. Milgram. They had to go and dig it up and then spill it to you. And you had to go and track him down. You drove right past his house, Spademan. The day after you turned up at Lesser's apartment. The day I first brought you in. No way I could let you follow that trail all the way to the end. So I sent you on an errand. Find Lesser. After that, you just became a kind of useful idiot. Plus, I will admit, I do feel some responsibility.

For Lesser?

No. For you.

What do you mean?

If you were born here, Spademan, then I created you. Right here. In Times Square.

But Boonce, I don't—

But then I do.

And I don't need to say it. I don't want to say it. Not to Boonce. Not to myself.

Don't even want to know it.

But I do.

And I say it.

You knew—

I do say it.

—you knew—

Because now I know.

—you knew about the plot against Times Square.

Boonce looks almost regretful. Then he shrugs.

Could we have stopped it? Would it have mattered?

And just like that, the regret, whatever I saw there in his eyes for a moment, whatever flared up and flickered briefly, is gone. Snuffed out. Extinguished. Like this city.

He knew about Times Square.

He knew beforehand and he let it happen.

Boonce gazes out the window. Says to me.

We didn't plan it, of course. Well, maybe we gave it a nudge. Mostly I just saw what was coming and simply stepped out of the way.

Why?

Because when you see chaos approaching, Spademan, you either prepare to perish or you prepare to prosper. I mean—

—and here he gestures again to the dead square below us—

—look what happened after Times Square. A new world flourished. The off-body world. A world I must now leave you in order to join.

The windows of the building are really thrumming now, singing like plucked strings.

Boonce grins.

More than join, actually, if all goes well.

He reaches out his hand.

Your box-cutter, Spademan.

Stands still with his hand out. Palm open. Says again.

Your box-cutter. I know it's in your pocket. Come on. You can see I'm unarmed.

You want me to give you my box-cutter?

No, Spademan. I want you to use it on me.

And now he drops his hand back to his side so that both arms are dangling, relaxed and loose, his head back, his throat exposed, and he closes his eyes calmly.

And he says.

I want you to use it on me, Spademan. Do the one thing you're good at. One last time.

I feel the box-cutter in my pocket and I grip it. My thumb traces the sharp edge of the extended blade. I slice my own skin. Draw blood. I can feel the blood pool, warm in my pocket. Then I take my sliced thumb and slide the blade shut. Pull my hand from my pocket. Tell Boonce.

No.

He doesn't even open his eyes. The windows are trembling now, shaking, as though they're about to implode. Shower us both in a cascade of shearing glass.

He says again.

Use it, Spademan. End this.

You want me to.

Yes, I do.

But it won't end this.

He opens his eyes.

No, it won't.

Then he reaches his own hand into his suit-pant pocket.

Well, if you won't do that, there is one last thing you can do for me, Spademan.

What's that, Boonce?

He smiles.

Watch this.

Then he pulls a short curved blade from his pocket.

What's that phrase? The one your wife was so fond of saying?

Thinks a moment. Recalls it.

Ah yes.

Then he says it.

See you on the other side.

And he swipes his own blade cleanly across his neck, opening his throat, quick and steady and without hesitation, and the blood comes suddenly, and he stands for a moment, blade in his hand, bleeding, like he's both the priest and the sacrifice being offered, and then the knife falls from his hand, and his body drops.

39.

Hoboken.

Puchs glides forward into the apartment, pistol drawn, silent, sighting targets, moving quickly, without hesitation. He's been sitting in that squad car too long, coiled up, waiting all week for this part. Boonce promised him that this is how they would end it. That they would get to do this, if they just waited patiently.

The living room's empty, so Puchs signals all-clear to Luckner, who's still standing in the apartment doorway. Then Puchs turns and looks toward the bedroom door, which is open.

Sees Persephone standing in the doorway.

Just behind the doorway, actually.

Just out of sight.

Glock leveled.

Persephone doesn't wait.

Doesn't really aim either.

Just unloads.

She left Hannah in her crib, in the closet, in the dark, with all the blankets she could grab draped over the top of the crib, hoping they would muffle the sound, hoping they would hide her, protect her, a little bit at least.

Then she positioned herself a foot back in the doorway, just enough so she couldn't be seen from the sightlines of the apartment's front door. Stood right where Simon showed her to stand, before he left, in case there was any trouble. Told her to wait until whoever came in was dead in her sights. Told her how to hold the Glock. Showed her how to pull the trigger if the time came.

The waiting will be the hardest part, he told her.

They'll buzz up, and when they do, you should let them in, Simon said. Then stand right here, just back from the doorway, just out of sight, and wait.

So she buzzed them up.

Stood in the doorway.

Gripped the gun.

Elbows loose, not locked.

Finger gentle on the trigger.

And waited.

Until now.

Persephone unloads.

Not sure how many times she hit the guy, but enough that the guy is down.

Felt easy.

Automatic.

Just like Simon said it would.

That's two times Simon's saved her now.

Just be a machine, he told her. Just breathe, stay calm, and be a machine.

She can do that, she thought. Be just like her baby.

A machine for staying alive.

Simon and Mark stand ready in the train car as Boonce strides toward them, the dropped mound of Do-Best lying behind him on the floor.

Joseph Boonce. Still standing. Still alive. In the limn, at least.

Simon looks him up and down and says to Boonce.

Why are you red, Boonce? You look like a baboon's ass.

Boonce smirks.

I like you, Simon. So I apologize in advance for this.

Puts his hand lightly on Simon's forehead like a faith healer.

Simon drops.

Slumps to the floor without a word.

Mark raises his sword, which bursts into flame with a soft, barely audible pop like a gas burner catching.

As he does this, Boonce says.

You're a pastor, Mark, right? So you know your scripture. Well, here's a favorite of mine.

His voice like a hive of insects. A sound that swarms into Mark's ears and seems to devour his eardrums.

Boonce says.

He that killeth with the sword must be killed with the sword—

Boonce says.

—and something something something I forget the rest—

And then Boonce unhinges his red jaw, opening it wide like a snake, so that his mouth drops wide, and he reaches a red fist deep down into his own throat, and from his throat pulls a long sword from within himself, impossibly, but he does it, because he can now do anything, or so it seems.

Just a dream, Mark thinks. Just a dream.

And Mark raises his own flaming sword but his sword is suddenly lighter, it takes barely any strength to heft at all, and he realizes that, faster than Mark could follow, Boonce used his own blade to cut through Mark's sword in three quick strokes, leaving his sword in flaming sections on the subway floor, each of which now quickly sputters out, and Mark's left holding only the hilt.

Then Boonce raises his long thin impossible sword with both hands and readies the killing blow.

But Mark's disappeared.

Boonce's sword simply slices the air where Mark stood.

So in a rage Boonce swings the sword again and plunges it into Simon's body, again and again, which shudders on the subway floor, then stills, and the train roars on.

———

Hoboken.

Luckner in the doorway fires three shots toward the bedroom, but she doesn't have the angle. Just splinters doorframe.

Doesn't matter. She counted at least twelve shots, and with the way that woman was firing, just unloading wildly, no way that clip isn't empty, or very close.

Amateur mistake.

Luckner adjusts her sunglasses. Steps into the apartment.

Behind Persephone, Hannah is bawling now. Even in the closet, even under all those blankets, Persephone can hear her, wailing, all alone.

Persephone knows the gun is empty because she heard the click-click-click the last few times she squeezed the trigger, but her finger kept pulling and she couldn't stop herself. A machine to stay alive.

Squeeze squeeze squeeze squeeze squeeze click click click shit.

It won't end like this, she thinks, then starts to cry, finally, because she knows it very well could end like this. After the cabin. After today. After the camps in Central Park. After the van in Red Hook. After what she saw in her father's heaven.

After her father.

After everyone left her here alone, again, with Hannah, in Hoboken.

I'm sorry, Hannah, she thinks. I promise I will hold you and you won't feel pain. I promise—

Luckner appears in the doorway. Gun drawn.

Spots Persephone. Sights her slowly. Hint of a grin.

Persephone backs up until she's standing in front of the closet door. Shuts her eyes.

Does what she used to do once as a habit. As a reflex. As a refuge.

She prays.

If ever You loved me, save Hannah. Take me but save Hannah at least. Save Hannah—

Persephone's still praying when she hears a single shot and startles.

Opens her eyes just in time to see Luckner fall.

Brain matter on the doorjamb.

Luckner slumped in the doorway.

Sunglasses askew.

Then Persephone hears a voice from the livingroom.

Hello? Are you okay in there?

A long man pokes his long face around the corner. Gives her a long look. Then stows his snub-nose in a shoulder holster.

I'm sorry if I frightened the baby, ma'am. My name's Dandy. Detective James Dandy. NYPD.

It takes her a minute. She's about to say it but he cuts her off.

—I prefer James. I'm looking for a Mr Spade Man?

He's not here.

Okay, well, could you tell him I stopped by? And let him know I decided to run a check on those two cops that Boonce had watching you. Good thing I did. Turns out they're no good.

He glances down at Luckner's body.

But I guess you figured that out.

Persephone opens the closet and pulls Hannah from her crib. Clutches her close. Calms her. Whispers to her.

Let's go home.

Then turns to the detective.

I'm sorry. What did you say your name was again?

Dandy. Detective Dandy.

Well, Detective Dandy, would you please come in here and help us get packed?

40.

One Times Square.

I run.

Down the hall. Past the Teuton.

Away from Boonce's body.

Jam elevator buttons.

Then I plummet toward the earth like the New Year's ball.

Ten.

Nine.

Left Boonce's body bleeding out. Boonce is dead. So I assume.

Eight.

Seven.

Saw his blood swallowed up by the gray wall-to-wall carpet. Soak it through.

Six.

Five.

But I know it's not over. I don't know what he's doing, but I do know that.

Four.

Three.

He said he writes stories. Writes endings. And this story hasn't ended. Not yet.

Two.

Hit the ground floor.

One.

Run.

Through Times Square. Down Broadway. The long blocks

south toward the safe perimeter. Where the first of the craziest cabbies might be foolhardy enough to nibble for a fare.

Forty-First.

Fortieth.

Keep running.

Thirty-Ninth.

No cabs. And little time.

Thirty-Eighth.

So I do something strange.

Thirty-Seventh.

I pray.

Please—

Never done this before.

—if you can hear me—

Thirty-Sixth.

—I know I never—

Then I spot it.

Blocks away.

Dab of yellow against the ashtray gray of the streetscape. Lone cab prowling.

Whisper thank you. To Whoever.

Then flag it.

Cab slows.

I climb inside. Tell the driver.

Atlantic Avenue. In Brooklyn.

He waves a hand frantically.

No no no no no no no Atlantic Avenue no Brooklyn—

He's brave enough to trawl Times Square, but he's not that brave, apparently.

I consider hijacking the cab. Another cab. Like I'm collecting them.

But then I remember something.

Check my pocket. Find the box-cutter. And still there, next to the box-cutter.

Van keys.

So I pull out the last of my wad of cash. Toss it into the front seat.

Tell the driver.

Take me to Chinatown instead.

In the cab, I call Persephone's cellphone.

Hope she'll answer.

Curse myself while the phone rings and rings. And rings.

Then finally.

She picks up. No hello. Her voice cold.

Don't worry. We're safe. Both of us. And we're already gone. Don't come after us, Spademan. Tell Simon to join us when he can. Tell him we're all going home.

Then Persephone hangs up on me.

Cab pulls up to the Kakumu Lounge.

Inside, the flop-shop is dark and smells of sweat and vomit and panic. It takes my eyes a minute to adjust, and when they do, I'm greeted by this tableau.

Mina, pale and spent.

Mark sitting up in his bed, tubes half-detached, shirt soaked through thoroughly, faintly dazed and silent but tapped out.

Nurse hovering at Simon's bedside, hand clutched over her mouth.

Simon in his bed. Not moving.

I ask Mark, though I know the answer.

You find Lesser?

He shakes his head. Tries to speak. Forgets his jaw's still broken out here. Then he grabs a scrap of paper. Scribbles quickly.

A TRAP. JUST BOONCE. MINA YANKED ME OUT.

Boonce is dead.

Mark looks up at me. Scribbles again.

NO HE'S NOT.

Mark, I just saw it with my own eyes. He's dead. I watched him die. Ten minutes ago in Times Square.

Mark scribbles.

NOT DEAD.

Scribbles again.

NOT IN THERE.

This I did not expect. I look to Mina and she seems about to speak, then realizes she has nothing to add, so she tends instead to Mark's last few sensors, pulling them free.

So I say to Mark.

But that's not possible. Maybe who you saw wasn't Boonce.

Mark scribbles.

MAYBE.

But Mark knows. And I know too.

Meanwhile Simon still hasn't moved.

I ask Nurse.

Why haven't you tapped him out?

She pulls her hand from in front of her mouth, where it's been hovering, helpless.

I'm afraid to.

Why?

I don't know if he'll make it.

What do you mean?

Whatever they did, whatever Boonce did to him, in there, Simon's not responding. He's completely shut down. I can't—I've never seen this, Spademan. But his vitals are all so marginal, it's like—it's like he's only still alive in there. So if I tap him out—I don't know—

Well, you have to tap him out.

I don't know—

What other choice do we have?

She has nothing more to say. I nod to Simon.

All right. Watch over him. I have to get to Brooklyn.

Then I say to Mark.

Stay here. Watch these three. Wait for my call.

He nods.

Then I say to Mina.

Lock up. Don't let anyone in. Not anyone. You have a basement?

She nods.

Then everyone who can, get in the basement.

Nurse asks.

What about you?

I need to get to Brooklyn. Atlantic Avenue. Quickly.

Why? What's at Atlantic—

Boonce's final act.

You don't think he's coming here for us?

I say to Nurse.

No. Not us.

Fingers on triggers.

Waiting to pull.

I head out to the street in Chinatown.

Canal Street.

Where Puchs first picked me up.

Head down an alleyway.

Air still thrumming. Air's alive.

Buzzing, like a swarm is coming.

Just like in Times Square.

Figure I have maybe twenty minutes, tops.

————

Think about what Mark just told me. About Boonce.

Think about the only answer that makes sense.

What Lesser found. What Lesser had. It wasn't a way to kill someone in the limn. Not exactly.

It was a way to live in the limn. Regardless of what happens to your body out here.

To live forever in the limn, detached from any body.

When I was talking to Boonce, he was in the limn too. In both worlds. Without a bed, without sensors, without sedatives, without tubes. Without needing to tap in.

That was Lesser's secret. That's what Lesser had found.

Who needs to live at all in this world when you can live forever in that one?

Mark knew it too. He wouldn't say it. But he knew it.

Boonce is alive.

Just not out here.

Head down the alleyway.

Turn left.

Say another prayer. What the hell? First one worked.

Hello. It's me again—

Turn another corner. Hope it's still here.

It's still here.

Rental minivan is covered from stem to stern in graffiti and a window's broken, but at least it's not up on blocks. Still has tires. So it's drivable. In theory.

And when I beep-beep the rental fob the doors unlock.

I climb in and the van starts on the first twist too.

Magic wagon.

Hit the wipers, which smear fresh graffiti just enough that I can see. Back out of the alley, U-turn, then head toward the Brooklyn Bridge.

Hope it's open.

Because I've got maybe five minutes left.

On the side panel of the minivan, the name of the rental company's all but covered by the handiwork of vandals. Barely visible, though. If you squint.

Check-Off's minivan. Waiting in the wings.

I flatten the pedal and drive.

Hit the bridge. No traffic.

Sail over unimpeded.

Then I spot them. Over the East River.

Four of them.

Flying in formation.

Noses down. For extra speed.

Rotors set the air to thrumming. Sound like a thousand hoof beats. Thundering toward Brooklyn.

Toward Atlantic Avenue.

Toward Shaban.

Attack copters.

Military. Look like well-armed wasps.

The pilots' faces just barely visible in the windows of the choppers' wide glass. Heading for their target.

Fingers on their triggers.

Waiting to pull.

Floor the magic wagon.

Exit the bridge.

Squeal past what few cars sit with startled drivers as I speed by.

Hit Atlantic.

Spin the wheel left.

Tires keening.

Keep the pedal jammed.

Crunch the brakes.

Pull up to the scent shop, van halfway up the curb.

Spot the Closed sign swinging on the locked door.

Jump out.

Shout and pound the glass.

In the silence of the street, the call to prayer is heard.

Sounded by the nearby mosque, newly reopened.

I'm standing, pounding on the glass door, shouting, sure that no one inside can hear me. From inside, I'm sure, I look like a crazy man, no sound, just fists pummeling and my mouth moving wildly.

And outside, the call to prayer is deafening, a low drone that rolls out and blankets Atlantic Avenue and muffles every other street noise.

Keep pounding.

One of the clerks finally appears inside, behind the counter.

I scream through the locked door.

Shaban!

Clerk looks startled. Walks slowly toward the door. Looks like he's wondering whether he should bring the shotgun with him. This crazy man, outside, drumming on the glass.

Then behind him, Shaban appears, and he knows.

Behind me.

In the air.

Hoof beats. Rising louder. Getting closer.

Not hoof beats.

Helicopters.

The roar of the rotor blades shreds the morning air.

All but drowning out the call to prayer.

———

I motion to Shaban, who's in some kind of long robe, like he's probably on his way out to the mosque, hooking his wire-rimmed glasses around his ears so he can see better who's at the door. And he walks up and unlocks the door and opens it and is about to ask me something but whatever look is on my face at that moment answers all his questions.

Then he barks something urgently over his shoulder to the clerk and motions the clerk to come, come, come, and when the clerk turns to go upstairs and retrieve a few things, Shaban barks again, no time, just come, and the clerk abandons his thought and follows us outside. And I hurry them both to the minivan parked halfway up on the curb, where I slide the side door open and they climb inside.

And after they climb in and I slide the door shut and I get into the driver's seat, the second clerk appears up the block, turning a corner on his way to the mosque, and he stops in the street, sees the two of them being hurried into the van by me, and the second clerk startles, like he fears maybe they're being arrested or kidnapped or worse. And the second clerk shouts something, and Shaban, inside the van, shouts something to me and slaps at the window from the inside, and the first clerk beside him reaches for the door, and slides it open again and we're already moving but the first clerk jumps free, to run and warn his fellow clerk, to gather him up, but it's too late, because I've jammed the gas and swerved into a wild U-turn into the center of Atlantic and turned the van the wrong way down a one-way side street, because there's no more time, and I jack the gas and we've left the two clerks behind, there's no time, there's no time, and we're gone, we're gone, and Shaban looks back out of the gaping side door and shouts something but we have to leave them now, leave them in the street, and in the end, I can only take one.

Just one.

Just Shaban.

Just the target.

We drive quietly for a moment down a derelict block, side door still hanging wide-open, past dead brownstones, the two of us weirdly silent, like we're in the first leg of some long dreary road trip we're both dreading.

And then behind us we hear the first thump and then a great whoosh and the van jolts forward and we jolt forward too, straining against our seat belts, and Shaban won't look behind but just slides the door quickly closed, but I can see it, behind us, this fiery tongue licking Atlantic Avenue clean, I can see it all behind us brightly in the rearview mirror of the van.

And then the next three copters follow.

Fire sidewinders into slumping tenements.

Each missile sinks into brick with a fiery orange blossom. The tired buildings sag and shudder, then buckle in a brick-dust cloud.

And in this loud crush of rubble, a billowing red cloud rises, and the rotors of the four copters suck up the red dust and send it swirling skyward, wild red dervishes loosed as the copters sweep low and speed down the block, skirting the avenue, their landing rails kissing asphalt and their up-tilted rotors thundering and swallowing any frail human sounds that aren't already buried under the rumble of the blocks' collapse.

Choppers sweep the street.

Then circle back.

Coming round for a second pass.

Sidewinders loosed with a finger-pull, once, twice, payloads sent spiraling, trailing corkscrew tails of smoke.

Hitting home.

And the four choppers unload the last of their munitions into what's left of Atlantic Avenue, a once-dead street that tried to rise, but which now slumps in a last sigh of fire and smoke like a gravely wounded dragon, found sleeping in its cave and slain for good.

I just drive.

    Leave the carnage behind us. Playing out in the rearview.

    The Atlantic Avenue sweep. The second one.

    First one ended in riots.

    Second one ended in fire.

    Both end in rubble.

    And we drive.

41.

I take Shaban the long way round to Hoboken. Figure I can hide him there for now.

Hope they'll think they killed him, at least for a little while.

That's the upside of rubble.

Hides its secrets for weeks.

Persephone's gone once we get back to my apartment, of course. I knew she wouldn't be there but it still stings. Place is empty, save for two more bodies, Puchs and Luckner, to go with the two Pushbroom stiffs. All left behind for the host to take care of, which I do.

Bodies, I can deal with.

Dead ones, anyway.

Live bodies I've been having some trouble with lately.

Shaban told me too. The whole story. In the van.

While we were driving.

We didn't take the Holland Tunnel. Holland's closed again now, maybe for good. They're all closed, all the tunnels and bridges, no one gets into the city and no one gets out. It's all over the news. Mayor declared a lockdown in the chaos right after Bellarmine was killed. Called in the National Guard. Shutting everything down. Sealing the city off.

Shaban and I barely made it over the Verrazano Bridge in south Brooklyn before the soldiers closed that too. Hobbled minivan covered in spray paint, Shaban ducking down to the floorboards in the back, inching past a roadblock that was only just being set up. Some peach-fuzzed private, no older than eighteen, stopped us and cupped his hands on the window but couldn't see inside for all the graffiti, and the line of traffic behind us was honking and cursing, also eager to leave before the lockdown, so he waved us past.

After all, we were heading out of the city anyway, so why worry about us?

Honestly, it was just the confusion that saved us.

As we inched in traffic past cops arguing over conflicting commands. Past soldiers hastily assembling barricades. Past superiors shouting instructions at grunts. All of them still waiting for final orders that weren't coming. Sorting through the confusion. Still struggling, while chaos spread.

Chaos.

Just like Boonce promised.

Though if we'd arrived ten minutes later, we would have been caught in the teeth of the siege, and Shaban would now be in prison or dead and who knows where I'd be.

But we didn't, and we weren't, and we slipped away.

And we drove.

Crossed the Verrazano to Staten Island, then took the long way round through south Jersey, then doubled back toward the north. Before long, we were deep into Jersey and well out of sight of the city. The towers of Manhattan are taller than any building for a hundred miles, but if you drive long enough, even they eventually drop out of sight.

Then it's just Shaban and me out on a Sunday drive. Passing long pastoral stretches that still feel like farmland. Gas needle at one-eighth of a tank but there's no way we're stopping for gas.

Shaban tells me his story as we drive.

Says it softly. Starting with a confession.

I knew. What Lesser had. I knew.

Shaban is still in the backseat, while I'm up front like a chauffeur, glancing every so often in the rearview, while he sits and watches the farm fields pass.

How did you know, Shaban?

I was his roommate, after all. At Near Enemy. We shared everything. But it was more than that.

What do you mean?

I knew because I built it. At least in theory. I imagined it.

Imagined what? You'll have to excuse me, Shaban, but I'm not an expert in IT.

He smiles. Watches more fields pass.

Please. Call me Sam.

Imagined what, Sam?

The code. That Lesser had. That Boonce used. The code that lets you live inside the limn. I wrote that code. Or, rather, I imagined that it might be possible. I wrote it, yes, but only on a blackboard. Then I erased it. I knew it was a mistake the moment it came out of the tip of the chalk. Lesser was the one who took it and tested it. Who made it real. Then Boonce took it from him.

So how does it work?

You know about the loop, yes?

Sure. The loop. People get trapped in their final moments in the limn if they're killed out here.

Shaban starts to continue, and I can tell he is figuring out just how technical to get. So I help him out.

Just speak slowly, Sam. I'll follow.

The theory of the loop is that your brain produces a last neural burst, right at the moment of your death. And that this burst can accidentally persist in the limn. Become part of the code of the construct. Even if your body is buried or carted away. Your consciousness persists, perpetually experiencing that one last moment, forever.

Sure.

So that's what I wrote on the blackboard. A question, in the form of numbers.

What was the question, Sam?

What if it wasn't a loop?

But you're dead out here. Your brain's dead. Your body's dead. You're all dead. Just like Boonce.

Of course. But you can persist in there. In theory, anyway. And that's all it was. A theory. I was just a brat, showing off. Then I gave that all up. But I left Lesser with the idea.

And Lesser took it.

Yes. He took it. Never tried it himself, as far as I know. I heard he got so spooked by the whole idea that he just went back to full-time hopping. He was always more comfortable doing that, just hovering unseen in other people's dreams. Felt safer, just being someone else's ghost. But Boonce knew Lesser had something, some new hack, but he didn't know what, and he was determined to find out. And I knew Lesser. I knew the idea wasn't safe with him.

Sure. But Lesser is dead now. And Boonce is dead.

Not really. Not in the limn.

How did Boonce do that? How did he tap in with no bed?

I have no idea, Spademan. I don't know what Boonce is capable of now.

Well, at least you're still alive, Shaban.

Yes. Thanks to you.

You'll have to disappear, you know.

Shaban's damaged voice barely even audible. His eyes still on the passing fields.

I know.

I'm serious, Sam. Anything you left back there, anyone, all

those things are gone. Because what they think you're responsible for? They won't stop coming after you. You'll have to disappear. No trace. Like Salem Shaban never existed.

I know. Don't worry. I understand.

And you can do that?

Oh yes. I've done it before.

When he says this, something in his damaged, sandpaper voice starts to change. Something drops away, that coarse edge to his voice that he'd blamed on burned vocal cords. So when he speaks again, it is his same voice, but different.

Softer. Like his true voice.

Unveiled.

When he says.

It was me. Who called you.

What?

I called you. To kill Lesser. It was me. I was the one who hired you. Because I knew what he knew, and I knew he could never be trusted with it. I tried to reason with him, but he called me a fanatic. Called me worse. And I knew that, no matter what, it could never get out. Not to someone like Boonce. So I called you. To kill Lesser. I guess in the end we both failed.

But it was a woman who called me, Sam. A woman who hired me to kill Lesser.

Shaban speaks again from the backseat. That new voice. Not hindered now.

I know, Spademan. But trust me. It was me.

I look again at Shaban in the rearview, wondering what kind of game this is. Notice his wire-rimmed glasses are gone. Notice his clipped black hair, slicked back from the soft face, one cheek rippled with terrible burns. The rest of the face smooth and hairless, though. No beard. No hint of whiskers.

And then I know.

Salem Shaban never had a sister.

And Hussein el-Shaban never had a son.

Just a daughter.

As we drive, Salem Shaban tells me everything.

The rest of it.

She spills it all.

Alia Shaban was a genius programmer, a prodigy, and she was killed as a teenager in that drone strike, for all intents and purposes. Yes, she was pulled out alive, barely alive, and then she was sent to the United States, under the protection of a millionaire named Langland, and somewhere during that overseas midnight flight she was reborn as the brother she never had.

Alia Shaban died in the drone strike and was reborn as Salem Shaban. Langland knew, and had just enough pull to fudge the paperwork, and record-keeping back in Egypt was so chaotic that no one got too worked up if there was a gap in the official record here and there. All easily explained, and Langland stepped up as the sponsor, arranged asylum for Shaban as an extraordinary alien. This teenage boy plucked from the crisis zone. His father's enemies now on the rise back home, looking to fill the power vacuum left behind by a missile strike.

And Alia knew too. She knew she had to disappear.

She also knew, in some part of her damaged heart, even if she hadn't quite figured it out yet, that if she was to become the person she wanted to be in America, the leader she wanted to be, that they would never follow a woman. Especially not a teenage girl. Her experiences later only confirmed this. When Salem Shaban started his campaign to repopulate Atlantic Avenue. As the male heir, he commanded respect beyond his years.

No daughter could have led that movement.

Of course, normally someone like Salem Shaban would never even sniff a visa, but Langland moved quickly and convinced a spook named Joseph Boonce to help. Boonce, who could work back channels. Who could arrange for a military escort and a secret midnight airlift. Who worked secretly and quickly and discreetly.

Off the books.

And Shaban, Salem Shaban, the only son, the living heir, the hacker whiz, the special child, was considered enough of an asset to Boonce and his fledgling project, Near Enemy, that together he and Langland marshaled the forces to spirit this special child to the USA.

Reborn in an air transport, somewhere over the Atlantic.

In the bathroom. Looking at herself in a round, warped mirror.

Her face half-burned and scarred and bandaged anyway.

Souvenirs of the missile strike. And once she arrived in America, she knew no one would think twice to ask how she got them.

They always expect anyone from over there to arrive with scars.

And Langland was right.

Shaban was special.

A prodigy.

Chopped her hair off in that air-transport bathroom and flushed it by the handful down the toilet.

Got fitted for a tweed suit on the day that he arrived.

Baggy tweed suit. Two sizes too big.

Became a trademark.

Tweed and wire-rimmed glasses.

A shy aspect, but with a brilliance behind his eyes.

Salem Shaban.

Please, just call me Sam.

Chewed khat all the time for the pain.

Became known to his friends as Sam the Khat.

Kind of like a Cheshire cat.

Eventually everything disappeared but the smile.

By the time he met Lesser, his new roommate at Near Enemy, Salem Shaban had arrived with a reputation for brilliance, shyness, and extraordinary modesty. Never showered with the other kids. Never even spoke of sex. Very pious and never had a girlfriend that anyone could remember. Most people chalked all that up to him coming from an extremely religious household.

And there were rumors too. About a sister left behind.

A sister killed in an honor killing. By her brother.

He let those rumors go unremarked.

Sometimes rumors are useful. Keep people at a distance. From this soft-spoken boy, Salem Shaban, the one with the sandpaper voice and the hideous scars.

Hard to believe what he'd been through, everyone said.

This soft-cheeked boy with ripples of burns on his face. Who could never grow a beard. Even later when he embraced religion.

Even when he left Near Enemy to become the Moses of Atlantic Avenue.

The kind of man that other men would follow.

Later, Salem Shaban, Sam to his friends, khat addict and fledgling radical, did his best to bury the last remnants of his work at Near Enemy. Starting with the theory he'd devised, the one he scribbled on a chalkboard, then quickly erased.

The one that lets you live forever in the limn, without any body out here.

He hoped to destroy all trace of it, and cripple the limn so it could never be used, thinking only then would he be free to leave his old life behind.

So he set out on an errand.

An errand done in disguise. Burns hidden. Voice obscured.

A black burqa was the perfect subterfuge.

Walking out in the world as a woman again. One last time.

And in her burqa she knocked on the oaken door of the Cloisters, where she would give a sect of Wakers the secrets they'd need to clear out the limn for good.

After that, there was only one last loose end.

Only one other person who knew.

So Shaban called me. Dropped the sandpaper voice.

Said a single name.

Lesser.

Hung up quickly.

Money cleared an hour later.

They'd been best friends once, so Shaban hated to make that call. But he knew that Lesser couldn't be trusted with his secret.

With his two secrets, actually.

After all, Lesser even spilled it to me, that night in Stuyvesant Town.

Not her. Not here.

All that is gone now.

Lesser is gone.

Atlantic Avenue is gone.

New York is gone, locked down, receding and vanished in our rearview.

A moment ago, Salem Shaban was sitting in the backseat of my magic wagon.

But soon, Salem Shaban will be gone too.

42.

I leave Shaban in my apartment in Hoboken and lug the bodies of Luckner and Puchs, and the two Pushbroom flunkies, out back of the building to where the minivan sits idling. Toss them all in the back, then drive the van to an out-of-the-way place I know by the waterfront, where I park it, tires half-deep in the filthy water, and torch the whole thing.

Abracadabra.

Magic wagon goes up in a flash.

Check-Off can bill me.

As for everyone else in the world who might care about four dead bodies and a bonfire, they've got too many other things to worry about.

I stand in the heat of the minivan burning and look across the river at New York.

Most of the lights of the city are out now.

All the bridges and tunnels are closed.

Cops and National Guard have sealed off every entrance and exit.

Tanks turning back traffic. Gunboats patrolling the Hudson.

So it's all I can do, an hour later, to zip across the river and nab Nurse under cover of night.

Meet her at a pier west of Chinatown.

Just me and the outboard motor, still chugging, waiting in the black water.

I take her hand as she steps her pristine white nurse shoes off the pier and into the boat.

Mark's still back at Mina's, but he's tapped into his own dream now. I'm not surprised, given he'd been in-body, trapped out here in the real-time world, for a week. Things he saw, up at the cabin, then in the train with Simon, he needs to drift in oblivion, or whatever chosen fantasy, for a while. I call Mina and tell her, let him drift, open-ended, I'll cover the fees. She answers, don't be silly, it's on the house.

And Mina's watching Simon now.

We still can't bring him out and no one wants to move him. Mina swears she'll take good care of him, despite their history. Sit vigil at his bedside until something happens. Wait and watch him, with her cross-shaped memento carved into her forehead. I'd rather leave Nurse but I need her with me now, and Nurse says there's nothing she can do for Simon anyway. Simon's motionless, in some kind of coma, neither here nor there, but worse. Boonce did something to him, but we don't know what. Nothing Nurse has ever seen before.

So for now we watch and wait.

I haven't told Persephone. Don't know how to reach her even if I wanted to. Tried her phone again and it was dead.

So we leave Simon in the limn.

And who knows what Boonce is doing to him in there right now.

Nurse and I skip across the water with New York shrinking behind us.

Spray of the Hudson soaks us both as the gunboats circle, spotlights sweeping, but it's not like I've never dodged a spotlight sweep before.

I'd left Shaban at my apartment, told him I don't have a TV, but he should feel free to entertain himself otherwise.

Told her.

Told her she should feel free.

That's going to take some getting used to.

She was too absorbed in her handheld anyway, when I left, watching the scrolling newsfeed. Looking for word. Finding word. All the word was bad. Especially for her.

—the fires on Atlantic Avenue now under control as police report they are confident the terrorists—

—make no mistake those responsible for Commissioner Bellarmine's death will be found and brought to—

—a cell headed by known agitator Salem Bhukrat Shaban, now believed to have been killed in this morning's counteractions—

—continue the temporary lockdown as officials work to determine the extent—

—Shaban, who it's now believed may have played a role in the attack on Times Square—

—go to our national correspondent live at the State Department, where officials are expected to answer questions as to how Shaban, a US citizen—

—and police are asking all Islamic New Yorkers to report to their local precinct—

—want to stress that this registration program is completely and entirely voluntary. However—

—mayor continues to be confident that the measures will be temporary, though declined to speculate as to—

—officials confirmed the election will be postponed indefinitely in light of these disturbing and tragic—

—stopped short of describing it as martial law—

—new reports of another tragic death, as law enforcement officials located the body of former NYPD security consultant Joseph Boonce—

—being hailed as a hero, Lieutenant Boonce was apparently slain as part of a wider terrorist—

—go live now to the mayor's remarks—

—this great malignant threat, living right in our midst, like a tumor in the body of our city, who've taken advantage time and again of our hospitality, but we can no longer—

Shaban switches the handheld off.

43.

It takes us a couple days to get our hands on a bed.

Slightly used, but in good shape, and relatively high-end. It's a bit of a shady backdoor deal, but a good find on short notice for what we can afford with what little cash the three of us can scrape together.

As for me, I'm dead broke. Left the last of my money roll on the front seat of that cab. Nurse lives in a nunnery, so she's not much help. But thankfully, Shaban's been amassing donations for a while. And had the foresight to amass them in cash.

In the hours while we wait for delivery, we watch more of the news, and it's nothing good. Turns out the two cops, from Boonce's detail, the ones who assassinated Bellarmine, both left flagrant electronic trails of apparent Islamist sympathies. Google searches. Emails. Damning wire transfers that revealed their concocted pasts. All of it expertly forged and impossible to overlook. Most notably, their supposed ties to Salem Shaban. Even planted those brochures, the ones Shaban was mailing out, in their apartments for the cops to find.

Shaban is now the city's most wanted fugitive.

Face all over the *Post*.

Perfectly framed.

We turn the TV off and then Shaban tells us not to worry about her. She tells us instead.

Worry about Boonce.

Then Shaban explains to me and Nurse what it means if Boonce is alive in there.

If he's loose in the limn.

Not tethered to a body.

Free to roam. Visit any dream.

Build an empire.

Spread panic.

Spread chaos.

Spread worse.

The delivery guys arrive and assemble the bed in my livingroom while Shaban keeps out of sight, Nurse makes coffee, and I make small talk.

Delivery guy jokes it's a perfect time to start tapping in full-time.

You know, what with—

He gestures toward Manhattan. I nod, like we're in total agreement. Say to him.

Crazy times, right?

Delivery guy nods.

End times, my friend. Believe it. Between the ragheads and the lunatics? End times.

Then the delivery guy mentions he saw the bullet holes down in the lobby. Denting the mailbox. Nowhere's safe, he says with a sympathetic shrug.

I shrug back. Thankfully, he doesn't notice the bullet holes in my apartment. I spackled them.

Delivery guy is one of those types who, once you get him going, he'll just keep going, like a wind-up toy. Says to me, as he's on one knee, hooking up hoses under the bed.

I mean, I used to think it was safe over there in Manhattan. But it ain't safe over there. Then I used to think it was safe over here. But it ain't safe over here no more either. Nowhere's safe.

Nods to the bed. Pats it.

Except maybe in there.

I shrug again.

We'll see.

Like I said. Small talk.

He and his partner take another hour to set it up, run the tests, make sure we're hooked in, signal's strong, plugs us in to a quasi-legal patch-in, which will cost us an extra thousand, cash, just to thank him for looking the other way. Whole thing winds up running into five figures, assembly included, and that's the bought-from-the-back-of-a-truck rate.

Then we shake hands and he pats the bed and says.

You're ready to go.

I thank him and hand him an overstuffed envelope, then give them whatever loose cash I have left in my pocket as a tip.

It's a few bills. He takes it happily.

In any case, I won't be needing the cash.

Not where I'm going.

Once the delivery guys leave, Shaban gives the bed a once-over. Makes a couple of adjustments. A few modifications. Fine-tunes.

Then steps back. Says.

This will do.

I look at Shaban and Nurse and think, It's funny that this is my support team. A Muslim fugitive hacker prodigy who found religion and swore off the limn, and a nurse who's part of some secret sisterhood sworn to spread the holy truth of wakefulness.

And me, a former tap-in junkie.

A terrorist, a nurse, and a garbageman.

I've never had a bed in my own home before. Never once. Not even close.

Could never afford it, for starters, but I didn't want one either.

Not in my own home. I was always happy to head out and haunt Chinatown. Live that part of my life out there, try to live some other life back home.

Back in the days when I was on the tap, daily.

Back before my Stella died. Before Times Square. Back when I'd sneak off to deep-dive for an hour at a flop-shop, as just the easiest way to escape all the garbage in this world.

And then after my Stella. After Times Square.

When I'd go and just tap into nothing.

One full hour.

Start the clock.

Oblivion.

Nothingness.

Bought my sessions in bulk.

Until eventually I spent my money on a box-cutter instead and gave up the limn for good.

I lie back.

Still have that box-cutter.

Stashed in my pants pocket.

Just for luck.

I figure it's like how they used to put pennies on the eyes of dead men before they put them in the tomb.

Just in case you might need it on the other side.

Nurse looms over me.

Holds the needle.

All the sensors already attached.

She's about to slide it in, then she pauses. Says nothing.

So I answer the questions I know she wants to ask but won't ask.

Yes, I'm sure. And yes, I'll be back soon.

The first part I am sure about. The second, not so much. But I make them both sound convincing, just for her.

She smiles, but it's a smile that has no acquaintance with happiness.

Then she kisses my forehead.

Then she slides the needle in.

Boonce went looking for a secret he could steal. He thought the secret was a way to kill someone through the limn, but he was wrong.

The secret was better.

To live in the limn.

And he stole it.

Fucked with me. Chased away what passed for my family. Not to mention his part in Times Square.

Took everything from me, then kept on taking.

He did all that, then laughed about it, then loosed chaos in the real-time world.

Then disappeared.

All while I stood and watched him do it.

Watched him slip away.

Scot-free.

Now Boonce could be anywhere.

In there.

In the limn.

In any construct.

Any dream.

Even yours.

As best I know, the rule still stands.

First rule.

You can't kill someone in the limn.

Cannot be broken.

But then again, why not try?

Because as someone once told me, there are no rules or laws in the limn. Not really.

No rules.

No laws.

Just problems to be solved.

Fair enough.

Let's find out.

I tap in.

ACKNOWLEDGMENTS

Only after you write a book do you understand just how many people it takes to make one. Thank you to my agent, David Mc-Cormick, to Molly Stern at Crown, and to my indispensable editor, Zachary Wagman, without whom there would be no second Spademan novel. Thank you to Sarah Bedingfield, Sarah Breivogel, Kayleigh George, Rachelle Mandik, and the team at Crown, without whom this book would not be in your hands. Thank you to Mark Leyner and Professor Peter Ohlin. Thank you to Megan Abbott, Toby Barlow, Lauren Beukes, Kelly Braffet, Austin Grossman, Lev Grossman, Nick Harkaway, Roger Hobbs, and Ian Rankin. Many books influenced this novel in many ways, but three should be mentioned by name: *Securing the City* by Christopher Dickey, *God's Jury* by Cullen Murphy, and *The Looming Tower* by Lawrence Wright. Thank you to my parents, again and always. And thank you to Julia, my treasured collaborator in all things, to whom I say: I confess. I'm biased. But best I can tell, she is the perfect child.